The Shadow of the Rope

E. W. Hornung

Complete & Unabridged

Tutis Digital Publishing Private Limited

First published in 1906 as *The Shadow of the Rope*.

This edition published by
Tutis Digital Publishing Pvt Ltd, 2008.

CHAPTER I

The End of their Life

"It is finished," said the woman, speaking very quietly to herself. "Not another day, nor a night, if I can be ready before morning!"

She stood alone in her own room, with none to mark the white-hot pallor of the oval face, the scornful curve of quivering nostrils, the dry lustre of flashing eyes. But while she stood a heavy step went blustering down two flights of stairs, and double doors slammed upon the ground floor.

It was a little London house, with five floors from basement to attic, and a couple of rooms upon each, like most little houses in London; but this one had latterly been the scene of an equally undistinguished drama of real life, upon which the curtain was even now descending. Although a third was whispered by the world, the persons of this drama were really only two.

Rachel Minchin, before the disastrous step which gave her that surname, was a young Australian lady whose apparent attractions were only equalled by her absolute poverty; that is to say, she had been born at Heidelberg, near Melbourne, of English parents more gentle than practical, who soon left her to fight the world and the devil with no other armory than a good face, a fine nature, and the pride of any heiress. It is true that Rachel also had a voice; but there was never enough of it to augur an income. At twenty, therefore, she was already a governess in the wilds, where women are as scarce as water, but where the man for Rachel did not breathe. A few years later she earned a berth to England as companion to a lady; and her fate awaited her on board.

Mr. Minchin had reached his prime in the underworld, of which he also was a native, without touching affluence, until his fortieth year. Nevertheless, he was a travelled man, and no mere nomad of the bush. As a mining expert he had seen much life in South Africa as well as in Western Australia, but at last he was to see more in Europe as a gentleman of means. A wife had no place in his European scheme; a husband was the last thing Rachel wanted; but a long sea voyage, an uncongenial employ, and the persistent chivalry of a handsome, entertaining, self-confident man of the world, formed a combination as fatal to her inexperience as that of so much poverty, pride, and beauty

1

proved to Alexander Minchin. They were married without ceremony on the very day that they arrived in England, where they had not an actual friend between them, nor a relative to whom either was personally known. In the beginning this mattered nothing; they had to see Europe and enjoy themselves; that they could do unaided; and the bride did it only the more thoroughly, in a sort of desperation, as she realized that the benefits of her marriage were to be wholly material after all.

In the larger life of cities, Alexander Minchin was no longer the idle and good-humored cavalier to whom Rachel had learned to look for unfailing consideration at sea. The illustrative incidents may be omitted; but here he gambled, there he drank; and in his cups every virtue dissolved. Rachel's pride did not mend matters; she was a thought too ready with her resentment; of this, however, she was herself aware, and would forgive the more freely because there was often some obvious fault on her side before all was said. Quarrels of infinite bitterness were thus patched up, and the end indefinitely delayed.

In the meantime, tired of travelling, and impoverished by the husband's follies, the hapless couple returned to London, where a pure fluke with some mining shares introduced Minchin to finer gambling than he had found abroad. The man was bitten. There was a fortune waiting for special knowledge and a little ready cash; and Alexander Minchin settled down to make it, taking for the nonce a furnished house in a modest neighborhood. And here it was that the quarrelling continued to its culmination in the scene just ended.

"Not another day," said Rachel, "nor a night – if I can be ready before morning!"

Being still a woman with some strength of purpose, Mrs. Minchin did not stop at idle words. The interval between the slamming of doors below and another noise at the top of the house was not one of many minutes. The other noise was made by Rachel and her empty trunk upon the loftiest and the narrowest flight of stairs; one of the maids opened their door an inch.

"I am sorry if I disturbed you," their mistress said. "These stairs are so very narrow. No, thank you, I can manage quite well." And they heard her about until they slept.

It was no light task to which Rachel had set her hand; she was going back to Australia by the first boat, and her packing must be done that night. Her resolve only hardened as her spirit cooled. The sooner her departure, the less his opposition; let her delay, and the callousness of the passing brute might give place to the tyranny of the normal man. But she was going, whether or no; not another day – though she would doubtless see its dawn. It was the month of September. And she was not going to fly empty-handed, nor fly at all; she was going deliberately away, with a trunk containing all that she should want upon the voyage. The selection was not too easily made. In his better moods the creature had been lavish enough; and more than once did Rachel snatch from drawer or wardrobe that which remained some moments in her hand, while the incidents of purchase and the first joys of possession, to one who had possessed so little in her life, came back to her with a certain poignancy.

But her resolve remained unshaken. It might hurt her to take his personal gifts, but that was all she had ever had from him; he had never granted her a set allowance; for every penny she must needs ask and look grateful. It would be no fault of hers if she had to strip her fingers for passage-money. Yet the exigency troubled her; it touched her honor, to say nothing of her pride; and, after an unforeseen fit of irresolution, Rachel suddenly determined to tell her husband of her difficulty, making direct appeal to the capricious generosity which had been recalled to her mind as an undeniably redeeming point. It was true that he had given her hearty leave to go to the uttermost ends of the earth, and highly probable that he would bid her work her own way. She felt an impulse to put it to him, however, and at once.

She looked at her watch – it at least had been her mother's – and the final day was already an hour old. But Alexander Minchin was a late sitter, as his young wife knew to her cost, and to-night he had told her where he meant to sleep, but she had not heard him come up. The room would have been the back drawing-room in the majority of such houses, and Rachel peeped in on her way down. It was empty; moreover, the bed was not made, nor the curtains drawn. Rachel repaired the first omission, then hesitated, finally creeping upstairs again for clean sheets. And as she made his bed, not out of any lingering love for him, but from a sense of duty and some consideration for his comfort, there was yet something touching in her instinctive care, that breathed the wife she could have been.

He did not hear her, though the stairs creaked the smallness of the hour – or if he heard he made no sign. This discouraged Rachel as she stole down the lower flight; she would have preferred the angriest sign. But there were few internal sounds which penetrated to the little study at the back of the dining-room, for the permanent tenant was the widow of an eminent professor lately deceased, and that student had protected his quiet with double doors. The outer one, in dark red baize, made an alarming noise as Rachel pulled it open; but, though she waited, no sound came from within; nor was Minchin disturbed by the final entry of his wife, whose first glance convinced her of the cause. In the professor's armchair sat his unworthy successor, chin on waistcoat, a newspaper across his knees, an empty decanter at one elbow. Something remained in the glass beside the bottle; he had tumbled off before the end. There were even signs of deliberate preparations for slumber, for the shade was tilted over the electric light by which he had been reading, as a hat is tilted over the eyes.

Rachel had a touch of pity at seeing him in a chair for the night; but the testimony of the decanter forbade remorse. She had filled it herself in the evening against her husband's return from an absence of mysterious length. Now she understood that mystery, and her face darkened as she recalled the inconceivable insult which his explanation had embraced. No, indeed; not another minute that she could help! And he would sleep there till all hours of the morning; he had done it before; the longer the better, this time.

She had recoiled into the narrow hall, driven by an uncontrollable revulsion; and there she stood, pale and quivering with a disgust that only deepened as she looked her last upon the shaded face and the inanimate frame in the chair. Rachel could not account for the intensity of her feeling; it bordered upon nausea, and for a time prevented her from retracing the single step which at length enabled her to shut both doors as quietly as she had opened them, after switching off the light from force of habit. There was another light still glowing in the hall, and, again from habit, Rachel put it out also before setting foot upon the stairs. A moment later she was standing terror-stricken in the dark.

It was no sound from the study, but the tiniest of metallic rattles from the flap of the letter-box in the front door. The wind might have done it, for the flap had lost its spring; and, though the noise was not repeated, to the wind Rachel put it down, as she mounted the stairs at last in a flutter that caused her both shame and apprehension. Her nerve was going, and she needed it so! It should not go; it should not; and as if to steady it, she opened the landing window, and spent some minutes gazing out into the cool and starry night. Not that she could see very far. The backs of houses hid half the stars in front and on either hand, making, with the back of this house and its fellows, a kind of square turned inside out. Miserable little gardens glimmered through an irregular network of grimy walls, with here and there a fair tree in autumnal tatters; but Rachel looked neither at these nor at the stars that lit them dimly. In a single window of those right opposite a single lamp had burnt all night. It was the only earthly light that Rachel could see, the only one of earth or heaven upon which she looked; and she discovered it with thanksgiving, and tore her eyes away from it with a prayer.

In time the trunk was packed, and incontinently carried downstairs, by an effort which left Rachel racked in every muscle and swaying giddily. But she could not have made much noise, for still there was no sign from the study. She scarcely paused to breathe. A latchkey closed the door behind her very softly; she was in the crisp, clean air at last.

But it was no hour for finding cabs; it was the hour of the scavenger and no other being; and Rachel walked into broad sunlight before she spied a solitary hansom. It was then she did the strangest thing; instead of driving straight back for her trunk, when near the house she gave the cabman other directions, subsequently stopping him at one with a card in the window.

A woman answered the bell with surprising celerity, and a face first startled and then incensed at the sight of Mrs. Minchin.

"So you never came!" cried the woman, bitterly.

"I was prevented," Rachel replied coldly. "Well?"

And the monosyllable was a whisper.

"He is still alive," said the woman at the door.

"Is that all?" asked Rachel, a catch in her voice.

"It is all I'll say till the doctor has been."

"But he has got through the night," sighed Rachel, thankfully. "I could see the light in his room from hour to hour, even though I could not come. Did you sit up with him all night long?"

"Every minute of the night," said the other, with undisguised severity in her fixed red eyes. "I never left him, and I never closed a lid."

"I am so sorry!" cried Rachel, too sorry even for renewed indignation at

5

the cause. "But I couldn't help it," she continued, "I really could not. We – I am going abroad – very suddenly. Poor Mr. Severino! I do wish there was anything I could do! But you must get a professional nurse. And when he does recover – for something assures me that he will – you can tell him – "

Rachel hesitated, the red eyes reading hers.

"Tell him I hope he will recover altogether," she said at length; "mind, altogether! I have gone away for good, tell Mr. Severino; but, as I wasn't able to do so after all, I would rather you didn't mention that I ever thought of nursing him, or that I called last thing to ask how he was."

And that was her farewell message to the very young man with whom a hole-and-corner scandal had coupled Rachel Minchin's name; it was to be a final utterance in yet another respect, and one of no slight or private significance, as the sequel will show. Within a minute or two of its delivery, Rachel was on her own doorstep for the last time, deftly and gently turning the latchkey, while the birds sang to frenzy in a neighboring garden, and the early sun glanced fierily from the brass knocker and letter-box. Another moment and the door had been flung wide open by a police officer, who seemed to fill the narrow hall, with a comrade behind him and both servants on the stairs. And with little further warning Mrs. Minchin was shown her husband, seated much as she had left him in the professor's chair, but with his feet raised stiffly upon another, and the hand of death over every inch of him in the broad north light that filled the room.

The young widow stood gazing upon her dead, and four pairs of eyes gazed yet more closely at her. But there was little to gather from the strained profile with the white cheek and the unyielding lips. Not a cry had left them; she had but crossed the threshold, and stopped that instant in the middle of the worn carpet, the sharpest of silhouettes against a background of grim tomes. There was no swaying of the lissome figure, no snatching for support, no question spoken or unspoken. In moments of acute surprise the most surprising feature is often the way in which we ourselves receive the shock; a sudden and complete detachment, not the least common of immediate results, makes us sometimes even conscious of our failure to feel as we would or should; and it was so with Rachel Minchin in the first moments of her tragic freedom. So God had sundered whom God had joined together! And this was the man whom she had married for love; and she could look upon his clay unmoved! Her mind leapt to a minor consideration, that still made her shudder, as eight eyes noted from the door; he must have been dead when she came down and found him seated in shadow; she had misjudged the dead, if not the living. The pose of the head was unaltered, the chin upon the chest, the mouth closed in death as naturally as in sleep. No wonder his wife had been deceived. And yet there was something unfamiliar, something negligent and noble, and all unlike the living man; so that Rachel could already marvel that she had not at once detected this dignity and this distinction, only too foreign to her husband as she had learnt to know him best, but unattainable in the noblest save by death. And her eyes had risen to the slice of sky in the upper half of the window, and at last the tears were rising in her eyes, when they filled instead with sudden horror and enlightenment.

There was a jagged hole in the pane above the hasp; an upset of ink on the desk beneath the window; and the ink was drying with the dead man's blood, in which she now perceived him to be soaked, while the newspaper on the floor beside him was crisp as toast from that which it had hidden when she saw him last.

"Murdered!" whispered Rachel, breaking her long silence with a gasp. "The work of thieves!"

The policemen exchanged a rapid glance.

"Looks like it," said the one who had opened the door, "I admit."

There was a superfluous dryness in his tone; but Rachel no more noticed this than the further craning of heads in the doorway.

"But can you doubt it?" she cried, pointing from the broken window to the spilled ink. "Did you think that he had shot himself?"

And her horror heightened at a thought more terrible to her than all the rest. But the constable shook his head.

"We should have found the pistol – which we can't," said he. "But shot he is, and through the heart."

"Then who could it be but thieves?"

"That's what we all want to know," said the officer; and still Rachel had no time to think about his tone; for now she was bending over the body, her white hands clenched, and agony enough in her white face.

"Look! look!" she cried, beckoning to them all. "He was wearing his watch last night; that I can swear; and it has gone!"

"You are sure he was wearing it?" asked the same constable, approaching.

"Absolutely certain."

"Well, if that's so," said he, "and it can't be found, it will be a point in your favor."

Rachel sprang upright, her wet eyes wide with pure astonishment.

"In my favor?" she cried. "Will you have the goodness to explain yourself?"

The constables were standing on either side of her now.

"Well," replied the spokesman of the pair, "I don't like the way that window's broken, for one thing, and if you look at it you'll see what I mean. The broken glass is all outside on the sill. But that's not all, ma'am; and, as you have a cab, we might do worse than drive to the station before more people are about."

CHAPTER II

The Case for the Crown

It was years since there had been a promise of such sensation at the Old Bailey, and never, perhaps, was competition keener for the very few seats available in that antique theatre of justice. Nor, indeed, could the most enterprising of modern managers, with the star of all the stages at his beck for the shortest of seasons, have done more to spread the lady's fame, or to excite a passionate curiosity in the public mind, than was done for Rachel Minchin by her official enemies of the Metropolitan Police.

Whether these gentry had their case even more complete than they pretended, when the prisoner was finally committed for trial, or whether the last discoveries were really made in the ensuing fortnight, is now of small account – though the point provided more than one excuse for acrimony on the part of defending counsel during the hearing of the case. It is certain, however, that shortly after the committal it became known that much new evidence was to be forthcoming at the trial; that the case against the prisoner would be found even blacker than before; and that the witnesses were so many in number, and their testimony so entirely circumstantial, that the proceedings were expected to occupy a week.

Sure enough, the case was accorded first place in the November Sessions, with a fair start on a Monday morning toward the latter end of the month. In the purlieus of the mean, historic court, it was a morning not to be forgotten, and only to be compared with those which followed throughout the week. The prisoner's sex, her youth, her high bearing, and the peculiar isolation of her position, without a friend to stand by her in her need, all appealed to the popular imagination, and produced a fascination which was only intensified by the equally general feeling that no one else could have committed the crime. From the judge downward, all connected with the case were pestered for days beforehand with more or less unwarrantable applications for admission. And when the time came, the successful suppliant had to elbow every yard of his way from Newgate Street or Ludgate Hill; to pass three separate barriers held by a suspicious constabulary; to obtain the good offices of the Under Sheriff, through those of his liveried lackeys; and finally to occupy the least space, on the narrowest of seats, in a varnished stall filled with curiously familiar faces, within a few feet of the heavily veiled prisoner in the dock, and not many more from the red-robed judge upon the bench.

The first to take all this trouble on the Monday morning, and the last to escape from the foul air (shot by biting draughts) when the court adjourned, was a white-headed gentleman of striking appearance and stamina to match; for, undeterred by the experience, he was in like manner first and last upon each subsequent day. Behind him came and went the well-known faces, the authors and the actors with a semi-professional interest in the case; but they were not well known to the gentleman with the white head. He heard no more than he could help of their constant whisperings, and, if he knew not at whom he more than once had occasion to turn and frown, he certainly did not look the man to care. He had a well-preserved reddish face, with a small mouth of extraordinary strength, a canine jaw, and singularly noble forehead; but his most obvious distinction was his full head of snowy hair. The only hair upon his face, a pair of bushy eyebrows, was so much darker as to suggest a dye; but the eyes themselves were black as midnight, with a glint of midnight stars, and of such a subtle inscrutability that a certain sweetness of expression came only as the last surprise in a face full of contrast and contradiction.

No one in court had ever seen this man before; no one but the Under Sheriff learnt his name during the week; but by the third day his identity was a subject of discussion, both by the professional students of the human countenance, who sat behind him (balked of their study by the prisoner's veil), and among the various functionaries who had already found him as free with a sovereign as most gentlemen are with a piece of silver. So every day he was ushered with ceremony to the same place, at the inner end of the lowest row; there he would sit watching the prisoner, a trifle nearer her than those beside or behind him; and only once was his attentive serenity broken for an instant by a change of expression due to any development of the case.

It was not when the prisoner pleaded clearly through her veil, in the first breathless minutes of all; it was not a little later, when the urbane counsel for the prosecution, wagging his pince-nez at the jury, thrilled every other hearer with a mellifluous forecast of the new evidence to be laid before them. The missing watch and chain had been found; they would presently be produced, and the jury would have an opportunity of examining them, together with a plan of the chimney of the room in which the murder had been committed; for it was there that they had been discovered upon a second search instituted since the proceedings before the magistrates. The effect of this announcement may be conceived; it was the sensation of the opening day. The whole case of the prosecution rested on the assumption that there had been, on the part of some inmate of the house, who alone (it was held) could have committed the murder, a deliberate attempt to give it the appearance of the work of thieves. Thus far this theory rested on the bare facts that the glass of the broken window had been found outside, instead of within; that no other mark of foot or hand had been made or left by the supposititious burglars; whereas a brace of revolvers had been discovered in the dead man's bureau, both loaded with such bullets as the one which had caused his death, while one of them had clearly been discharged since the last cleaning. The discovery of the missing watch and chain, in the very chimney of the same room, was a piece of ideal evidence of the confirmatory kind. But it was not the point that made an impression on the man with the white hair; it did not increase his attention, for that would have been impossible; he was perhaps the one spectator who was not, if only for the moment, perceptibly thrilled.

Thrilling also was the earlier evidence, furnished by maid-servants and police constables in pairs; but here there was no surprise. The maids were examined not only as to what they had seen and heard on the night of the murder – and they seemed to have heard everything except the fatal shot – but upon the previous relations of their master and mistress – of which they showed an equally extensive knowledge. The constables were perforce confined to their own discoveries and observations when the maids had called them in. But all four witnesses spoke to the prisoner's behavior when shown the dead body of her husband, and there was the utmost unanimity in their several tales. The prisoner had exhibited little or no surprise; it was several minutes before she had uttered a syllable; and then her first words had been to point out that burglars alone could have committed the murder.

In cross-examination the senior counsel for the defence thus early showed his hand; and it was not a strong one to those who knew the game. A Queen's Counsel, like the leader for the Crown, this was an altogether different type of lawyer; a younger man, with a more engaging manner; a more brilliant man, who sought with doubtful wisdom to blind the jury with his brilliance. His method was no innovation at the Old Bailey; it was to hold up every witness in turn to the derision and contempt of the jury and the court. So both the maids were reduced to tears, and each policeman cleverly insulted as such. But the testimony of all four remained unshaken; and the judge himself soothed the young women's feelings with a fatherly word, while wigs were shaken in the well of the court. That was no road to the soft side of a decent, conscientious, hard-headed jury, of much the same class as these witnesses themselves; even the actors and authors had a sound opinion on the point, without waiting to hear one from the professional gentlemen in the well. But the man in front with the very white hair – the man who was always watching the prisoner at the bar – there was about as much expression of opinion upon his firm, bare face as might be seen through the sable thickness of her widow's veil.

It was the same next day, when, for some five hours out of a possible five and a half, the attention of the court was concentrated upon a point of obviously secondary significance. It was suggested by the defence that the watch and chain found up the study chimney were not those worn by the deceased at the time he met his death. The contention was supported by photographs of Alexander Minchin wearing a watch-chain that might or might not be of another pattern altogether; expert opinions were divided on the point; and experts in chains as well as in photography were eventually called by both sides. Interesting in the beginning, the point was raised and raised again, and on subsequent days, until all were weary of the sight of the huge photographic enlargements, which were handed about the court upon each occasion. Even the prisoner would droop in her chair when the "chain photograph" was demanded for the twentieth time by her own unflagging counsel; even the judge became all but inattentive on the point, before it was finally dropped on an intimation from the jury that they had made up their minds about the chains; but no trace of boredom had crossed the keen, alert face of the unknown gentleman with the snowy hair.

So the case was fought for Mrs. Minchin, tooth and nail indeed, yet perhaps with more asperity than conviction, and certainly at times upon points which were hardly worth the fighting. Yet, on the Friday afternoon, when her counsel at last played his masterstroke, and, taking advantage of the then new Act, put the prisoner herself in the witness-box, it was done with the air of a man who is throwing up his case. The truth could be seen at a glance at the clean-cut, handsome, but too expressive profile of the crushing cross-examiner of female witnesses and insolent foe to the police. As it had been possible to predict, from the mere look with which he had risen to his feet, the kind of cross-examination in store for each witness called by the prosecution, so it was obvious now that his own witness had come forward from her own wilful perversity and in direct defiance of his advice.

It was a dismal afternoon, and the witness-box at the Old Bailey is so situated that evidence is given with the back to the light; thus, though her heavy veil was raised at last, and it could be seen that she was very pale, it was not yet that Rachel Minchin afforded a chance to the lightning artists of the half-penny press, or even to the students of physiognomy behind the man with the white hair. This listener did not lean forward an inch; the questions were answered in so clear a voice as to render it unnecessary. Yet it was one of these questions, put by her own counsel, which caused the white-headed man to clap a sudden hand to his ear, and to incline that ear as though the answer could not come without some momentary hesitation or some change of tone. Rachel had told sadly but firmly of her final quarrel with her husband, incidentally, but without embarrassment, revealing its cause. A neighbor was dangerously ill, whom she had been going to nurse that night, when her husband met her at the door and forbade her to do so.

"Was this neighbor a young man?"

"Hardly more than a boy," said Rachel, "and as friendless as ourselves."

"Was your husband jealous of him?"

"I had no idea of it until that night."

"Did you find it out then?"

"I did, indeed!"

"And where had your husband been spending the evening?"

"I had no idea of that either – until he told me he had been watching the house – and why!"

Though the man was dead, she could not rid her voice of its scorn; and presently, with bowed head, she was repeating his last words to her. A cold thrill ran through the court.

"And was that the last time you saw him alive?" inquired counsel, his face lightening in ready apprehension of the thrill, and his assurance coming back to him on the spot, as though it were he who had insisted on putting his client in the box.

But to this there was no immediate answer; for it was here that the white-haired man raised his hand to his ear; and the event was exactly as he seemed to have anticipated.

"Was that the last time you saw your husband alive?" repeated Rachel's counsel, in the winning accents and with the reassuring face that he could assume without an effort at his will.

"It was," said Rachel, after yet another moment's thought.

It was then that the white-headed man dropped his eyes for once; and for once the thin, hard lines of his mouth relaxed in a smile that seemed to epitomize all the evil that was in his face, and to give it forth in one sudden sour quintessence.

CHAPTER III

Name and Nature

The prisoner's evidence concluded with a perfectly simple if somewhat hesitating account of her own doings during the remainder of the night of her husband's murder. That story has already been told in greater detail than could be extracted even by the urbane but deadly cross-examiner who led for the Crown. A change had come over the manner in which Rachel was giving her evidence; it was as though her strength and nerve were failing her together, and henceforth the words had to be put into her mouth. Curiously enough, the change in Mrs. Minchin's demeanor was almost coincident with the single and rather sinister display of feeling upon the part of the white-haired gentleman who had followed every word of the case. On the whole, however, her story bore the stamp of truth; and a half-apologetic but none the less persistent cross-examination left it scarcely less convincing than before.

There was one independent witness for the defence, in addition to the experts in photography and chains. The landlady of the house at which Rachel called, in the early morning, on her way home with the cab, was about five minutes in the witness-box, but in those five minutes she supplied the defence with one of its strongest arguments. It was at least conceivable that a woman who had killed her husband might coolly proceed to pack her trunk, and thereafter fetch the cab which was to remove herself and her effects from the scene of the tragedy. But was it credible that a woman of so much presence of mind, to whom every minute might make the difference between life and death, would, having found her cab, actually drive out of her way to inquire after a sick friend, or even a dying lover, before going home to pick up her luggage and to ascertain whether her crime was still undetected? Suppose it were a lover, and inquire one must: would one not still leave those inquiries to the last? And having made them, last or first; and knowing the grim necessity of flight; would one woman go out of her way to tell another that she "had to go abroad very suddenly, and was going for good?"

"Inconceivable!" cried the prisoner's counsel, dealing with the point; and the word was much upon his lips during the course of a long and very strenuous speech, in which the case for the Crown was flouted from beginning to end, without, perhaps, enough of concentration on its more obvious weaknesses, or of respect for its undoubted strength.

For the prisoner's proceedings on the night of the murder, however, supposing she had committed it, and still more on the morning after, it would have been difficult to find a better epithet; the only drawback was that this one had seen service in the cause of almost every murderer who ever went to the gallows – as counsel for the prosecution remarked in his reply, with deadly deference to his learned friend.

"On the other hand," he went on, wagging his eyeglasses with leisurely deliberation, and picking his words with a care that enhanced their effect, after the unbridled rhetoric of the defence – "on the other hand, gentlemen, if criminals never made mistakes, inconceivable or not as we may choose to consider them – if they never made those mistakes, they would never stand in that dock."

It was late on the Saturday afternoon when the judge summed up; but a pleasant surprise was in store for those who felt that his lordship must speak at greater length than either of the counsel between whom he was to hold the scales. The address from the bench was much the shortest of the three. Less exhaustive than the conventional review of a complicated case, it was a disquisition of conspicuous clearness and impartiality. Only the salient points were laid before the jury, for the last time, and in a nutshell, but with hardly a hint of the judge's own opinion upon any one of them. The expression of that opinion was reserved for a point of even greater import than the value of any separate piece of evidence. If, said the judge, the inferences and theory of the prosecution were correct; if this unhappy woman, driven to desperation by her husband, and knowing where he kept his pistols, had taken his life with one of them, and afterwards manufactured the traces of a supposititious burglary; then there was no circumstance connected with the crime which could by any possibility reduce it from murder to manslaughter. The solemnity of this pronouncement was felt in the farthest corner of the crowded court. So they were to find her guilty of wilful murder, or not guilty at all! Every eye sped involuntarily to the slim black figure in the dock; and, under the gaze of all, the figure made the least little bow – a movement so slight and so spontaneous as to suggest unconsciousness, but all the more eloquent on that account.

Yet to many in court, more especially to the theatrical folk behind the man with the white hair, the gesture was but one more subtle touch in an exhibition of consummate art and nerve.

"If they do acquit her," whispered one of these wiseacres to another, "she will make her fortune on the stage!"

Meanwhile the judge was dealing at the last with the prisoner's evidence in her own behalf, and that mercifully enough, though with less reticence than had characterized the earlier portions of his address. He did not think it possible or even desirable to forget that this was the evidence of a woman upon trial for her life. It must not be discredited on that account. But it was for the jury to bear in mind that the story was one which admitted of no corroboration, save in unimportant details. More than that he would not say. It was for them to judge of that story as they had heard it for themselves, on its own merits, but also in relation to the other evidence. If the jury believed it, there was an end of the case. If they had any reasonable doubt at all, the prisoner was entitled to the full benefit of that doubt, and they must acquit her. If, on the other hand, the facts taken together before and after the murder brought the jury to the conclusion that it was none other than the prisoner who had committed the murder – though, of course, no one was present to see the act committed – they must, in duty to their oaths, find her guilty.

During the judge's address the short November day had turned from afternoon to night, and a great change had come over the aspect of the dim and dingy court. Opaque globes turned into flaring suns; incandescent burners revealed unsuspected brackets; the place was warmed and lighted for the first time during the week. And the effect of the light and warmth was on all the faces that rose as one while the judge sidled from the bench, and the jury filed out of their box, and the prisoner disappeared down the dock stairs for the last time in ignorance of her fate. Next moment there was the buzz of talk that you expect in a theatre between the acts, rather than in a court of justice at the solemn crisis of a solemn trial. It was like a class-room with the master called away. Hats were put on again in the bulging galleries; hardly a tongue was still. On the bench a red-robed magnate and another in knee-breeches exchanged views upon the enlarged photographs which had played so prominent a part in the case; in the well the barristers' wigs nodded or shook over their pink blotters and their quill pens; gentlemen of the Press sharpened their pencils and indulged in prophecy; and on their right, between the reporters and the bench, the privileged few, the literary and theatrical elect, discussed the situation with abnormal callousness, masking emotion with a childlike cynicism of sentiment and phrase.

And for once the stranger in their midst, the man with more outward distinction than any one of them, the unknown man with the snowy hair, could afford to listen to what they had to say.

"No chance, my dear man. Not an earthly!"

"I'm not so sure of that."

"Will you bet?"

"No, hang it! What a beast you are! But I thought the woman was speaking the truth."

"You heard what the judge said. Where's your corroboration? No, they ought never to have let her go into the box. I hear she insisted. But it hasn't saved anybody yet."

"The new law? Then it shows her pluck!"

"But not necessarily her innocence, dear boy."

Thus one shaven couple. Others had already exhausted the subject.

"Yes, I finished it down at Westgate last week."

"Satisfied?"

"In a way. It depends so much on the cast."

"These actor-managers – what?"

"More or less. I must be off. Dining out."

"What! Not going to wait for the end of the fourth act?"

"No, I'm late as it is. Ta-ta!"

The white-haired man was amused. He did not turn round, nor, if he had, would he have known the retreating gentleman for the most eminent of living playwrights; but he knew the reason for his sudden retreat. A hush had fallen, and some one had whispered, "They're coming!" The light-hearted chatter had died away on the word; perhaps it was not so light-hearted after all. But the alarm was false, there was no sign of the jury, and the talk rose again, as the wind will in a storm.

"We shall want a glass when this is over," whispered one of the pair who had argued about the case.

"And we'll have it, too, old man!" rejoined his friend.

The white-haired man was grimly interested. So this was the way men talked while waiting to hear a fellow-creature sentenced to death! It was worth knowing. And this was what the newspaper men would call a low buzz – an expectant hush – this animated babble! Yet the air was charged with emotion, suppressed perhaps, but none the less distinguishable in every voice. Within earshot a perspiring young pressman was informing his friends that to come there comfortably you should commit the murder yourself, then they gave you the Royal Box; but his teeth could be heard chattering through the feeble felicity. The white-headed listener curled a contemptuous nostril. They could joke, and yet they could feel! He himself betrayed neither weakness, but sat waiting patiently and idly listening, with the same grim jaw and the same inscrutable eye with which he had watched the prisoner and the jury alternately throughout the week. And when the latter at last returned, and then the former, it was the same subtle stare that he again bent upon them both in turn.

The jury had been absent but forty minutes after all; and their expedition seemed as ill an omen as their nervous and responsible faces. There was a moment's hush, another moment of prophetic murmurs, and then a stillness worthy of its subsequent description in every newspaper. The prisoner was standing in the front of the dock, a female warder upon either hand. The lightning pencil of the new journalist had its will of her at last. For Mrs. Minchin had dispensed not only with the chair which she had occupied all the week, but also with the heavy veil which she had but partially lifted during her brief sojourn in the witness-box, and never once in the dock. The veil was now flung back over the widow's bonnet, peaking and falling like a sable cowl, against which the unearthly pallor of her face was whiter far then that of the merely dead, just as mere death was the least part of the fate confronting her. Yet she had raised her veil to look it fairly in the face, and the packed assembly marvelled as it gazed.

Was that the face that had been hidden from them all these days? It was not what they had pictured beneath the proud, defiant carriage of its concealing veil. Was that the face of a determined murderess?

Beautiful it was not as they saw it then, but the elements of beauty lay unmistable beneath a white mist of horror and of pain, as a lovely landscape is still lovely at its worst. The face was a thin but perfect oval, lengthened a little by depth of chin and height of forehead, as now also by unnatural emaciation and distress. The mouth was at once bloodless, sweet, and firm; the eyes of a warm and lustrous brown, brilliant, eloquent, brave – and hopeless!

Yes, she had no hope herself! It was plain enough at the first glimpse of the deadly white, uncovered face, in the cruel glare of gas. But it became plainer still as, with sad, unflinching eyes, she watched and listened while, for the last time, the jurymen answered to their names.

Now they were done. The foreman shifted nervously in his place. In the overstain of the last dread pause, the crowded court felt hotter and lighter than ever. It seemed to unite the glare of a gin palace with the temperature of a Turkish bath.

"Gentlemen, are you greed upon your verdict?"

"We are."

"Do you find the prisoner guilty or not guilty?"

"Not guilty."

There was a simultaneous gasp from a hundred throats – a distinct cry from some. Then the Clerk of Arraigns was seen to be leaning forward, a hand to his ear, for the foreman's voice had broken with excitement. And every soul in court leaned forward too.

But this time his feelings had a different effect upon the excited foreman.

"*Not* guilty!" he almost bawled.

Dead silence then, while the clock ticked thrice.

"And that is the verdict of you all?"

"Of every one of us!"

The judge leant back in his place, his eyes upon the desk before him, without a movement or a gesture to strike the personal note which had been suppressed with such admirable impartiality throughout the trial. But it was several moments before his eyes were lifted with his voice.

"Let her be discharged," was all he said even then; but he would seem to have said it at once gruffly, angrily, thankfully, disgustedly, with emotion, and without any emotion at all. You read the papers, and you take your choice.

So Rachel Minchin was supported from the court before the round eyes of a hundred or two of her fellow-creatures, in the pitiable state of one who has been condemned to die, and not set free to live. It was as though she still misunderstood a verdict which had filled most faces with incredulity, but none with an astonishment to equal her own. Her white face had leaped alight, but not with gladness. The pent-up emotion of the week had broken forth in an agony of tears; and so they half led, half carried her from the court. She had entered it for the last time with courage enough; but it was the wrong kind of courage; and, for the one supreme moment, sentence of life was harder to bear than sentence of death.

In a few minutes the court was empty – a singular little theatre of pale varnish and tawdry hangings, still rather snug and homely in the heat and light of its obsolete gas, and with as little to remind one of the play as any other theatre when the curtain is down and the house empty. But there was clamor in the corridors, and hooting already in the street. Nor was the house really empty after all. One white-haired gentleman had not left his place when an attendant returned to put out the lights. The attendant pointed him out to a constable at the door; both watched him a few moments. Then the attendant stepped down and touched him on the shoulder.

The gentleman turned slowly without a start. "Ah, you're the man I want to see," said he. "Was that the Chief Warder in the dock?"

"Him with the beard," said the attendant, nodding.

"Well, give him this, and give it him quick. I'll wait up there till he can see me."

And he pressed his card into the attendant's palm, with a couple of sovereigns underneath.

"Wants to see the Chief Warder," explained the attendant to the constable at the door.

"He's been here all the week," mused the constable aloud. "I wonder who he is?"

"Name of Steel," whispered the other, consulting the card, as the gentleman advanced up the steps toward them, the gaslight gleaming in his silver hair, and throwing his firm features into strong relief.

"And not a bad name for him," said the constable at the door.

CHAPTER IV

The Man in the Train

Rachel fought her weakness with closed eyes, and was complete mistress of herself when those about her thought that consciousness alone was returning. She recognized the chamber at a glance; it was the one in which generations of metropolitan malefactors, and a few innocent persons like herself, had waited for the verdict of life or death. For her it was life, life, life! And she wondered whether any other of the few had ever come back to life with so little joy.

The female warders were supporting her in a chair; the prison doctor stood over her with a medicine glass.

"Drink this," said he, kindly.

"But I have been conscious all the time."

"Never mind. You need it."

And Rachel took the restorative without more words.

It did its work. The color came back to her face. The blood ran hot in her veins. In a minute she was standing up without assistance.

"And now," said Rachel, "I shall not trespass further on your kindness, and I am sure that you will not wish to detain me."

"We cannot," said the doctor, with a broad smile and a bow; "you are as free as air, and will perhaps allow me to be the first to congratulate you. At the same time, my dear madam, and quite apart from your condition – which is wonderful to me after what you've been through – at the same time, and even with your fortitude, I think it would be advisable to – to wait a little while."

The doctor raised his eyes, and all at once Rachel heard. Overheard – outside – in the world – there was the brutal hooting of a thoughtless mob.

"So that is for me!"

Rachel set her teeth.

"On the contrary," said the kindly doctor, "it may be for the witnesses; but crowds are fickle things; and I should strongly urge you not to court a demonstration of one sort or the other. You are best where you are for the time being, or at all events somewhere within the precincts. And meanwhile your solicitor is waiting to add his congratulations to mine."

"Is he, indeed!" cried Rachel, in a voice as hard as her eye.

"Why, to be sure," rejoined the other, taken somewhat aback. "There must be many matters for discussion between you, and he at least seems very anxious to discuss them. In fact, I may say that he is only awaiting my permission for an immediate interview."

"Then let him await mine!" exclaimed Rachel, in a vindictive voice for which she was apologizing in the next breath. "I owe you much," she added, "if only for your kindness and sympathy during these few minutes. But to him I owe nothing that I cannot pay in cash. He tried to keep me from telling my own story in the box – they all did – but he was the worst of all. So I certainly do not owe him my life. He came to me and he said what he liked; he may have forgotten what he said, but I never shall."

"He would be the first to admit his error now."

"Perhaps; but he believed me guilty to the very end; and I utterly refuse to see him to-night."

"Then I shall tell him so."

And the good doctor disappeared for the nonce, but was back in a couple of minutes, full of the lawyer's expostulations. What did Mrs. Minchin intend to do? Where did she propose to go? There were a hundred matters for explanation and arrangement. Her solicitor said she had no friends, and seemed himself most anxious to act in that capacity. Rachel's lips curled at the thought.

"At least," said she, "I have the friends who guaranteed his bill, if that has anything to say to his anxiety! But what I mean to do and where I may go, are entirely my own affair. And as for the hundred matters he mentions, he might have spoken of them during the week. Perhaps he thought it would be waste of breath, but I should have appreciated the risk."

So her solicitor was beaten off, with all the spirit which was one of Rachel's qualities, but also with the rashness which was that quality's defect. The man was indeed no ornament to his profession, but a police-court practitioner of the pushing order, who had secured the case for notoriety and nothing else. Rachel's soul sickened when she thought of her interviews, and especially her most recent interviews, with one whom she had never seen before her trouble, and whom she devoutly hoped never to see again. She did not perceive that the time had come when the lawyer might have been really useful to her. Yet his messages left her more alive to the difficulties that lay before her as a free woman, and to the immediate necessity of acting for herself once more.

After all there had been a silver lining to the cloud under which she had lain so long. Others had acted for her. It had been a rest. But, conscious of her innocence, and serene in that consciousness, she had prepared herself rather for another life than for a new lease of this one; and, while seeking to steel her soul to the awful sequel of a conviction, in the other direction she had seldom looked beyond the consummate incident of an acquittal. Life seems a royal road when it is death that stares one in the face; but already Rachel saw the hills and the pitfalls; for indeed they began under her nose.

She had no plans, nor a single soul to help her to make any. In all the world she had no real friend. And yet, with the very independence to which this isolation was largely due, she must pick and choose, and reject, in the hour when any friend would have been better than none!

In the first ten minutes of the new life which Rachel Minchin began with her acquittal, she had refused to see her own solicitor, and an unknown gentleman whose card was brought to her by the Chief Warder himself. With the card was a message which might have inspired confidence, and the same might be said of the address. But it was enough for Rachel that she knew no one of the name. The Chief Warder, one of the kindliest mortals, displayed no little irritation under her repeated refusals; but it was the agent, and not the principal, who was so importunate; and the message was not repeated once the former could be induced to bear Mrs. Minchin's answer. The Chief Warder did indeed return, but it was not to make any further reference to the mysterious Mr. Steel who had craved an interview with Mrs. Minchin. And now the good fellow was all smiles.

"Feeling more yourself?" said he; and, when Rachel said she was, he asked her to listen now; and there was nothing to listen to. "The coast's as clear as the Criminal Court," explained this pleasant official. "A closed cab did it, with an officer on the box; and I'll call you another as soon as you like."

Rachel rose at once.

"It was kind of you to let me stay so long," she said. "But I don't think I will take a cab, thank you, if there's an underground station within reach, and you will kindly tell me the way."

"There's Blackfriars Bridge within five minutes. But you will have more than you can carry – "

"I have nothing worth taking away with me," said Rachel, "except the things I stand up in; but you may give what I leave to any poor woman who cares to have them. And I hope you will accept this trifle for yourself, with my deep gratitude for all your kindness."

Indeed, the man had been kind, and his kindness would have continued to the last had the trial ended differently. Nevertheless, Rachel's trifle was a piece of gold, and one of her last. Nor was this pure generosity. There was an untold joy in being able to give again. It was the first real taste of freedom; and in another minute Rachel was free.

Oh, but what a miracle to hear her feet on the now deserted pavement, to see her breath in the raw November night, and the lights of Ludgate Hill beyond! Rachel raised her veil to see them better. Who would look for her afoot so near the scene of her late ordeal? And what did it matter who saw her and who knew her now? She was innocent; she could look the whole world in the face once more. Oh, to rub shoulders with the world again!

A cab came tinkling up behind her, and Rachel half thought of hailing it, and driving through the lighted town after all; but the hansom was occupied, and the impulse passed. She put down her veil and turned into the stream without catching a suspicious eye. Why should they suspect her? And again, what did it matter if they did?

"Trial an' verdic'! Trial an' verdic'! Acquittal o' Mrs. Minchin! Trial an' verdic'!"

Everybody was buying the damp, pink sheets. Rachel actually bought one herself; and overheard the opinion of the man in the street without a pang. So she might think herself lucky! But she did, she did; in the reaction that had come upon her with the first mouthful of raw air, in the intoxication of treading the outer world again, she thought herself the luckiest woman in London, and revelled rather than otherwise in the very considerations which had appalled her in the precincts of the court. How good, after all, to be independent as well as free! How great to drift with the tide of innocent women and law-abiding men, once more one of themselves, and not even a magnet for morbid curiosity! That would come soon enough; the present was all the more to be enjoyed; and even the vagueness of the immediate future, even the lack of definite plans, had a glamor of their own in eyes that were yet to have their fill of street lamps and shop windows and omnibuses and hansom cabs.

The policeman under the bridge was a joy in himself; he refreshed Rachel's memory as to the way, without giving her an unnecessary look; and he called her "madam" into the bargain! After all, it was not every policeman who had been on duty at the Old Bailey, nor one in many thousands of the population who had gained admission to the court.

Yet if Rachel had relieved the tedium of her trial by using her eyes a little more; if, for example, she had condescended to look twice at the handful of mere spectators beyond the reporters on her right, she could scarcely have failed to recognize the good-looking, elderly man who was at her heels when she took her ticket at Blackfriars Bridge. His white hair was covered by his hat, but the face itself was not one to be forgotten, with its fresh color, its small, grim mouth, and the deep-set glitter beneath the bushy eyebrows. Rachel, however, neither recognized nor looked again.

In a few minutes she had a better chance, when, having entered an empty compartment in the first class, she was joined by this gentleman as the train began to move.

Rachel hid herself behind the newspaper which she had bought, not that she had looked twice at her companion, but because at such close quarters, and in the comparatively fierce light of the first-class compartment, she was terribly afraid that he might look once too often at her. But this fear passed from her in the matchless fascination of reading and re-reading five words in the stop-press column: – "MINCHIN CASE – Verdict, Not guilty."

Not guilty! Not guilty! And to see it in print! Her eyes filled at the sight, and she dried them to gloat again. There were columns and columns about the case, embellished with not unskilful sketches of counsel addressing the jury, and of the judge in the act of summing up. But Rachel had listened to every word from all three; and the professional report was less full and less accurate than the one which she carried in her brain and would carry to her grave. Not that the speeches mattered now. It was no speech that had saved her; it was her own story, from her own lips, that the lawyers would have closed! Rachel forgave them now; she was almost grateful to them for having left it to her to save herself in spite of them all: so should her perfect innocence be impressed upon the whole country as on those twelve fair minds. And once more she pored upon the hurriedly added and ill-printed line which gave their verdict to the world, while the train stopped and started, only to stop and start again.

"And what do you think of it, madam?"

The voice came from the opposite corner of the compartment, and Rachel knew it for that of the gentleman who had jumped in at the last moment at Blackfriars Bridge. It was Charing Cross that they were leaving now, and the door had not opened at that station or the last. Rachel sat breathless behind her evening paper. Not to answer might be to fasten suspicion upon her widow's weeds; and, for all her right to look mankind in the face, she shrank instinctively from immediate recognition. Then in a clap came the temptation to discuss her own case with the owner of a voice at once confident and courtly, and subtly reminiscent of her native colony, where it is no affront for stranger to speak to stranger without introduction or excuse.

Rachel's hesitation lasted perhaps a couple of seconds, and then her paper lay across her lap.

"Of what?" she asked, with some presence of mind, for she had never an instant's doubt that the question referred to the topic of the hour.

"We were reading the same paper," replied the questioner, with perfect courtesy; "it only struck me that we might both be reading the same thing, and feeling equally amazed at the verdict."

"You mean in the Minchin case," said Rachel steadily, and without the least interrogation in her tone. "Yes, I was reading it, as I suppose everybody is. But I disagree with you about the verdict."

The young widow's manner was as downright as her words. There was a sudden raising of the bushy eyebrows in the opposite corner, a brief opening of the black eyes underneath.

"Pardon me," said the gentleman, breaking into a smile; "I was not aware that I had expressed an opinion on that point."

"I understood you were amazed," said Rachel, dryly.

"And are not you?" cried the other point-blank. "Do you mean to tell me that you were prepared for an acquittal?"

"I was prepared for anything," replied Rachel, returning a peculiarly penetrating stare with one at least as steady, and yet holding her breath for very fear lest this stranger had found her out, until his next words allayed the suspicion.

"Madam, have you followed the case?"

"Indeed I have," sighed honest Rachel.

"And as a woman you believe this woman innocent?"

"I do."

It was hard enough to say no more than that; but Rachel was very fresh from her great lesson in self-control.

"It is easy to see that you do not," she merely permitted herself to add.

"On the contrary," said he, with great precision; "on the contrary, my dear madam, I believe this poor lady to be as innocent as yourself."

Again their eyes were locked; again Rachel drew the only inference from so pointed a pronouncement, and yet again was the impression shaken by her companion's next words.

"But I really have no right to an opinion," said he; "since, unlike you, I cannot claim to have read the case. Nor is that the interesting thing now." The stations had come and gone, until now they were at Victoria. The speaker looked out of the window, until they were off again, and off by themselves as before. "The interesting thing, to me, is not what this poor lady has or has not done, but what on earth she is going to do now!"

He looked at her again, and now Rachel was sure. But there was a kindness in his look that did away both with resentment and regret.

"They say she has literally no friends in England," he went on, with unconcealed concern. "That is incredible; and yet, if there be any truth in it, what a terrible position! I fear that everybody will not share your conviction, and, I may add, my own. If one can judge thus early by what one has heard and seen for oneself, this verdict is a personal disappointment to the always bloodthirsty man in the street. Then, God help the poor lady if he spots her! I only hope she will not give him a chance."

And now Rachel not only knew that he knew, but that he wished to apprise her of his knowledge without confessing it in so many words. So he would spare her that embarrassment, and would help her if he could, this utter stranger! Yet she saw it in his face, she heard it in his voice; and becoming gradually alive to his will to help her, as she instinctively was to his power, she had herself the will to consult one whose good intention and better tact were alike obvious. Mystery there was in her meeting with this man; something told her that it was no accident on his side; she began to wonder whether she had not seen him before; and while she wondered he came and sat opposite to her, and went on speaking in a lower voice, his dark eyes fixed on hers.

"If Mrs. Minchin wants a friend – and to-night I think she must – if ever she did or will! Well, if she does, I for one would be her friend – if she would trust me!"

The last words were the lowest of all; and in the tone of them there was a timbre which thrilled Rachel as the dark eyes fascinated her. She began to feel a strange repugnance – and yet more strange attraction. But to the latter her independence gave instant battle – a battle the easier to fight since the next station was Rachel's destination.

"Do you think she would trust me?" he almost whispered leaning towards her. "As a woman – don't you think she might?"

As Rachel hesitated the carriages began to groan beneath the brake; and her hesitation was at an end. So also was her limited capacity for pretence. She sat more upright in her corner, her shoulders fell in angles, and beneath the veil, which she had raised to read her paper, her eyes carried the war of interrogation into the enemy's country.

"I seem to have seen you before," said Rachel, cool of tongue but hot at heart.

"I think it very possible that you have."

"Were you at the trial?"

"From first to last!"

The pause that followed was really broken by the lights of Sloane Square station.

"You know me," said Rachel, hurriedly; "I have seen that for some time. May I ask if you are Mr. Steel?"

"I am."

"The Mr. Steel who sent me his card after the trial?"

Steel bowed.

"As a perfect stranger?"

"As a perfect stranger who had watched you for a whole long week in court."

Rachel ignored the relative clause.

"And because I would not see you, Mr. Steel, you have followed me, and forced yourself upon me!"

The train stopped, and Rachel rose.

"You will gather my motives when you recall our conversation," observed Steel; and he opened the door for her. But Rachel turned to him before alighting.

"Mr. Steel," said she, "I am quite sure that you mean kindly and well, and that I above all women should feel supremely grateful; but I cannot help thinking that you are unjust to the man in the street!"

"Better give him a trial," said Steel, coldly enough in his turn.

"I should prefer to," rejoined Rachel, getting out; and there was no little sting in the intonation of the verb; but Mr. Steel was left smiling and nodding very confidently to himself.

CHAPTER V

The Man in the Street

Rachel's perturbation was only the greater from her success in concealing, or at least suppressing it, during the actual process of this singular interview. You may hold your breath without moving a muscle, but the muscles will make up for it when their turn comes, and it was so with Rachel and her nerves; they rose upon her even on the platform, and she climbed the many stairs in a tremor from head to foot. And at the top, in the open night, and at all the many corners of a square that is nothing of the kind, from hoarse throat and on fluttering placard, it was "Trial and Verdict," or "Sensational Verdict at the Old Bailey," here as at the other end of the town.

But now all Rachel's thoughts were of this mysterious Mr. Steel; of his inexplicable behavior towards her, and of her own attitude towards him. Yet, when all was said, or when all that had been said could be remembered, would his behavior be found so very inexplicable? Rachel was not devoid of a proper vanity, albeit that night she had probably less than most women with a tithe of her personal attractions; and yet upon reflection she could conceive but one explanation of such conduct in an elderly man.

"There is no fool like an old fool," quoted Rachel to herself; and it was remarkable that until this moment she had never thought of Mr. Steel as either elderly or old. His eyes were young; his voice was young; she could hear him and see him still, so the strong impression was not all on one side. No more, it would seem, was the fascination. Rachel, indeed, owned to no such feeling, even in her inmost heart. But she did begin to blame herself, alike for her reception of advances which might well have been dictated by mere eccentric benevolence, and for her readiness now to put another construction upon them. And all this time she was threading the streets of Chelsea at a pace suggestive of a destination and a purpose, while in her mind she did nothing but look back.

Impulsive by nature, Rachel had also the courage of each impulse while it lasted; on the other hand, if quick to act, she was only too ready to regret. Like many another whose self-reliance is largely on the surface, an achievement of the will and not the gift of a temperament, she usually paid for a display of spirit with the most dispiriting reaction;

and this was precisely the case in point. Rachel was ashamed alike of her rudeness and her vanity; the latter she traced to its source. It was inspired by vague memories of other women who had been through the same ordeal as herself. One had been handed a bouquet in the dock; another had been overwhelmed by proposals of marriage. Rachel herself had received letters of which the first line was enough. But there had been no letter from Mr. Steel. Ah! but he had attended her trial; she remembered him now, his continual presence had impressed itself very subtly upon her mind, without the definite memory of a single glance; and after the trial he sent her his card, he dogged her in the train! What was she to think? There was the voice in which he had offered her his aid; there was the look in his eyes; there was the delicate indirectness of that offer.

A year or two ago, with all her independence, Rachel would not have been so ready to repel one whose advances, however unwarrantable in themselves, were yet marked by so many evidences of sympathy and consideration. She had not always been suspicious and repellent; and she sighed to think how sadly she must have changed, even before the nightmare of the last few weeks.

But a more poignant reminder of her married life was now in store for Rachel Minchin. She had come to Chelsea because it was the only portion of the town in which she had the semblance of a friend; but there did live in Tite Street a young couple with whom the Minchins had at one time been on friendly terms. That was in the day of plenty and extravagance; and the acquaintance, formed at an hotel in the Trossachs, had not ripened in town as the two wives could have wished. It was Mrs. Carrington, however, who had found the Minchins their furnished house, while her husband certainly interested himself in Rachel's defence. Carrington was a barrister, who never himself touched criminal work, but he had spoken to a friend who did, to wit the brilliant terror of female witnesses, and caustic critic of the police, to whom Rachel owed so little. But to Carrington himself she owed much – more indeed than she cared to calculate – for he was not a man whom she liked. She wished to thank him for his kindness, to give certain undertakings and to ask his advice, but it was Mrs. Carrington whom she really hoped to see. There was a good heart, or Rachel was much mistaken. They would have seen more of each other if Mrs. Carrington had had her way. Rachel remembered her on the occasion of the solitary visit she had received at Holloway – for Mrs. Carrington had been the visitor.

"Don't tell Jim," she had said, "when you get off and come to see us."

And she had kissed her captive sister in a way that made poor Rachel sometimes think she had a friend in England after all; but that was before her committal; and thereafter from that quarter not a word. It was not Mrs. Carrington whom Rachel blamed, however, and those last words of hers implied an invitation which had never been withdrawn. But invitation or no invitation, friend or no friend, Mrs. Carrington she would have to see. And even he would be different now that he knew she was innocent; and if it was easy to see what he had believed of her before, well, so much the more credit to him for what he had done.

So Rachel had decided before quitting the precincts of the Old Bailey; but her subsequent experiences in street and train so absorbed her that she was full of the interview that was over when she ought to have been preparing for the one still before her. And, in her absence of mind, the force of habit had taken advantage of her; instead of going on to Tite Street, she turned too soon, and turned again, and was now appalled to find herself in the very street in which her husband had met his death.

The little street was as quiet as ever; Rachel stood quite still, and for the moment she was the only person in it. She stole up to the house. The blinds were down, and it was in darkness, otherwise all was as she remembered it only too well. Her breath came quickly. It was a strange trick her feet had played her, bringing her here against her will! Yet she had thought of coming as a last resort. The furnished house should be hers for some months yet; it had been taken for six months from July, and this was only the end of November. At the worst − if no one would take her in −

She shuddered at the unfinished thought; and yet there was something in it that appealed to Rachel. To go back there, if only for the shortest time − to show her face openly where it was known − not to slink and hide as though she were really guilty! That might give her back her self-respect; that might make others respect her too. But could she do it, even if she would? Could she bring herself to set foot inside that house again?

Rachel felt tremulously in her pocket; there had been more keys than one, and that which had been in her possession when she was arrested was in it still. Nobody had asked her for it; she had kept it for this; dare she use it after all? The street was still empty; it is the quietest little street in Chelsea. There would never be a better chance.

Rachel crept up the steps. If she should be seen!

She was not; but a footstep rang somewhere in the night, and on that the key was fitted and the door opened without another moment's hesitation. Rachel entered, the door shut noisily behind her, and then her own step rang in turn upon the floor. It was bare boards; and as Rachel felt her way to the electric switches, beyond the dining-room door, her fingers missed the pictures on the walls. This prepared her for what she found when the white light sprang out above her head. The house had been dismantled; not a stick in the rooms, not so much as a stair-rod on the stairs, nor a blind to the window at their head.

The furniture removed while the use of it belonged legally to her! Had they made so sure of her conviction as all that? Rachel's blood came straight from zero to the boil; this was monstrous, this was illegal and wicked. The house was hers for other two months; and there were things of hers in it, she had left everything behind her. If they had been removed, then this outrage was little short of felony, and she would invoke the law from whose clutches she herself had escaped. Rachel had expected to be terrified in the house; she was filled insted with anger and indignation.

It was as she expected; not a trunk had been left; and the removal had taken place that very week. This would account for the electric light being still intact. Rachel discovered it by picking up a crumpled newspaper, which seemed to have contained bread and cheese; it did contain a report of the first day of the trial. They might have waited till her trial was over; they should suffer for their impatience, it was their turn. So angry was Rachel that her own room wounded her with no memories of the past. It was an empty room, and nothing more; and only on her return to the lower floor did that last dread night come back to her in all its horror and all its pitifulness.

The double doors of the late professor! Rachel forgot her grudge against his widow; she pulled the outer door, and pushed the inner one, just as she had done in the small hours of that fatal morning, but this time all was darkness within. She had to put on the electric light for herself. The necessity she could not have explained, but it existed in her mind; she must see the room again. And the first thing she saw was that the window was broken still.

Rachel looked at it more closely than she had done on the morning when she had given her incriminating opinion to the police, and the longer she looked the less reason did she see to alter that opinion. The broken glass might have been placed upon the sill in order to promote the very theory which had been so gullibly adopted by the police, and the watch and chain hidden in the chimney for the same purpose. They might have hanged the man who kept them; and surely this was not the first thief who had slunk away empty-handed after the committal of a crime infinitely greater than the one contemplated.

Rachel had never wavered in these ideas, but neither had she dwelt on them to any extent, and now they came one instant only to go the next. Her husband was dead – that was once more the paramount thought – and she his widow had been acquitted on a charge of murdering him. But for the moment she was thinking only of him, and her eyes hung over the spot where she had seen him sitting dead – once without dreaming it – and soon they filled. Perhaps she was remembering all that had been good in him, perhaps all that had been evil in herself; her lips quivered, and her eyes filled. But it was hard to pity one who was at rest, hard for her with the world to face afresh that night, without a single friend. The Carringtons? Well, she would see; and now she had a very definite point upon which to consult Mr. Carrington. That helped her, and she went, quietly and unseen as she had come.

There was still a light in the ground-floor windows of the Tite Street house, strong lights and voices; it was the dining-room, for the Minchins had dined there once; and the voices did not include a feminine one that Rachel could perceive. If there were people dining with them, the ladies must have gone upstairs, and Mrs. Carrington was the woman to see Rachel for five minutes, and the one woman in England to whom she could turn. It was an opportunity not to miss – she had not the courage to let it pass – and yet it required almost as much to ring the bell. And even as she rang – but not until that moment – did Rachel recognize and admit to herself the motive which had brought her to that door. It was not to obtain the advice of a clever man; it was the sympathy of another woman that she needed that night more than anything else in all the world.

She was shown at once into the study behind the dining-room, and immediately the voices in the latter ceased. This was ominous; it was for Mrs. Carrington that Rachel had asked; and the omen was instantly fulfilled. It was Mr. Carrington who came into the room, dark, dapper, and duskily flushed with his own hospitality, but without the genial front which Rachel had liked best in him. His voice also, when he had carefully shut the door behind him, was unnaturally stiff.

"I congratulate you," he said, with a bow but nothing more; and Rachel saw there and then how it was to be; for with her at least this man had never been stiff before, having indeed offended her with his familiarity at the time when her husband and he were best friends.

"I owe it very largely to you," faltered Rachel. "How can I thank you?"

Carrington said it was not necessary.

"Then I only hope," said Rachel, on one of her impulses, "that you don't disagree with the verdict?"

"I didn't read the case," replied Carrington glibly, and with neither more nor less of the contemptuous superiority with which he would have referred to any other Old Bailey trial; but the man himself was quick to see the brutality of such a statement, and quicker yet to tone it down.

"It wasn't necessary," he added, with a touch of the early manner which she had never liked; "you see, I knew you."

The insincerity was so obvious that Rachel could scarcely bring herself to confess that she had come to ask his advice. "What was the point?" he said to that, so crisply that the only point which Rachel could think of was the fresh, raw grievance of the empty house.

"Didn't your solicitor tell you?" asked Carrington. "He came to me about it; but I suppose – "

Rachel knew well what he supposed.

"He should have told you to-night," added Carrington, "at any rate. The rent was only paid for half the term – quite right – the usual way. The permanent tenant wanted to be done with the house altogether, and that entitled her to take her things out. No, I'm afraid you have no grievance there, Mrs. Minchin."

"And pray," demanded Rachel, "where are my things?"

"Ah, your solicitor will tell you that – when you give him the chance! He very properly would not care to bother you about trifles until the case against you was satisfactorily disposed of. By the way, I hope you don't mind my cigar? We were smoking in the next room."

"I have taken you from your guests," said Rachel, miserably. "I know I ought not to have come at such an hour."

Carrington did not contradict her.

"But there seemed so much to speak about," she went desperately on. "There are the money matters and – and – "

"If you will come to my chambers," said Carrington, "I shall be delighted to go into things with you, and to advise you to the best of my ability. If you could manage to come at half-past nine on Monday morning, I would be there early and could give you twenty minutes."

He wrote down the address, and, handing it to Rachel, rang the bell. This drove her to despair; evidently it never occurred to him that she was faint with weariness and hunger, that she had nowhere to go for the night, and not the price of a decent meal, much less a bed, in her purse. And even now her pride prevented her from telling the truth; but it would not silence her supreme desire.

"Oh!" she cried; "oh, may I not speak to your wife?"

"Not to-night, if you don't mind," replied Carrington, with his bow and smile. "We can't both desert our guests."

"Only for a minute!" pleaded Rachel. "I wouldn't keep her more!"

"Not to-night," he repeated, with a broader smile, a clearer enunciation, and a decision so obviously irrevocable that Rachel said no more. But she would not see the hand that he could afford to hold out to her now; and as for going near his chambers, never, never, though she starved!

"No, I wouldn't have kept her," she sobbed in the street; "but she would have kept me! I know her! I know her! She would have had pity on me, in spite of him; but now I can never go near either of them again!"

Then where was she to go? God knew! No respectable hotel would take her in without luggage or a deposit. What was she to do?

But while she wondered her feet were carrying her once more in the old direction, and as she walked an idea came. She was very near the fatal little street at the time. She turned about, and then to the left. In a few moments she was timorously knocking at the door of a house with a card in the window.

"It's you!" cried the woman who came, almost shutting the door in Rachel's face, leaving just space enough for her own.

"You have a room to let," said Rachel, steadily.

"But not to you," said the woman, quickly; and Rachel was not surprised, the other was so pale, so strangely agitated.

"But why?" she asked. "I have been acquitted – thanks partly to your own evidence – and yet you of all women will not take me in! Do you mean to tell me that you actually think I did it still?"

Rachel fully expected an affirmative. She was prepared for that opinion now from all the world; but for once a surprise was in store for her. The pale woman shifted her eyes, then raised them doggedly, and the look in them brought a sudden glow to Rachel's heart.

"No, I don't think that, and never did," said the one independent witness for the defence. "But others do, and I am too near where it happened; it might empty my house and keep it empty."

Rachel seized her hand.

"Never mind, never mind," she whispered. "It is better, ten thousand times, that you should believe in me, that any woman should! Thank you, and God bless you, for that!"

She was turning away, when she faced about upon the steps, gazing past the woman who believed in her, along the passage beyond, an unspoken question beneath the tears in her eyes.

"He is not here," said the landlady, quickly.

"But he did get over it?"

"So we hope; but he was at death's door that morning, and for days and weeks. Now he's abroad again – I'm sure I don't know where."

Rachel said good-night, and this time the door not only shut before she had time to change her mind again, but she heard the bolts shot as she reached the pavement. The fact did not strike her. She was thinking for a moment of the innocent young foreigner who had brought matters to a crisis between her husband and herself. On the whole she was glad that he was not in England – yet there would have been one friend.

And now her own case was really desperate; it was late at night; she was famished and worn out in body and mind, nor could she see the

39

slightest prospect of a lodging for the night.

And that she would have had in the condemned cell, with food and warmth and rest, and the blessed certainty of a speedy issue out of all her afflictions.

It was a bitter irony, after all, this acquittal!

There was but one place for her now. She would perish there of cold and horror; but she might buy something to eat, and take it with her; and at least she could rest, and would be alone, in the empty house, the house of misery and murder, that was yet the one shelter that she knew of in all London.

She crept to the King's road, and returned with a few sandwiches, walking better in her eagerness to break a fast which she had only felt since excitement had given place to despair. But now it was making her faint and ill. And she hurried, weary though she was.

But in the little street itself she stood aghast. A crowd filled it; the crowd stood before the empty house of sorrow and of crime; and in a moment Rachel saw the cause.

It was her own fault. She had left the light burning in the upper room, the bedroom on the second floor.

Rachel joined the skirts of the crowd – drawn by an irresistible fascination – and listened to what was being said. All eyes were upon the lighted window of the bedroom – watching for herself, as she soon discovered – and this made her doubly safe where she stood behind the press.

"She's up there, I tell yer," said one.

"Not her! It's a ghost."

"Her 'usband's ghost, then."

"But vere's a chap 'ere wot sore 'er fice to fice in the next street; an' followed 'er and 'eard the door go; an' w'en 'e come back wiv 'is pals, vere was vat light."

"Let's 'ave 'er aht of it."

"Yuss, she ain't no right there."

"No; the condemned cell's the plice for 'er!"

"Give us a stone afore the copper comes!"

And Rachel saw the first stone flung, and heard the first glass break; and within a very few minutes there was not a whole pane left in the front of the house; but that was all the damage which Rachel herself saw done.

A hand touched her lightly on the shoulder.

"Do you still pin your faith to the man in the street?" said a voice.

And, though she had heard it for the first time that very evening, it was a voice that Rachel seemed to have known all her life.

CHAPTER VI

A Peripatetic Providence

"Do you still pin your faith to the man in the street?"

It was Mr. Steel who stood at Rachel's elbow, repeating his question word for word; but he did not repeat it in the same tone. There was an earnest note in the lowered voice, an unspoken appeal to her to admit the truth and be done with proud pretence. And indeed the pride had gone out of Rachel at sight of him; a delicious sense of safety filled her heart instead. She was as one drowning, and here was a strong swimmer come to her rescue in the nick of time. What did it matter who or what he was? She felt that he was strong to save. Yet, as the nearly drowned do struggle with their saviours, so Rachel must fence instinctively with hers.

"I never did pin my faith to him," said she.

"Yet see the risk that you are running! If he turns round – if any one of them turns round and recognizes you – listen to that!"

It was only the second window, but a third and a fourth followed like shots from the same revolver. Rachel winced.

"For God's sake, come away!" he whispered, sternly.

And Rachel did come a few yards before a flicker of her spirit called a halt.

"Why should I run away?" she demanded, in sudden tears of mortification and of weakness combined. "I am innocent – so why should I?"

"Because they don't like innocent people; and there appear to be no police in these parts; and if you fall into their hands – well, it would be better for you if you had been found guilty and were safe and sound in Newgate now!"

That was exactly what Rachel had felt herself; she took a few steps more, but still with reluctance and irresolution; and once round the nearest corner, and out of that hateful street for ever, she turned to her companion in unconcealed despair.

"But what am I to do?" she cried. "But where am I to turn?"

"Mrs. Minchin," said Steel, "can you not really trust me yet?"

He stood before her under a street lamp, handsome still, upright for all his years, strong as fate itself, and surely kinder than any fate which Rachel Minchin had yet met with in the course of her short but checkered life. And yet – and yet – she trusted and distrusted him too!

"I can and I cannot," she sighed; and even with the words one reason occurred to her. "You have followed me, you see, after all!"

"I admit it," he replied, "and without a particle of shame. My dear lady, I was not going to lose sight of you to-night!"

"And why not?"

"Because I foresaw what might happen, and may happen still! Nay, madam, it will, if you continue to let your pride sit upon your common sense. Do you hear them now? That means the police, and when they're dispersed they'll come this way to King's Road. Any moment they may be upon us. And there's a hansom dropped from heaven!"

He raised his umbrella, the bell tinkled, the two red eyes dilated and widened in the night, then with a clatter the horse was pulled up beside the curb, and Steel spread his hand before the muddy wheel.

"Be sensible," he whispered, "and jump in! In a hansom you can see where you are going; in a hansom you can speak to the driver or attract the attention of any decent person on the sidewalk. Ah! you will trust me so far at last – I thank you from my heart!"

"Where to, sir?" asked the cabman through the roof.

And Rachel listened with languid curiosity; but that was all. She had put herself in this man's hands; resistance was at an end, and a reckless indifference to her fate the new attitude of a soul as utterly overtaxed and exhausted as its tired tenement of clay.

"Brook Street," said Steel, after a moment's pause – "and double-quick for a double fare. We shall be there in a quarter of an hour," he added reassuringly as the trap-door slammed, "and you will find everything ready for you, beginning with something to eat. I, at all events, anticipated the verdict; if you don't believe me, you will when we get there, for they have been ready for you all day. Do you know Claridge's Hotel, by the way?"

"Only by name," said Rachel, wearily.

"I'm glad to hear it," pursued Mr. Steel, "for I think you will be pleased. It is not like the ordinary run of hotels. Your rooms are your castle – regular self-contained flat – and you needn't see another soul if you don't like. I am staying in the hotel myself, for example, but you shall not set eyes on me for a week unless you wish to."

"But I don't understand," began Rachel, roused a little from her apathy. She was not suffered to proceed.

"Nor are you to attempt to do so," said her companion, "until to-morrow morning. If you feel equal to it then, I shall crave an audience, and you shall hear what I have got to say. But first, let me beg of you, an adequate supper and a good night's rest!"

"One thing is certain," said Rachel, half to herself: "they can't know who I am, or they never would have taken me in. And no luggage!"

"That they are prepared for," returned Steel; "and in your rooms you will find a maid who is also prepared and equipped for your emergency. As to their not knowing who you are at the hotel, there you are right; they do not know; it would have been inexpedient to tell them."

"Then at least," said Rachel, "I ought to know who I am supposed to be."

And she smiled, for interest and curiosity were awakened within her, with the momentary effect of stimulants; but Mr. Steel sat silent at her side. The cab was tinkling up Park Lane. The great park on the left, the great houses on the right, the darkness on the one hand, the lights on the other, had all the fascination of sharp contrasts – that very fascination which was Mr. Steel's. Rachel already discovered it in his face, and divined it in his character, without admitting to herself that there was any fascination at all. Yet otherwise she would have dropped rather than have done what she was doing now. The man had cast a spell upon her; and for the present she did feel safe in his hands. But with that unmistakable sense of immediate security there mingled a subtler premonition of ultimate danger, to which Rachel had felt alive from the first. And this was the keenest stimulus of all.

What was his intention, and what his object? To draw back was to find out neither; and to say the truth, even if she had not been friendless and forlorn, Rachel would have been very sorry to draw back now.

The raw air in her face had greatly revived her; the sights and lights of the town were still new and dear to her; she had come back to the world with a vengeance, to a world of incident and interest, with an adventure ready waiting to take her out of her past self!

But it was only her companion's silence which enabled Rachel to realize her strange fortune at this stage, and she had to put her question point-blank before she obtained any answer at all.

"If you insist upon hearing all the little details to-night," said Steele, with a good-humored shrug, "well, I suppose you must hear them; but I hope you will not insist. I have had to make provisions which you may very possibly resent, but I thought it would be time enough for us to quarrel about them in the morning. To-night you need rest and sustenance, but no excitement; of that God knows you have had enough! No one will come near you but the maid of whom I spoke; no questions will be put to you; everything is arranged. But to-morrow, if you feel equal to it, you shall hear all about me, and form your own cool judgment of my behavior towards you. Meanwhile won't you trust me – implicitly – until then?"

"I do," said Rachel, "and I will – until to-morrow."

"Then there are one or two things that I can promise you," said Steel, with the heartiness of a man who has gained his point. "You will not be compromised in any sort or kind of way; your self-respect shall not suffer; nothing shall vex or trouble you, if I can help it, while you remain at this hotel. And this I guarantee – whether you like it or not – unless you tell them, not a single soul in the place shall have the faintest inkling as to who you are. Now, only keep your why and wherefore till to-morrow," he concluded cheerily, "and I can promise you almost every satisfaction. But here we are at the hotel."

He thrust his umbrella outside, pointing to a portico and courtyard on the right; and in another moment Rachel was receiving the bows of powdered footmen in crimson plush, while Steel, hat in hand, his white hair gleaming in the electric light, led the way to the lift.

Rachel's recollection of that night was ever afterwards disjointed and involved as that of any dream; but there were certain features that she never forgot. There was the beautiful suite of rooms, filled with flowers that must have cost a small fortune at that time of year, and in one of them a table tastefully laid. Rachel remembered the dazzle of silver and the glare of napery, the hot plates, the sparkling wine, the hot-house fruit, and the deep embarrassment of sitting down to all this in solitary state. Mr. Steel had but peeped in to see that all was in accordance with his orders; thereafter not even a waiter was allowed to enter, but only Rachel's attendant, to whose charge she had been committed; a gentle and assiduous creature, quiet of foot and quick of hand, who spoke seldom but in a soothing voice, and with the delicate and pretty accent of the French-Swiss.

Rachel used to wonder whether she had shocked this mannerly young woman by eating very ravenously; she remembered a nervous desire to be done with that solitary repast, and to get to bed. Yet when she was there, in the sweetest and whitest of fine linen, with a hot bottle at her feet, and a fire burning so brightly in the room that the brass bedstead seemed here and there red-hot, then the sound sleep that she sorely needed seemed further off than ever, for always she dreamt she was in prison and condemned to die, till at length she feared to close her eyes. But nothing had been forgotten; and Rachel's last memory of that eventful day, and not less eventful night, was of a mild, foreign face bending over her with a medicine-glass and a gentle word.

And the same good face and the same soft voice were waiting for her when she awoke after many hours; the fire still burned brightly, also the electric-light, though the blind was up and the window filled with a dull November sky. It was a delicious awakening, recollection was so slow to come. Rachel might have been ill for days. She experienced the peace that is left by illness of sufficient gravity. But all she ailed was a slight headache, quickly removed by an inimitable cup of tea, that fortified her against the perplexing memories which now came swarming to her mind. This morning, however, enlightenment was due, and meanwhile Rachel received a hint, though a puzzling one, from the Swiss maid, as to the new identity which had been thrust upon her for the time being in lieu of her own.

"It was very sad for madame to lose all her things," cooed the girl, as she busied herself about the room.

"It was irritating," Rachel owned, beginning to wonder how much the other knew.

"But it was better than losing your life, madame!" the girl added with a smile.

And now Rachel lay silent. Could this amiable young woman know all? In one way Rachel rather hoped it was the case; it would be something to have received so much kindness and attention, even though bought and paid for, from one of her own sex who knew all there was to know, and yet did not shrink from her. But the young woman's next words dismissed this idea.

"When so many poor people were drowned!" said she. And the mystification increased.

Presently there was a knock at the outer door, which the maid answered, returning with Mr. Steele's card.

"Is he there?" asked Rachel, hastily.

"No, madame, but one of the servants is waiting for an answer. I think there is something written on the back, madame."

Rachel read the harmless request on the back of the card; nothing could have been better calculated to turn away suspicion of one sort or another, and there was obvious design in the absence of an envelope. But Rachel was not yet in the secret, and she was determined not to wait an hour longer than she need.

"What is the time, please?"

"I will see, madame."

The girl glided out and in.

"Well?"

"A quarter to ten, madame."

"Then order my breakfast for a quarter past, and let Mr. Steele be told that I shall be delighted to see him at eleven o'clock."

CHAPTER VII

A Morning Call

"The way to conceal one's identity," observed Mrs. Steel, "is to assume another as distinctive as one's own."

This oracular utterance was confidentially delivered from the leathern chair at the writing-table, in an inner recess of Rachel's sumptuous sitting-room. The chair had been wheeled aloof from the table, on which were Steel's hat and gloves, and such a sheaf of book-stall literature as suggested his immediate departure upon no short journey, unless, indeed, the magazines and the Sunday newspapers turned out to be another offering to Mrs. Minchin, like the nosegay of hothouse flowers which she still held in her hand. Rachel herself had inadvertently taken the very easy-chair which was a further feature of the recess; in its cushioned depths she already felt at a needless disadvantage, with Mr. Steel bending over her, his strong face bearing down, as it were, upon hers, and his black eyes riddling her with penetrating glances. But to have risen now would have been to show him what she felt. So she trifled with his flowers without looking up, though her eyebrows rose a little on their own account.

"I know what you are thinking," resumed Steel; "that you had no desire to assume any new identity, or for a single moment to conceal your own, and that I have taken a great deal upon myself. That I most freely admit. And I think you will forgive me when you see the papers!"

"Is there so much about me, then?" asked Rachel, with a sigh of apprehension.

"A leading article in every one of them. But they will keep. Indeed, I would much rather you never saw them at all."

"Was that why you brought them in, Mr. Steel?"

The question was irresistible, its satire unconcealed; but Steel's disregard of it steered admirably clear of contempt.

"That was why I bought them, certainly," he admitted. "But I brought them with me for quite a different purpose, for which one would indeed have been enough. I was saying, however, that the best way to sink one's identity is to assume another, provided that the second be as distinctive as the first. We will leave for a moment the question of my officiousness in the matter, and we'll suppose, for the sake of argument, that I was authorized by you to do what in fact I have done. All last week the papers were literally full of your trial, but on Saturday there was a second sensation as well, and this morning it is hard to say which is first and which second; they both occupy so many columns. You may not know it, but the Cape liner due on Saturday was lost with scores of lives, off Finisterre, on Friday morning last."

Rachel failed to see the connection, and yet she felt vaguely that there was one, if she could but recall it; meanwhile she said nothing, but listened with as much attention as a mental search would permit.

"I heard of it first," continued Steel, "late on Friday afternoon, as I came away from the Old Bailey. Now, it was on Friday afternoon, if you recollect, that you gave evidence yourself in your own defence. When you left the witness-box, Mrs. Minchin, and even before you left it, I knew that you were saved!"

Rachel remembered the Swiss maid's remark about the loss of her clothes and the number of persons who had fared so much worse and lost their lives. But Steel's last words dismissed every thought but that of their own import. And in an instant she was trembling upright in the easy-chair.

"You believed me!" she whispered. "You believed me at the time!"

And for nothing had he earned such gratitude yet; her moist eyes saw the old-fashioned courtesy of his bow in answer, but not the subtlety of the smile that bore it company in the depths of the dark eyes: it was a smile that did not extend to the short, tight mouth.

"What is more to the point, my dear lady," he went on in words, "the jury believed you, and I saw that they did. You made a tremendous impression upon them. The lawyer against you was too humane to try very hard to remove it, and the judge too just – though your own man did his best. But I saw at once that it would never be removed. It was between you and the jury – human being to human beings – and no third legal party intervening. That was where you scored; you went straight as a die to those twelve simple hearts. And I saw what you had done – what the lawyers between them could not undo – and took immediate measures."

49

Rachel looked up with parted lips, only to shut them firmly without a word.

"And who was I to take measures on your behalf?" queried Steel, putting the question for her. "What right or excuse had I to mix myself up in your affairs? I will tell you, for this morning is not last night, and at least you have one good night's rest between you and the past. My dear Mrs. Minchin, I had absolutely no right at all; but I had the excuse which every man has who sees a woman left to stand alone against the world, and who thrusts himself, no matter how officiously, into the breach beside her. And then for a week I had seen you all day and every day, upon your trial!"

At last there something with a ring of definite insincerity, something that Rachel could take up; and she gazed upon her self-appointed champion with candid eyes.

"Do you mean to say that you never saw me before – my trouble, Mr. Steel?"

"Never in my life, my dear lady."

"Then you knew something about me or mine!"

"What one read in the newspapers – neither more nor less – upon my most solemn word – if that will satisfy you."

And it did; for if there had been palpable insincerity in his previous protestations, there was sincerity of a still more obvious order in Mr. Steel's downright assurances on these two points. He had never ever seen her before. He knew nothing whatever about her up to the period of notoriety; he had no special and no previous knowledge of his own. It might not be true, of course; but there was that in the deep-set eyes which convinced Rachel once and for all. There was a sudden light in them, a light as candid as that which happened to be shining in her own, but a not too kindly one, rather a glint of genuine resentment. It was his smooth protestations that Rachel distrusted and disliked. If she could ruffle him, she might get at the real man; and with her questions she appeared to have done so already.

"I am more than satisfied, in one way," replied Rachel, "and less in another. I rather wish you had known something about me; it would have made it more natural for you to come to my assistance. But never mind. What were these immediate measures?"

"I took these rooms; I had spoken of taking them earlier in the week."

"For me?"

"Yes, on the chance of your getting off."

"But you did not say they were for me!"

"No; and I was vague in what I had said until then. I had a daughter – a widow – whom I rather expected to arrive from abroad towards the end of the week. But I was quite vague."

"Because you thought I had no chance!"

"I had not heard your evidence. The very afternoon I did hear it, and had no longer any doubt about the issue in my own mind, I also heard of this wreck. The very thing! I waited till next morning for the list of the saved; luckily there were plenty of them; and I picked out the name of a married woman travelling alone, and therefore very possibly a widow, from the number. Then I went to the manager. The daughter whom I expected had been wrecked, but she was saved, and would arrive that night. As a matter of fact, the survivors were picked up by a passing North German Lloyd, and they did reach London on Saturday night. Meanwhile I had impressed it upon the manager to keep the matter as quiet as possible, for many excellent reasons, which I need not go into now."

"But the reason for so elaborate a pretence?"

And the keen, dark face was searched with a scrutiny worthy of itself. Steel set his mouth in another visible resolution to tell the truth.

"I thought you might not be sorry to cease being Mrs. Minchin – the Mrs. Minchin who had become so cruelly notorious through no fault of her own – if only for a day or two, or a single night. That was most easily to be effected by your arriving here minus possessions, and plus a very definite story of your own."

"You made very sure of me!" said Rachel, dryly.

"I trusted to my own powers of persuasion, and it was said you had no friends. I will confess," added Steel, "that I hoped the report was true."

"Did it follow that I could have no pride?"

"By no means; on the contrary, I knew that you were full of pride; it is, if I may venture to say so, one of your most salient characteristics. Nothing was more noticeable at your trial; nothing finer have I ever seen! But," added Steel, suppressing a burst of enthusiasm that gained by the suppression, "but, madam, I hoped and prayed that you would have the sense to put your pride in the second place for once."

"Well," said Rachel, "and so far I have done so, Heaven knows!"

"And that is something," rejoined Steel, impressively. "Even if it ends at this – even if you won't hear me out – it is something that you have had one night and one morning free from insult, discomfort, and annoyance."

Rachel felt half frightened and half indignant. Steel was standing up, looking very earnestly down upon her. And something that she had dimly divined in the very beginning – only to chide herself for the mere thought – that thing was in his face and in his voice. Rachel made a desperate attempt to change the subject, but, as will be seen, an unlucky one.

"So I am supposed to be your daughter!" she exclaimed nervously. "May I ask my new name?"

"If you like; but I am going to suggest to you a still newer name, Mrs. Minchin."

Rachel tried to laugh, though his quietly determined and serious face made it more than difficult.

"Do you mean that I am not to be your daughter any longer, Mr. Steel?"

"Not if I can help it. But it will depend upon yourself."

"And what do you want to make me now?"

"My wife!"

CHAPTER VIII

The Dove and the Serpent

Rachel was bereft of speech; and yet a certain sense of relief underlay the natural embarrassment caused by a proposal so premature and so abrupt. Nor was the deeper emotion very difficult to analyze. Here at last was a logical explanation of the whole behavior of this man; it was the first that had occurred to her, and, after all, it was the only possible one.

"I want you to be my wife," repeated Mr. Steel, with enough of respect in his tone, yet none the less with the air of a man who is accustomed to obtain what he wants.

And Rachel, looking at the wiry, well-knit, upright figure, and at the fresh, elderly, but virile face, with its sombre eyes and its snowy hair, thought once again of the ancient saw which she had quoted to herself the night before, only to dismiss it finally from her mind. This man was no fool, nor was he old. He might be eccentric, but he was eminently sane; he might be elderly, in the arbitrary matter of mere years; but an old man he was not, and never would be with those eyes.

She tried to tell him it was absurd, but before the word could come she saw that it was the last one to apply; he was so confident, so quiet, so sure of himself, if not of Rachel. At last she told him she could not think of it, he had seen nothing of her, and could not possibly care for her, even supposing that she cared for him.

"By 'caring,'" said he, "do you mean being 'in love,' as they say, and all that?"

"Naturally," said Rachel, with great ease and irony, but with a new misgiving every moment.

"And have I said I was in love with you?" inquired Mr. Steel, with a smile as indulgent as his tone. "It might, perhaps, be no more than the truth; but have I had the insolence to tell you so?"

"It is a greater insult if you are not," returned Rachel, speaking hotly and quickly, but with lowered eyes.

"What! To offer to marry a person whom one does not – as yet – pretend to love?"

Rachel vouchsafed no reply.

"Whom one only – but tremendously – admires?"

Rachel felt bound to answer him, for at least there was no insult in his tone. She raised her candid eyes, a sweet brown blush upon her face.

"Yes," she said, "I think there is absolutely no excuse for a proposal of marriage, if it is not founded upon love and nothing else!"

"Or its pretence and nothing else," amended Steel, with a bow and a smile of some severity. "That is a hard saying," he went on, resuming his chair, and wheeling it even nearer to Rachel's than it had been before; "moreover," he added, "since I have already insulted you, let me tell you that it is an exceedingly commonplace saying, into the bargain. It depends, you must admit, upon the commonplace conception of marriage; and before we go any further I should like to give you my own conception, not of the institution, but of the particular marriage which I have in view."

So he had it in view! It was not an inspiration, but already quite a prospect! Rachel made an acid little note of this; but there was no acidity in her permission to him to proceed; her turn was coming last.

"The marriage that I propose to you," continued Steel, "is simply the most convenient form of friendship of which I can think. I want to be your friend; indeed, that much I mean to be, if necessary, in spite of you. I was interested in your case, so I came up to hear your trial. I was more interested in your trial, but most interested of all in yourself. There, indeed, the word is too weak; but I will not vex your spirit with a stronger. My attraction you know; my determination you know; even the low wiles to which your pride reduced me, even my dodging and dogging, have been quite openly admitted to you on the first reasonable opportunity. All this business of the shipwrecked daughter was of course a crude device enough; but I had very little time to think, and my first care was that you should not be recognized here or elsewhere in my society. That was essential, if there was the slightest chance of your even listening to my proposition, as indeed you are doing now. Last night I told you nothing, because that's always easier than telling only a little; moreover, you were so distraught that you would possibly have gone right away without benefiting even to the slight extent of the comfortable night's rest you so badly needed; but this morning I am prepared to put it to the touch. And let me begin by saying, that if circumstances would permit me to continue the paternal imposture, that would be quite enough for me; unluckily, I am known in my own country as an old bachelor; so that I cannot suddenly produce a widowed daughter, without considerable unpleasantness for us both. What I can do, however," and Steel bent further forward, with eyes that held Rachel's in their spell; "what I can do, and will, is to go back with a lady who shall be my wife in name, my daughter in effect. We should, I trust, be the best of friends; but I will give you my word, and not only my word but my bond, that we never need be anything more."

He had spoken rapidly; the pause that followed lasted longer than this lengthy speech. And through it all they sat with eyes still locked, until he spoke again.

"You believe, at least, in the bona fides of my offer?"

And Rachel, still looking in his eyes, murmured that she did.

"You will bear in mind how essentially it differs from the ordinary offer of the kind; also, that I have never for a moment pretended to be in love with you?"

"I will."

Steel had risen as if to go; the keen scrutiny was withdrawn, a distinct spell as distinctly broken; and yet he lingered, with a smile.

"That," said he, "was a poor compliment to pay twice over! But it is human to err, and in my anxiety not to do so on the side of sentiment I own myself in danger of flying to the other extreme. Well, you know which is the common extreme in such cases; and at all events we shall avoid the usual pitfall. I am going to give you a few minutes to think it over; then, if you care to go into it further, I shall be most happy; if not, the matter is at an end."

A few minutes! Rachel felt very angry, without knowing that she was most angry with herself for not feeling angrier still. She had heard quite enough; it were weakness to listen to another word; and yet – and yet –

"Don't go," said Rachel, with some petulance; "that is quite unnecessary. Anything more extraordinary – but I owe you too much already to be your critic. Still, I do think I am entitled to go a little further into the matter, as you said, without committing myself."

"To be sure you are."

But this time he remained standing; and for once he kept those mesmeric eyes to himself. Obviously, Rachel was to have a chance.

"You spoke of your own country," she began. "Do you live abroad?"

There was the least suspicion of eagerness in the question. Rachel herself was unaware of it; not so Mr. Steel, and he sighed.

"A mere figure," he said; "what I meant was my own country-side."

"And where is that?"

"In the north," he replied vaguely. "Did you look twice at my card? Well, here is another, if you will do me that honor now. The initials J. B. stand for no very interesting names – John Buchanan. A certain interest in the Buchanan, perhaps; it comes out in the flesh, I fancy, though not on the tongue. As for the address, Normanthorpe House is the rather historic old seat of the family of that name; but they have so many vastly superior and more modern places, and the last fifty years have so ruined the surroundings, that I was able to induce the Duke to take a price for it a year or two ago. He had hardly slept a night there in his life, and I got it lock-stock-and-barrel for a song. The Northborough which, you will observe, it is 'near' – a good four miles, as a matter of fact – is the well-known centre of the Delverton iron-trade. But you may very well have spent a year in this country without having heard of it; they would be shocked at Northborough, but nowhere else."

Rachel had dropped the card into her lap; she was looking straight at Mr. John Buchanan Steel himself.

"You are very rich," she said gravely.

"I am nothing of the kind," he protested. "The Duke is rich, if you like, but I had to scrape together to pay him what would replenish his racing-stud, or stand him in a new yacht."

But Rachel was not deceived.

"I might have known you were very rich," she murmured, as much to herself as to him; and there was a strange finality in her tone, as though all was over between them; a still more strange regret, involuntary, unconscious, and yet distinct.

"Granting your hypothesis, for the sake of argument," he went on, with his simplest smile; "is it as difficult as ever for the poor rich man to get to heaven?"

Rachel spent some moments in serious thought. He was wonderfully honest with her; of his central motive alone was she uncertain, unconvinced. In all else she felt instinctively that he was telling her the truth, telling her even more than he need. His generous candor was a challenge to her own.

"It may be very small of me," she said at length, "but – somehow – if you had been comparatively poor – I should have been less – ashamed!"

And candor begot candor, as it generally will.

"Upon my word," he cried, "you make me sigh for the suburbs and six hundred a year! But you shall know the worst. I meant you to know it when I came in; then I changed my mind; but in for a penny, in for the lot!"

He caught up the magazine which he had brought in with the sheaf of newspapers, and he handed it to Rachel, open at an article quite excellently illustrated for an English magazine.

"There," he cried, "there's a long screed about the wretched place, before it came into my hands. But it's no use pretending it isn't quite the place it was. I took over the whole thing – every stick outside and in – and I've put in new drainage and the electric light."

His tone of regret was intentionally ludicrous. Had Rachel been listening, she would once more have suspected a pose. But already she was deep in the article in the two-year-old magazine, or rather in its not inartistic illustrations.

"The House from the Tennis Lawn," "In the Kitchen Garden," "The Drawing-room Door," "A Drawing-room Chimney-piece," "A Corner of the Chinese Room," "A Portion of the Grand Staircase" – of such were the titles underneath the process pictures. And (in all but their production) each of these was more beautiful than the last.

"That," observed Steel, "happens to be the very article from which I first got wind of the place, when I was looking about for one. And now," he added, "I suppose I have cut my own throat! Like the devil, I have taken you up to a high place-"

It was no word from Rachel that cut him short, but his own taste, with which she at least had very little fault to find. And Rachel was critical enough; but her experience was still unripe, and she liked his view of his possessions, without perceiving how it disarmed her own.

Presently she looked up.

"Now I see how much I should have to gain. But what would you gain?"

The question was no sooner asked than Rachel foresaw the pretty speech which was its obvious answer. Mr. Steel, however, refrained from making it.

"I am an oldish man," he said, "and – yes, there is no use in denying that I am comfortably off. I want a wife; or rather, my neighbors seem bent upon finding me one; and, if the worst has to come to the worst, I prefer to choose for myself. Matrimony, however, is about the very last state of life that I desire, and I take it to be the same with you. Therefore – to put the cart before the horse – you would suit me ideally. One's own life would be unaltered, but the Delverton mothers would cease from troubling, and at the head of my establishment there would be a lady of whom I should be most justly proud. And even in my own life I should, I hope, be the more than occasional gainer by her society; may I also add, by her sympathy, by her advice? Mrs. Minchin," cried Steel, with sudden feeling, "the conditions shall be very rigid; my lawyer shall see to that; nor shall I allow myself a loophole for any weakness or nonsense whatsoever in the future. Old fellows like myself have made fools of themselves before to-day, but you shall be safeguarded from the beginning. Let there be no talk or thought of love between us from first to last! But as for admiration, I don't mind telling you that I admire you as I never admired any woman in the world before; and I hope, in spite of that, we shall be friends."

Still the indicative mood, still not for a moment the conditional! Rachel did not fail to make another note; but now there was nothing bitter even in her thoughts. She believed in this man, and in his promises; moreover, she began to focus the one thing about him in which she disbelieved. It was his feeling towards her – nothing more and nothing else. There he was insincere; but it was a pardonable insincerity, after all.

Of his admiration she was convinced; it had been open and honest all along; but there was something deeper than admiration. He could say what he liked. The woman knew. And what could it be but love?

The woman knew; and though the tragedy of her life was so close behind her; nay, though mystery and suspicion encompassed her still, as they might until her death, the woman thrilled.

It was a thrill of excitement chiefly, but excitement was not the only element. There was the personal factor, too; there was the fascination which this man had for her, which he could exert at will, and which he was undoubtedly exerting now.

To escape from his eyes, to think but once more for herself, and by herself, Rachel rose at last, and looked from the window which lit this recess.

It was the usual November day in London; no sun; a mist, but not a fog; cabmen in capes, horses sliding on the muddy street, well-dressed women picking their way home from church – shabby women hurrying in shawls – hurrying as Rachel herself had done the night before – as she might again to-night. And whither? And whither, in all the world?

Rachel turned from the window with a shudder; she caught up the first newspaper of the sheaf upon the writing-table. Steel had moved into the body of the room; she could not even see him through the alcove. So much the better; she would discover for herself what they said.

Leading articles are easily found, and in a Sunday paper they are seldom long. Rachel was soon through the first, her blood boiling; the second she could not finish for her tears; the third dried her eyes with the fires of fierce resentment. It was not so much what they said; it was what they were obviously afraid to say. It was their circumlocution, their innuendo, their mild surprise, their perfunctory congratulations, their assumption of chivalry and their lack of its essence, that wounded and stung the subject of these effusions. As she raised her flushed face from the last of them, Mr. Steel stood before her once more, the incarnation of all grave sympathy and consideration.

"You must not think," said he, "that my proposal admits of no alternative but the miserable one of making your own way in a suspicious and uncharitable world. On the contrary, if I am not to be your nominal and legal husband, I still intend to be your actual friend. On the first point you are to be consulted, but on the second not even you shall stand in my way. Nor in that event would I attempt to rob you of the independence which you value so highly; on the other hand, I would point the way to an independence worth having. I am glad you have seen those papers, though to-morrow they may be worse. Well, you may be shocked, but, if you won't have me, the worse the better, say I! Your case was most iniquitously commented upon before ever it came for trial; there is sure to be a fresh crop of iniquities now; but I shall be much mistaken if you cannot mulct the more flagrant offenders in heavy damages for libel."

Rachel shivered at the thought. She was done with her case for ever and for ever. People could think her guilty if they liked, but that the case should breed other cases, and thus drag on and on, and, above all, that she should make money out of all that past horror, what an unbearable idea!

On second thoughts, Mr. Steel agreed.

"Then you must let me send you back to Australia." No, no, no; she could never show her face there again, or anywhere else where she was known. She must begin life afresh, that was evident.

"It was evident to me," said Steel, quietly, "though not more so than the injustice of it, from the very beginning. Hence the plans and proposals that I have put before you."

Rachel regarded him wildly; the Sunday papers had driven her to desperation, as, perhaps, it was intended that they should.

"Are you sure," she cried, "that they would not know me – up north?"

"Not from Eve," he answered airily. "I should see to that; and, besides, we should first travel, say until the summer."

"If only I *could* begin my life again!" said Rachel to herself, but aloud, in a way that made no secret of her last, most desperate inclination.

"That is exactly what I wish you to do," Steel rejoined quietly, even gently, his hand lying lightly but kindly upon her quivering shoulder. How strong his touch, how firm, how reassuring! It was her first contact with his hand.

"I wish it so much," he went on, "that I would have your past life utterly buried, even between ourselves; nay, if it were possible, even in your own mind also! I, for my part, would undertake never to ask you one solitary question about that life – on one small and only fair condition. Supposing we make a compact now?"

"Anything to bury my own past," owned Rachel; "yes, I would do anything – anything!"

"Then you must help me to bury mine, too," he said. "I was never married, but a past I have."

"I would do my best," said Rachel, "if I married you."

"You will do your best," added Steel, correcting her; "and there is my compact cut and dried. I ask you nothing; you ask me nothing; and there is to be no question of love between us, first or last. But we help each other to forget – from this day forth!"

Rachel could not speak; his eyes were upon her, black, inscrutable, arrestive of her very faculties, to say nothing of her will. She could only answer him when he had turned away and was moving towards the door.

"Where are you going?" she cried.

"To send to my solicitor," replied Steel, "as I warned him that I might. It has all to be drawn up; and there is the question of a settlement; and other questions, perhaps, which you may like to put to him yourself without delay."

CHAPTER IX

A Change of Scene

The Reverend Hugh Woodgate, Vicar of Marley-in-Delverton – a benefice for generations in the gift of the Dukes of Normanthorpe, but latterly in that of one John Buchanan Steel – was writing his sermon on a Friday afternoon just six months after the foregoing events. The month was therefore May, and, at either end of the long, low room in which Mr. Woodgate sat at work, the windows were filled with a flutter of summer curtains against a brilliant background of waving greenery. But a fire burned in one of the two fireplaces in the old-fashioned funnel of a room, for a treacherous east wind skimmed the sunlit earth outside, and whistled and sang through one window as the birds did through the other.

Mr. Woodgate was a tall, broad-shouldered, mild-eyed man, with a blot of whisker under each ear, and the cleanest of clerical collars encompassing his throat. It was a kindly face that pored over the unpretentious periods, as they grew by degrees upon the blue-lined paper, in the peculiar but not uncommon hand which is the hall-mark of a certain sort of education upon a certain order of mind. The present specimen was perhaps more methodical than most; therein it was characteristic of the man. From May to September, Mr. Woodgate never failed to finish his sermon on the Friday, that on the Saturday he might be free to play cricket with his men and lads. He was a poor preacher and no cricketer at all; but in both branches he did his best, with the simple zeal and the unconscious sincerity which redeemed not a few of his deficiencies.

So intent was the vicar upon his task, so engrossed in the expression of that which had already been expressed many a million times, that he did not hear wheels in his drive, on the side where the wind sang loudest; he heard nothing until the door opened, and a girl in her twenties, trim, slim, and brown with health, came hurriedly in.

"I'm sorry to disturb you, dear, but who do you think is here?"

Hugh Woodgate turned round in his chair, and his honest ox-eyes filled with open admiration of the wife who was so many years younger than himself, and who had seen in him Heaven knew what! He never could look at her without that look first; and only now, after some years of marriage, was he beginning sometimes to do so without this thought next. But he had not the gift of expression, even in the perpetual matter of his devotion; and perhaps its perpetuity owed something to that very want; at least there was none of the verbal evaporation which comes of too much lovers' talk.

"Who is it?" he asked.

"Mrs. Venables!"

Woodgate groaned. Was he obliged to appear? His jaw fell, and his wife's eyes sparkled.

"Dear, I wouldn't even have let you know she was here – you shouldn't have been interrupted for a single instant – if Mrs. Venables wasn't clamoring to see you. And really I begin to clamor too; for she is full of some mysterious news, which she won't tell me till you are there to hear it also. Be an angel, for five minutes!"

Woodgate wiped his pen in his deliberate way.

"Probably one of the girls is engaged," said he; "if so I hope it's Sybil."

"No, Sybil is here too; she doesn't look a bit engaged, but rather bored, as though she had heard the story several times already, whatever it may be. They have certainly paid several calls. Now you look quite nice, so in you come."

Mrs. Venables, a stout but comely lady, with a bright brown eye, and a face full of character and ability, opened fire upon the vicar as soon as they had shaken hands, while her daughter looked wistfully at the nearest books.

"He is married!" cried Mrs. Venables, beginning in the middle like a modern novelist.

"Indeed?" returned the matter-of-fact clergyman, with equal directness – "and who is he?"

"Your neighbor and your patron – Mr. Steel!"

"Married?" repeated Mrs. Woodgate, with tremendous emphasis. "Mr. Steel?"

"This is news!" declared her husband, as though he had expected none worthy of the name. And they both demanded further particulars, at which Mrs. Venables shook her expensive bonnet with great relish.

"Do you know Mr. Steel so well – so much better than we do – and can you ask for particulars about anything he ever does? His marriage," continued Mrs. Venables, "like everything else about him, is 'wrop in mystery,' as one of those vulgar creatures says in Dickens, but I really forget which. It was never announced in the *Times*; for that I can vouch myself. Was ever anything more like him, or less like anybody else? To disappear for six months, and then turn up with a wife!"

"But has he turned up?" cried the vicar's young wife, forgetting for a moment a certain preoccupation caused by the arrival of the tea-tray, and by a rapid resignation to the thickness of the bread and butter and the distressing absence of such hot things as would have been in readiness if Mrs. Venables had been expected for a single moment. It showed the youth of Morna Woodgate that she should harbor a wish to compete with the wealthiest woman in the neighborhood, even in the matter of afternoon tea, and her breeding that no such thought was legible in her clear-cut open-air face.

"I have heard nothing about it," said the vicar, in a tone indicative of much honest doubt in the matter.

"Nor is it the case, to my knowledge," rejoined Mrs. Venables; "but from all we hear it may become the case any moment. They were married in Italy last autumn – so he says – and are on their way home at this minute."

"If he says so," observed the vicar, with mild humor, "it is probably true. He ought to know."

"And who was she?" his young wife asked with immense interest, the cups having gone round, and the bread and butter been accepted in spite of its proportions.

"My dear Mrs. Woodgate," said Mrs. Venables, cordially, "you may well ask! Who was she, indeed! It was the first question I asked my own informant, who, by the way, was your friend, Mr. Langholm; but he knew no more than the man in the moon."

"And who told Mr. Langholm, of all people?" pursued Morna Woodgate. "It is not often that we get news of the real world from him!"

"Birds of a feather," remarked her caller: "it was Mr. Steel himself who wrote to your other eccentric friend, and told him neither more nor less than I have told you. He was married in Italy last autumn; not even the town – not even the month – let alone the lady's name – if, indeed – "

And Mrs. Venables concluded with a sufficiently eloquent hiatus.

"I imagine she is a lady," said the vicar to his tea.

"You are so charitable, dear Mr. Woodgate!"

"I hope I am," he said simply. "In this case I see no reason to be anything else."

"What – when you know really nothing about Mr. Steel himself?"

And the bright brown eyes of Mrs. Venables grew smaller and harder as they pinned Hugh Woodgate to his chair.

"I beg your pardon," said that downright person; "I know a great deal about Mr. Steel. He has done an immense amount for the parish; there are our new schoolrooms to speak for themselves. There are very few who would do the half of what Mr. Steel has done for us during the short time he has been at Normanthorpe."

"That may be," said the lady, with the ample smile of conscious condescension; "for he has certainly not omitted to let his light shine before men. But that is not telling us who or what he was before he came here, or how he made his money."

Then Hugh Woodgate gave the half boyish, half bashful laugh with which he was wont to preface his most candid sayings.

"And I don't think it's any business of ours," he said.

Morna went a trifle browner than she naturally was; her husband said so little that what he did say was often almost painfully to the point; and now Mrs. Venables had turned from him to her, with a smile which the young wife disliked, for it called attention to the vicar's discourtesy while it appealed to herself for prettier manners and better sense. It was a moment requiring some little tact, but Mrs. Woodgate was just equal to it.

"Hugh, how rude of you!" she exclaimed, with only the suspicion of a smile. "You forget that it's your duty to be friendly with everybody; there's no such obligation on anybody else."

"I should be friendly with Mr. Steel," said Hugh, "duty or no duty, after what he has done for the parish."

And his pleasant honest face and smile did away with the necessity for a set apology.

"I must say," added his wife to her visitor, "that it's the same with me, you know."

There was a pause.

"Then you intend to call upon her?" said Mrs. Venables, coming with directness to an obviously premeditated point.

"I do – I must – it is so different with us," said the vicar's young wife, with her pretty brown blush.

"Certainly," added the vicar himself, with dogmatic emphasis.

Mrs. Venables did not look at him, but she looked the harder at Morna instead.

"Well," said she, "I suppose you are right. In your position – yes – your position is quite different!" And the sudden, half accidental turn of her sentence put Mrs. Venables on good terms with herself once more; and so she rose all smiles and velvet. "No, not even half a cup; but it was really quite delicious; and I hope you'll come and see me soon, and tell me all about her. At his age!" she whispered as she went. "At sixty-five – if he's a day!"

A stranger would have imagined that this lady had quite decided not to call upon the newcomer herself; even Mrs. Woodgate was uncertain of her neighbor's intention as the latter's wheels ground the Vicarage drive once more, and she and her husband were left alone.

"It will depend upon the county," said she; "and Mrs. Venables is not the county pure and simple, she's half Northborough still, and she'll take her cue from the Invernesses and the Uniackes. But I do believe she's been round the whole country-side, getting people to say they won't call; as if it mattered to a man like Mr. Steel, or any woman he is likely to have chosen. Still, it is mysterious, isn't it? But what business of ours, as you say? Only, dear, you needn't have said it quite so pointedly. Of course I'll call as soon as I can in decency; she may let me be of use to her. Oh, bother Mrs. Venables! If she doesn't call, no doubt many others won't; you must remember that he has never entertained as yet. Oh, what a dance they could give! And did you hear what she said about his age? He is sixty-five, now!"

The vicar laughed. It was his habit to let his young wife rattle on when they were alone, and even lay down the law for him to her heart's content; but, though fifteen years her senior, and never a vivacious man himself, there was much in their life that he saw in the same light as she did, though never quite so soon.

"Sixty-five!" he suddenly repeated, with a fresh chuckle; "and last year, when Sybil was thought to be in the running – poor Sybil, how well she took it! – last year her mother told me she knew for a fact he was not a day more than five-and-forty! Poor Steel, too! He has done for them both in that quarter, I am afraid. And now," added Hugh, in his matter-of-fact way, as though they had been discussing theology all this time, "I must go back to my sermon if I am to get it done to-night."

CHAPTER X

A Slight Discrepancy

Mrs. Woodgate paid the promised call a few days later, walking briskly by herself along the woodland path that made it no distance from Marley Vicarage to Normanthorpe House, and cutting a very attractive figure among the shimmering lights and shadows of the trees. She was rather tall, and very straight, with the pale brown skin and the dark brown eye, which, more especially when associated with hair as light as Morna Woodgate's, go to make up one of the most charming and distinctive types of English womanhood. Morna, moreover, took a healthy interest in her own appearance, and had not only the good taste to dress well, but the good sense not to dress too well. Her new coat and skirt had just come home, and, fawn-colored like herself, they fitted and suited her to equal perfection. Morna thought that she might even go to church in the coat and skirt, now and again during the summer, and she had a brown straw hat with fine feathers of the lighter shade which she made peculiarly her own; but this she had discarded as too grand for an informal call, for Hugh had been summoned to a sick-bed at the last moment, and might be detained too late to follow. But the Steels had been back two days, and Morna could not wait another hour.

She was certainly consumed with curiosity; but that was not the only feeling which Mrs. Woodgate entertained towards the lady who was to be a nearer neighbor of her own sex and class than any she could count as yet. On the class question Morna had no misgivings; nevertheless, she was prepared for a surprise. Both she and her husband had seen a good deal of Mr. Steel. Morna had perhaps seen the best of him, since she was at once young and charming, and not even an unwilling and personally innocent candidate for his hand, like honest Sybil Venables. Yet Morna herself was not more attracted than repelled by the inscrutable personality of this rich man dropped from the clouds, who had never a word to say about his former life, never an anecdote to tell, never an adventure to record, and of whom even Mrs. Venables had not the courage to ask questions. What sort of woman would such a man marry, and what sort of woman would marry such a man? Morna asked herself the one question after the other, almost as often as she set her right foot in front of her left; but she was not merely inquisitive in the matter, she had a secret and instinctive compassion for the woman who had done this thing.

"She will not have a soul to call her own, poor thing!" thought Morna, as indignantly as though the imaginary evil was one of the worst that could befall; for the vicar's wife had her little weaknesses, not by any means regarded as such by herself; and this was one of the last things that could have been said about her, or that she would have cared to hear.

The woodland path led at last into the long avenue, and there was Normanthorpe House at the end of the vista; an Italian palace transplanted into the north of England, radiantly white between the green trees and blue sky, with golden cupola burning in the sun; perhaps the best specimen extant to mark a passing fashion in Georgian architecture, but as ill-suited to the Delverton district as an umbrella-tent to the North Pole. A cool grotto on a really hot day, the house was an ice-pit on any other; or so Mrs. Woodgate fancied, fresh from the cosey Vicarage, and warm from her rapid walk, as she stepped into another temperature, across polished marble that struck a chill through the soles of her natty brown shoes, and so into the lofty drawing-room with pilasters and elaborate architraves to the doors. What a place for a sane man to build in bleak old Delverton, even before there was any Northborough to blacken and foul the north-east wind on its way from the sea! What a place for a sane man to buy; and yet, in its cool white smoothness, its glaring individuality, its alien air – how like the buyer!

Though it was May, and warm enough for the month and place, Morna got up when the footman had left her, and thrust one brown shoe after the other as near as she could to the wood fire that glimmered underneath the great, ornate, marble mantelpiece. Then she sat down again, and wondered what to say; for Morna was at once above and below the conversational average of her kind. Soon she was framing a self-conscious apology for premature intrusion – Mrs. Steel was so long in coming. But at last there was a rustle in the conservatory, and a slender figure in a big hat stood for an instant on the threshold.

That was Morna's first impression of the new mistress of Normanthorpe, and it was never erased from her mind; a slender silhouette in an enormous hat, the light all behind her, the pilastered doorway for a frame, a gay background of hothouse flowers, and in the figure itself a nervous hesitancy which struck an immediate chord of sympathy in Morna. She also was shy; the touch of imperfect nature was mutually discernible and discerned; and the two were kin from the meeting of their hands.

Morna began her apology, nevertheless; but Rachel cut it very short.

"My dear Mrs. Woodgate, I think it is so kind of you!" she exclaimed, her low voice full of the frankest gratitude; and Morna was surprised at the time; it was as though she were the rich man's wife, and Mrs. Steel the vicar's.

They sat a little, talking of the time of year; and it was some minutes before Morna really saw her new neighbor's face, what with her great hat and the position of the chair which Mrs. Steel selected. And for these few minutes, after that first frank speech, the greater constraint was on the part of the hostess; then all at once she seemed to throw it off, rising impulsively, as though the great high room, with the Italian tiles and the garish gilt furniture, struck the same chill to her as to Morna before her.

"Come round the garden," said Rachel, quickly. "I am delighted with the garden, and I think it's really warmer than the house."

Delightful it certainly was, or rather they, for the Normanthorpe gardens were never spoken of in the singular number by those familiar with their fame; they had been reconstructed and enlarged by a dead duke with a fad for botany, and kept up by successors who could not endure the cold, uncomfortable house. It was said to have been a similar taste in Mr. Steel which had first attracted him to the place; but as he never confirmed or contradicted anything that was said of him, and would only smile when a rumor reached his ears, there was no real foundation for the report.

The ducal botanist had left behind him the rarest collection of plants and trees, and a tradition in scientific gardening which had not been allowed to die; it was neglected Normanthorpe that had loaded the tables and replenished the greenhouses of seats more favored by the family; and all this was the more wonderful as a triumph of art over some natural disadvantages in the way of soil and climate. The Normanthorpe roses, famous throughout the north of England, were as yet barely budding in the kindless wind; the blaze of early bulbs was over; but there were the curious alien trees, and the ornamental waters haunted by outlandish wildfowl, bred there on the same principle of acclimatization.

"I expect you know the way quite well," said Rachel, as they followed a winding path over a bank of rhododendrons near the lake; "to me every stroll is still a voyage of exploration, and I shall be rather sorry when I begin to know exactly what I am going to see next. Now, I have never been this way before, and have no idea what is coming, so you must tell me, if you know. What a funny scent! I seem to know it, too. Why, what have they got here?"

On the further side of the bank of rhododendrons the path had descended into a sheltered hollow, screened altogether from the colder winds, and, even in this temperate month of May, a very trap for the afternoon sun. And in this hollow was a clump of attenuated trees, with drooping leaves of a lacklustre hue, and a white bark peeling from the trunk; a pungent aroma, more medicinal than sylvan, hung rather heavily over the sequestered spot.

Rachel stood a moment with wide nostrils and round eyes; the look hardly lasted longer, and she said no more, but she was aware that Morna had made some answer to her question.

"What did you say?" inquired Rachel, turning politely to her visitor.

"I said they were blue gums from Australia."

Rachel made no immediate comment; secretive she might have to be, but to a deliberate pretence she would not stoop. So she did not even say, "Indeed!" but merely, after a pause, "You are something of a botanist yourself, then, Mrs. Woodgate?" For they had been talking of the gardens and of their history as they walked.

"I?" laughed Morna. "I only wish I was; but I happen to remember Mr. Steel telling me that one day when we were here last summer."

Rachel opened her eyes again, and her lips with them; but instead of speaking she went to the nearest gum-tree and picked a spray of the lacklustre leaves. "I like the smell of them," she said, as they went on; and the little incident left no impression upon Morna's mind.

Yet presently she perceived that Mrs. Steel had some color after all – at the moment Rachel happened to be smelling her gum-leaves – and that she was altogether prettier than Morna had fancied hitherto. The fact was that it was her first good look at Rachel, who had kept her back to the light indoors, and had literally led the way along the narrow paths, while her large hat had supplied a perpetual shadow of its own. It was a pathetic habit, which had become second nature with Rachel during the last six months; but now, for once, it was forgotten, and her face raised unguardedly to the sun, which painted it in its true and sweet colors, to Morna's surprise and real delight. The vicar's wife was one of those healthy-hearted young women who are the first to admire their own sex; she had very many friends among women, for whom marriage had not damped an enthusiasm which she hid from no one but themselves; and she was to be sufficiently enthusiastic about the thin but perfect oval of Rachel's face, the soft, sweet hazel of her eyes, the impetuous upper lip and the brave lower one, as she saw them now for an instant in the afternoon sun.

Moreover, she was already interested in Rachel on her own account, and not only as the wife of the mysterious Mr. Steel. There was an undoubted air of mystery about her also; but that might only be derived from him, and with all her reserve she could not conceal a sweet and sympathetic self from one as like her in that essential as they were different in all others. Not that the reserve was all on one side. Morna Woodgate had her own secrets too. One of them, however, was extracted during their stroll.

"May I make a personal remark?" asked Rachel, who had been admiring the pale brown face of Morna in her turn, as they came slowly back to the house across the lawns.

"You frighten me," said Morna, laughing. "But let me hear the worst."

"It's the ribbon on your hat," went on Rachel. "What pretty colors! Are they your husband's school or college?"

"No," said Morna, blushing as she laughed again. "No, they're my own college colors."

Rachel stood still on the grass.

"Have you really been at college?" said she; but her tone was so obviously one of envy that Morna, who was delightfully sensitive about her learning, did not even think of the short answer which she sometimes returned to the astonished queries of the intellectually vulgar, but admitted the impeachment with another laugh.

"Now, don't say you wouldn't have thought it of me," she added, "and don't say you would!"

"I am far too jealous to say anything at all," Rachel answered with a flattering stare. "And do you mean to tell me that you took a degree?"

"Of sorts," admitted Morna, whose spoken English was by no means undefiled. But it turned out to have been a mathematical degree; and when, under sympathetic pressure, Morna vouchsafed particulars, even Rachel knew enough to appreciate the honors which the vicar's wife had won. What was more difficult to understand was how so young a woman of such distinguished attainments could be content to hide her light under the bushel of a country vicarage; and Rachel could not resist some expression of her wonderment on that point.

"Did you do nothing with it all," she asked, "before you married?"

"No," said Morna; "you see, I got engaged in the middle of it, and the week after the lists came out we were married."

"What a career to have given up!"

"I would give it up again," said Morna, with a warmer blush; and Rachel was left with a deeper envy.

"I am afraid we shall have nothing in common," sighed Mrs. Steel, as they neared the house. "I have no education worthy the name."

Morna waxed all but indignant at the implication; she had a morbid horror of being considered a "blue-stocking," which she revealed with much girlish naïveté and unconscious simplicity of sentiment and praise. She was not so narrow as all that; she had had enough of learning; she had forgotten all that she had learnt; any dolt could be crammed to pass examinations. On the contrary, she was quite sure they would have heaps in common; for example, she was longing for some one to bicycle with; her husband seldom had the time, and he did not care for her to go quite alone in the country roads.

"But I don't bicycle," said Mrs. Steel, shaking her head rather sadly.

"Ah, I forgot! People who ride and drive never do." And it was Morna's turn to sigh.

"No, I should like it; but I have never tried."

"I'll teach you!" cried Morna at once. "What fun it will be!"

"I should enjoy it, I know. But – "

The sentence was abandoned – as was often the case in the subsequent intercourse between Rachel Steel and Morna Woodgate. From the beginning, Rachel was apt to be more off her guard with Morna than with any one whom she had met during the last six months; and, from the beginning, she was continually remembering and stopping herself in a manner that would have irritated Morna in anybody else. But then – yet again, from the beginning – these two were natural and immediate friends.

"You must learn," urged Morna, when she had waited some time for the sentence which had but begun. "There are people who scorn it – or pretend to – but I am sure you are not one. It may not be the finest form of exercise, but wait till you fly down these hills with your feet on the rests! And then you are so independent; no horses to consider, no coachman to consult; only your own bones and your own self! The independence alone – "

"May be the very thing for you, Mrs. Woodgate, but it wouldn't do for my wife!"

Mr. Steel had stolen a silent march upon them, on the soft, smooth grass; and now he was taking off his straw hat to Morna, and smiling with all urbanity as he held out his hand. But Morna had seen how his wife started at the sound of his voice, and her greeting was a little cool.

"I meant the bicycling," he was quick enough to add; "not the independence, of course!"

But there was something sinister in his smile, something quite sinister and yet not unkindly, that vexed and puzzled Morna during the remainder of her visit, which she cut somewhat short on perceiving that Mr. Steel had apparently no intention of leaving them to their own devices after tea. Morna, however, would have been still more puzzled, and her spirit not less vexed, had she heard the first words between the newly married couple after she had gone.

"What's that you have got?" asked Steel, as they turned back up the drive, after seeing Morna to her woodland path. Rachel was still carrying her spray of gum-leaves; he must have noticed it before, but this was the first sign that he had done so. She said at once what it was, and why she had pulled it from the tree.

"It took me back to Victoria; and, you know, I was born there."

Steel looked narrowly at his wife, a hard gleam in his inscrutable eyes, and yet a lurking sympathy too, nor was there anything but the latter in the tone and tenor of his reply.

"I don't forget," he said, "and I think I can understand; but neither must you forget that I offered to take you back there. So that's a sprig of gum-tree, is it?"

Rachel gave him a sudden glance, which for once he missed, being absorbed in a curious examination of the leaves.

"Did you never see one before?" she asked.

"A gum-tree?" said Steel, without looking up, as he sniffed and scrutinized. "Never in all my life – to my knowledge!"

CHAPTER XI

Another New Friend

The country folk did call upon the Steels, as indeed, they could scarcely fail to do, having called on him already as a bachelor the year before. Nor were the Uniackes and the Invernesses the bell-wethers of the flock. Those august families had returned to London for the season; but the taboo half-suggested by Mrs. Venables had begun and ended in her own mind. Indeed, that potent and diplomatic dame, who was the undoubted leader of society within a four-mile radius of Northborough town hall, was the first to recognize the mistake that she had made, and to behave as though she had never made it. Quite early in June, the Steels were bidden to a dinner-party in their honor at Upthorpe Hall.

"Mrs. Venables!" cried Rachel, in dismay. "Is that the gushing woman with the quiet daughters who called last Thursday?"

"That is the lady," said Steel, a gleam of humor in his grim eyes. He never expressed an opinion to his wife about any one of their neighbors, but when she let fall an impression of her own, he would look at her in this way, as though it was the very one that he had formed for himself a year ago.

"But need we go?" asked Rachel, with open apprehension.

"I think so," he said. "Why not?"

"A dinner-party, of all things! There is no cover at the dinner-table; you can't even wear a hat; you must sit there in a glare for hours and hours!" And Rachel shuddered. "Oh, don't let us go!" she urged; but her tone was neither pathetic nor despairing; though free from the faintest accent of affection, it was, nevertheless, the tone of a woman who has not always been denied.

"I am afraid we must go," he said firmly, but not unkindly. "You see, it is in our honor – as I happen to know; for Venables gave me a hint when I met him in the town the other day. He will take you in himself."

"And what is he like?"

"Fond of his dinner; he won't worry you," said Steel, reassuringly. "Nor need you really bother your head about all that any more. Nobody has recognized you yet; nobody is in the least likely to do so down here. Don't you see how delightfully provincial they are? There's a local lawyer, a pillar of all the virtues, who has misappropriated his own daughter-in-law's marriage portion and fled the country with the principal boy in their last pantomime; there are a lot of smart young fellows who are making a sporting thousand every other day out of iron warrants; the district's looking up after thirty years' bad times; and this is the sort of thing it's talking about. These are its heroes and its villains. All you hear from London is what the last man spent when he was up, and where he dined; and from all I can gather, the Tichborne trial made less impression down here than that of a Delverton parson who got into trouble about the same time."

"They must have heard of my trial," said Rachel, in a low voice. They were walking in the grounds after breakfast, but she looked round before speaking at all.

"They would glance at it," said Steel, with a shrug; "an occasional schoolboy might read it through; but even if you were guilty, and were here on view, you would command much less attention than the local malefactor in an infinitely smaller way. I am sorry I put it quite like that," added Steel, as Rachel winced, "but I feel convinced about it, and only wish I could convince you."

And he did so, more or less; but the fear of recognition had increased in Rachel, instead of abating, as time went on. It had increased especially since the rapid ripening of her acquaintance with Morna Woodgate into the intimacy which already subsisted between the two young wives. Rachel had told her husband that she would not have Morna know for anything; and he had appeared in his own dark way to sympathize with a solicitude which was more actual than necessary; but that was perhaps because he approved of Mrs. Woodgate on his own account. And so rare was that approval, as a positive and known quantity, yet so marked in this case, that he usually contrived to share Morna's society with his wife.

"You shall not monopolize Mrs. Woodgate," he would say with all urbanity as he joined them when least expected. "I was first in the field, you know!"

And in the field he would remain. There were no commands, no wishes to obey in the matter, no embargo upon the comings and goings between the two new friends. But Mr. Steel invariably appeared upon the scene as well. The good vicar attributed it to the elderly bridegroom's jealous infatuation for his beautiful young bride; but Morna knew better from the first.

"Are you going?" asked Rachel, eagerly, when she and Morna met again; indeed, she had gone expressly to the Vicarage to ask the question; and not until she had seen the Woodgates' invitation could Steel himself induce her to answer theirs.

The Woodgates were going. Morna was already in alternate fits of despair and of ideas about her dress.

"I wish I might dress you!" said Rachel, knowing her well enough already to say that. "I have wardrobes full of them, and yet my husband insists upon taking me up to London to get something fit to wear!"

"But not necessarily on your back!" cried Steel himself, appearing at that moment in his usual way, warm, breathless, but only playfully put out. "My dear Mrs. Woodgate, I must have a special wire between your house and ours. One thing, however, I always know where to find her! Did she tell you we go by the 12:55 from Northborough?"

It was something to wear upon her neck – a diamond necklet of superb stones, gradually swelling to one of the first water at the throat; and Rachel duly wore it at the dinner-party, with a rich gown of bridal white, whose dazzling purity had perhaps the effect of cancelling the bride's own pallor. But she was very pale. It was her first appearance at a gathering of the kind, not only there in Delverton, but anywhere at all since her second marriage. And the invitation had been of the correct, most ample length; it had had time to wind itself about Rachel's nerves.

Mr. Venables, who of course did take her in, by no means belied her husband's description of him; he was a rotund man with a high complexion, and his bulging eye was on the menu before his soft body had sunk into his chair. His conversation proved limited, but strictly to the point; he told Rachel what to eat, and once or twice what to avoid; lavished impersonal praise upon one dish, impartial criticisms upon another, and only spoke between the courses. It was a large dinner-party; twenty-two sat down. Rachel was at last driven to glancing at the other twenty.

To the man on her left she had not been introduced, but he had offered one or two civil observations while Mr. Venables was better engaged; and, after the second, Rachel had chanced to catch sight of the card upon which his name had been inscribed. He was, it seemed, a Mr. Langholm; and all at once Rachel leant back and looked at him. He was a loose-limbed, round-shouldered man, with a fine open countenance, and a great disorderly moustache; his hair might have been shorter, and his dress-coat shone where it caught the light. Rachel put the screw upon her courage.

"These cards," she said, with a glimpse of her own colonial self, "are very handy when one hasn't been introduced. Your name is not very common, is it?"

"Not very," he answered, "spelt like that."

"Yes it's spelt the same way as the Mr. Langholm who writes."

"It is."

"Then are you any relation?"

"I am the man himself," said Langholm, with quite a hearty laugh, accompanied by a flush of pleasurable embarrassment. He was not a particularly popular writer, and this did not happen to him every day.

"I hoped you were," said Rachel, as she helped herself to the first *entrée*.

"Then you haven't read my books," he chuckled, "and you never must."

"But I have," protested Rachel, quite flushed in her turn by the small excitement. "I read heaps of them in Tauchnitz when we were abroad. But I had no idea that I should ever meet you in the flesh!"

"Really?" he said. "Then that's funnier still; but I suppose Mr. Steel didn't want to frighten you. We saw quite a lot of each other last year; he wrote to me from Florence before you came over; and I should have paid my respects long ago, but I have been up in town, and only just come back."

The flush had died out of Rachel's face. Her husband told her nothing – nothing! In her indignation she was tempted to say so to the stranger; she had to think a moment what to say instead. A falsehood of any sort was always a peculiar difficulty to Rachel, a constitutional aversion, and it cost her an effort to remark at last that it was very stupid of her, she had quite forgotten, but now she remembered – of course! And with that she turned to her host, who was offering an observation across his empty plate.

"Strange thing, Mrs. Steel, but you can't get the meat in the country that you can in town. Those fillets, now – I wish you could taste 'em at my club; but we give our chef a thousand a year, and he drives up every day in his brougham."

The novels of Charles Langholm were chiefly remarkable for their intricate plots, and for the hope of better things that breathed through the cheap sensation of the best of them. But it was a hope that had been deferred a good many years. His manner was better than his matter; indeed, an incongruous polish was said by the literary to prevent Langholm from being a first favorite either with the great public or the little critics. As a maker of plots, however, he still had humble points; and Rachel assured him that she had burnt her candle all night in order to solve one of his ingenious mysteries.

"What!" he cried; "you call yourself a lady, and you don't look at the end before you reach it?"

"Not when it's a good book."

"Well, you have pitched on about the best of a bad lot; and it's a satisfaction to know you didn't cut the knot it took some months to tie."

Rachel was greatly interested. She had never before met a literary man; had no idea how the trick was done; and she asked many of those ingenuous questions which seldom really displease the average gentleman of this type. When not expatiating upon the heroine whom the exigencies of "serial rights" demanded in his books, Charles Langholm, the talker and the man, was an unmuzzled misogynist. But nobody would have suspected it from his answers to Rachel's questions, or from any portion of their animated conversation. Certainly the aquiline lady whom Langholm had taken in, and to whom he was only attentive by remorseful fits and penitential starts, had not that satisfaction; for her right-hand neighbor did not speak to her at all. There was thus one close and critical follower of a conversation which without warning took the one dramatic turn for which Rachel was forever on her guard; only this once, in an hour of unexpected entertainment, was she not.

"How do I get my plots?" said Langholm. "Sometimes out of my head, as they say in the nursery; occasionally from real life; more often a blend of the two combined. You don't often get a present from the newspaper that you can lift into a magazine more or less as it stands. Facts are stubborn things; they won't serialize. But now and then there's a case. There was one a little time ago. Oh, there was a great case not long since, if we had but the man to handle it, without spoiling it, in English fiction!"

"And what was that?"

"The Minchin case!"

And he looked straight at her, as one only looks at one's neighbor at table when one is saying or hearing something out of the common; he turned half round, and he looked in Rachel's face with the smile of an artist with a masterpiece in his eye. It was an inevitable moment, come at last when least expected; instinct, however, had prepared Rachel, just one moment before; and after all she could stare coldly on his enthusiasm, without a start or a tremor to betray the pose.

"Yes?" she said, her fine eyebrows raised a little. "And do you really think that would make a book?"

It was characteristic of Rachel that she did not for a moment – even that unlooked-for moment – pretend to be unfamiliar with the case.

"Don't you?" he asked.

"I haven't thought about it," said Rachel, looking pensively at the flowers. "But surely it was a very sordid case?"

"The case!" he cried. "Yes, sordid as you like; but I don't mean the case at all."

"Then what do you mean, Mr. Langholm?"

"Her after life," he whispered; "the psychology of that woman, and her subsequent adventures! She disappeared into thin air immediately after the trial. I suppose you knew that?"

"I did hear it."

Rachel moistened her lips with champagne.

"Well, I should take her from that moment," said Langholm. "I should

81

start her story there."

"And should you make her guilty or not guilty?"

"Ah!" said Langholm, as though that would require consideration; unluckily, he paused to consider on the spot.

"Who are you talking about?" inquired Mr. Venables, who had caught Rachel's last words.

"Mrs. Minchin," she told him steadily.

"Guilty!" cried Mr. Venables, with great energy. "Guilty, and I'd have gone to see her hanged myself!"

And Mr. Venables beamed upon Rachel as though proud of the sentiment, while the diamonds rose and fell upon her white neck, where he would have had the rope.

"A greater scandal," he went on, both to Rachel and to the lady on his other side (who interrupted Mr. Venables to express devout agreement), "a greater scandal and miscarriage of justice I have never known. Guilty? Of course she was guilty; and I only wish we could try her again and hang her yet! Now don't pretend you sympathize with a woman like that," he said to Rachel, with a look like a nudge; "you haven't been married long enough; and for Heaven's sake don't refuse that bird! It's the best that can be got this time of year, though that's not saying much; but wait till the grouse season, Mrs. Steel! I have a moor here in the dales, keep a cellar full of them, and eat 'em as they drop off the string."

"Well?" said Rachel, turning to Langholm when her host became a busy man once more.

"I should make her guilty," said the novelist; "and she would marry a man who believed in her innocence, and he wouldn't care two pins when she told him the truth in the last chapter, and they would live happily ever afterwards. Nobody would touch the serial rights. But that would be a book!"

"Then do you think she really was guilty?"

And Rachel waited while he shrugged, her heart beating for no good reason that she knew, except that she rather liked Mr. Langholm, and did not wish to cease liking him on the spot. But it was to him that the answer was big with fate; and he trifled and dallied with the issue of the moment, little dreaming what a mark it was to leave upon his life, while the paradox beloved of the literary took shape on his tongue.

"What does it matter what she was? What do the facts matter, Mrs. Steel, when one has an idea like that for fiction? Fiction is truer than fact!"

"But you haven't answered my question."

Rachel meant to have that answer.

"Oh, well, as a matter of fact, I read the case pretty closely, and I was thankful the jury brought in an acquittal. It required a little imagination, but the truth always does. It is no treason to our host to whisper that he has none. I remember having quite a heated argument with him at the time. Oh, dear, no; she was no more guilty than you or I; but it would be a thousand times more artistic if she were; and I should make her so, by Jove!"

Rachel finished heir dinner in great tranquillity after this; but there was a flush upon her face which had not been there before, and Langholm received an astonishing smile when the ladies rose. He had been making tardy atonement for his neglect of the aquiline lady, but Rachel had the last word with him.

"You will come and see us, won't you?" she said. "I shall want to hear how the plot works out."

"I am afraid it's one I can't afford to use," he said, "unless I stick to foolish fact and make her innocent."

And she left him with a wry face, her own glowing again.

"You looked simply great – especially towards the end," whispered Morna Woodgate in the drawing-room, for she alone knew how nervous Rachel had been about what was indeed her social debut in Delverton.

The aquiline lady also had a word to say. Her eyes were like brown beads, and her nose very long, which gave her indeed a hawk-like appearance, somewhat unusual in a woman; but her gravity was rather that of the owl.

"You talked a great deal to Mr. Langholm," said she, sounding her rebuke rather cleverly in the key of mere statement of fact. "Have you read his books, Mrs. Steel?"

"Some of them," said Rachel; "haven't you?"

"Oh, no, I never read novels, unless it be George Eliot, or in these days Mrs. Humphrey Ward. It's such waste of time when there are Browning, Ruskin, and Carlyle to read and read again. I know I shouldn't like Mr. Langholm's; I am sure they are dreadfully uncultured and sensational."

"But I like sensation," Rachel said. "I like to be taken out of myself."

"So you suggested he should write a novel about Mrs. Minchin!"

"No, I didn't suggest it," said Rachel, hurriedly; but the beady brown eyes were upon her, and she felt herself reddening horribly as she spoke.

"You seemed to know all about her," said the aquiline lady. "I'm not in the habit of reading such cases. But I must really look this one up."

CHAPTER XII

Episode of the Invisible Visitor

That was something like a summer, as the saying is, and for once they could say it even on the bleak northern spurs of the Delverton Hills. There were days upon days when that minor chain looked blue and noble as the mountains of Alsace and hackneyed song, seen with an envious eye from the grimy outskirts of Northborough, and when from the hills themselves the only blot upon the fair English landscape was the pall of smoke that always overhung the town. On such days Normanthorpe House justified its existence in the north of England instead of in southern Italy; the marble hall, so chill to the tread at the end of May, was the one really cool spot in the district by the beginning of July; and nowhere could a more delightful afternoon be spent by those who cared to avail themselves of a general invitation.

The Steels had not as yet committed themselves to formal hospitality of the somewhat showy character that obtained in the neighborhood, but they kept open house for all who liked to come, and whom they themselves liked well enough to ask in the first instance. And here (as in some other matters) this curious pair discovered a reflex identity of taste, rare enough in the happiest of conventional couples, but a gratuitous irony in the makers of a merely nominal marriage. Their mutual feelings towards each other were a quantity unknown to either; but about a third person they were equally outspoken and unanimous. Thus they had fewer disagreements than many a loving couple, and perhaps more points of insignificant contact, while all the time there was not even the pretence of love between them. Their lives made a chasm bridged by threads.

This was not seen by more than two of their acquaintance. Morna Woodgate had both the observation and the opportunities to see a little how the land lay between them. Charles Langholm had the experience and the imagination to guess a good deal. But it was little enough that Morna saw, and Langholm's guesses were as wide of the mark as only the guesses of an imaginative man can be. As for all the rest – honest Hugh Woodgate, the Venables girls, and their friends the young men in the various works, who saw the old-fashioned courtesy with which Steel always treated his wife, and the grace and charm of her consideration for him – they were every one receiving a liberal object lesson in matrimony, as some of them even realized at the time.

"I wish I could learn to treat my wife as Steel does his," sighed the good vicar, once when he had been inattentive at the table, and Morna had rebuked him in fun. "That would be my ideal – if I wasn't too old to learn!"

"Then thank goodness you are," rejoined his wife. "Let me catch you dancing in front of me to open the doors, Hugh, and I shall keep my eye on you as I've never kept it yet!"

But Rachel herself did not dislike these little graces, partly because they were not put on to impress an audience, but were an incident of their private life as well; and partly because they stimulated a study to which she had only given herself since their return to England and their establishment at Normanthorpe House. This was her study of the man who was still calmly studying her; she was returning the compliment at last.

And of his character she formed by degrees some remote conception; he was Steel by name and steel by nature, as the least observant might discern, and the least witty remark; a grim inscrutability was his dominant note; he was darkly alert, mysteriously vigilant, a measurer of words, a governor of glances; and yet, with all his self-mastery and mastery of others, there were human traits that showed themselves from time to time as the months wore on. Rachel did not recognize among these that studious consideration which she could still appreciate; it seemed rather part of a preconceived method of treating his wife, and the wary eye gleamed through it all. But it has been mentioned that Rachel at one time had a voice, of which high hopes had been formed by inexperienced judges. It was only at Normanthorpe that her second husband became aware of her possession, one afternoon when she fancied that she had the house to herself. So two could play at the game of consistent concealment! He could not complain; it was in the bond, and he never said a word. But he stood outside the window till she was done, for Rachel saw him in a mirror, and for many an afternoon to come he would hover outside the same window at the same time.

Why had he married her? Did he care for her, or did he not? What could be the object of that extraordinary step? Rachel was as far from hitting upon a feasible solution of these mysteries as she was from penetrating the deeper one of his own past life. Sometimes she put the like questions to herself; but they were more easily answered. She had been in desperate straits, in reckless despair; even if her second marriage had turned out no better than her first, she could not have been worse off than she was on the night of her acquittal; but she had been very well off ever since. Then there had been the incentive of adventure, the fascination of that very mystery which was a mystery still. And then – yes! – there had been the compelling will of a nature infinitely stronger than her own or any other that she had ever known.

Did she regret this second marriage, this second leap in the dark? No, she could not honestly pretend that she did; yet it had its sufficiently sinister side, its occasional admixture of sheer horror. But this was only when the mysteries which encompassed her happened to prey upon nerves unstrung by some outwardly exciting cause; it was then she would have given back all that he had ever given her to pierce the veil of her husband's past. Here, however, the impulse was more subtle; it was not the mere consuming curiosity which one in Rachel's position was bound to feel; it was rather a longing to be convinced that that veil hid nothing which should make her shudder to live under the same roof with this man.

Of one thing she was quite confident; wherever her husband had spent or misspent his life (if any part of so successful a whole could really have been misspent), it was not in England. He was un-English in a hundred superficial ways – in none that cut deep. With all his essential cynicism, there was the breadth and tolerance of a travelled man. Cosmopolitan on the other hand, he could not be called; he had proved himself too poor a linguist in every country that they had visited. It was only now, in their home life, that Rachel received hints of the truth, and it filled her with vague alarms, for that seemed to her to be the last thing he need have kept to himself.

One day she saw him ride a fractious horse, not because he was fond of riding, but because nobody in the stables could cope with this animal. Steel tamed it in ten minutes. But a groom remarked upon the shortness of his stirrups, in Rachel's hearing, and on the word a flash of memory lit up her brain. All at once she remembered the incident of the gum-leaves, soon after their arrival; he had told Morna what they were, yet to his wife he had pretended not to know. If he also was an Australian, why on earth should that fact, of all facts, be concealed from her? Nor had it merely been concealed; it was a point upon which Rachel had been deliberately misled, and the only one she could recall.

She was still brooding over it when a fresh incident occurred, which served not only to confirm her suspicions in this regard, but to deepen and intensify the vague horror with which her husband's presence sometimes inspired her.

Mr. Steel was an exceptionally early riser. It was his boast that he never went to sleep a second time; and one of his nearest approaches to a confidence was the remark that he owed something to that habit. Now Rachel, who was a bad sleeper, kept quite a different set of hours, and was seldom seen outside her own rooms before the forenoon. One magnificent morning, however, she was tempted to dress and make the best of the day which she had watched breaking shade by shade. The lawns were gray with dew; the birds were singing as they never sing twice in one summer's day. Rachel thought that for once she would like to be up and out before the sun was overpowering. And she proceeded to fulfil her wish.

All had been familiar from the window; all was unfamiliar on the landing and the stairs. No one had been down; the blinds were all drawn; a clock ticked like a sledge-hammer in the hall. Rachel ran downstairs like a mouse, and almost into the arms of her husband, whom she met coming out of the dining-room with a loaded tray. Another would have dropped it; with Steel there was not so much as a rattle of the things, but his color changed, and Rachel had not yet had such a look as he gave her with his pursed mouth and his flashing eyes.

"What does this mean?" he demanded, in the tone of distant thunder, with little less than lightning in his glance.

"I think that's for me to ask," laughed Rachel, standing up to him with a nerve that surprised herself. "I didn't know that you began so early!"

A decanter and a glass were among the things upon the tray.

"And I didn't know it of you," he retorted. "Why are you up?"

Rachel told him the simple truth in simple fashion. His tone of voice did not hurt her; there was no opposite extreme of tenderness to call to mind for the contrast which inflicts the wound. On the other hand, there was a certain satisfaction in having for once ruffled that smooth mien and smoother tongue; it was one of her rare glimpses of the real man, but as usual it was a glimpse and nothing more.

"I must apologize," said Steel, with an artificiality which was seldom so transparent; "my only excuse is that you startled me out of my temper and my manners. And I was upset to begin with. I have a poor fellow in rather a bad way in the boathouse."

"Not one of the gardeners, I hope?" queried Rachel; but her kind anxiety subsided in a moment, for his dark eyes were measuring her, his dark mind meditating a lie; and now she knew him well enough to read him thus far in his turn.

"No," replied Steel, deciding visibly against the lie; "no, not one of our men, or anybody else belonging to these parts; but some unlucky tramp, whom I imagine some of our neighbors would have given into custody forthwith. I found him asleep on the lawn; of course he had no business upon the premises; but he's so far gone that I'm taking him something to pull him together before I turn him off."

"I should have said," remarked Rachel, thoughtfully, "that tea or coffee would have been better for him than spirits."

Steel smiled indulgently across the tray.

"Most ladies would say the same," he replied, "but very few men."

"And why didn't you bring him into the house," pursued Rachel, looking her husband very candidly in the face, "instead of taking him all that way to the lake, and giving yourself so much more trouble than was necessary?"

The smile broadened upon Steel's thin lips, perhaps because it had entirely vanished from his glittering eyes.

"That," said he, "is a question you would scarcely ask if you had seen the poor creature for yourself. I don't intend you to see him; he is a rather saddening spectacle, and one of a type for which one can do absolutely nothing permanent. And now, if you are quite satisfied, I shall proceed, with your permission, to get rid of him in my own way."

It was seldom indeed that Steel descended to a display of sarcasm at his wife's expense, though few people who came much in contact with him escaped an occasional flick from a tongue that could be as bitter as it was habitually smooth. His last words were therefore as remarkable as his first; both were exceptions to a rule; and though Rachel moved away without replying, feeling that there was indeed no more to be said, she could not but dwell upon the matter in her mind. Satisfied she certainly was not; and yet there was so much mystery between them, so many instinctive reservations upon either side, that very little circumstance of the kind could not carry an ulterior significance, but many must be due to mere force of habit.

Rachel hated the condition of mutual secretiveness upon which she had married this man; it was antagonistic to her whole nature; she longed to repudiate it, and to abolish all secrets between them. But there her pride stepped in and closed her lips; and the intolerable thought that she would value her husband's confidence more than he would value hers, that she felt drawn to him despite every sinister attribute, would bring humiliation and self-loathing in its train. It was the truth, however, or, at all events, part of the truth.

Yet a more unfair arrangement Rachel had been unable to conceive, ever since the fatally reckless moment in which she had acquiesced in this one. The worst that could be known about her was known to her husband before her marriage; she had nothing else to hide; all concealment of the past, as between themselves, was upon his side. But matters were coming to a crisis in this respect; and, when Rachel deemed it done with, this incident of the tramp was only just begun.

It seemed that the servants knew of it, and that it was not Steel who had originally discovered the sleeping intruder, but an under-gardener, who, seeing his master also up and about, had prudently inquired what was to be done with the man before meddling with him.

"And the master said, 'leave him to me,'" declared Rachel's maid, who was her informant on the point, as she combed out her mistress's beautiful brown hair, before the late breakfast which did away with luncheon when there were no visitors at Normanthorpe.

"And did he do so?" inquired Rachel, looking with interest into her own eyes in the glass. "Did he leave him to your master?"

"He did that!" replied her maid, a simple Yorkshire wench, whom Rachel herself had chosen in preference to the smart town type. "Catch any on 'em not doin what master tells them!"

"Then did John see what happened?"

"No, m'm – because master sent him to see if the chap'd come in at t' lodge gates, or where, and when he got back he was gone, blanket an' all, an' master with him."

"Blanket and all!" repeated Rachel. "Do you mean to say he had the impudence to bring a blanket with him?"

"And slept in it!" cried her excited little maid. "John says he found him tucked up in a corner of the lawn, out of the wind, behind some o' them shrubs, sound asleep, and lapped round and round in his blue banket from head to heel."

Rachel saw her own face change in the glass; but she only asked one more question, and that with a smile.

"Did John say it was a blue blanket, Harris, or did your own imagination supply the color?"

"He said it, m'm; faded blue."

"And pray when did you see John to hear all this?" demanded Rachel, suddenly remembering her responsibility as mistress of this young daughter of the soil.

"Deary me, m'm," responded the ingenuous Harris, "I didn't see him, not more than any of the others; he just comed to t' window of t' servants' hall, as we were having our breakfasts, and he told us all at once. He was that full of it, was John!"

Rachel asked no more questions; but she was not altogether sorry that the matter had already become one of common gossip throughout the house. Meanwhile she made no allusion to it at breakfast, but her observation had been quickened by the events of the morning, and thus it was that she noticed and recognized the narrow blue book which was too long for her husband's breast-pocket, and would show itself as he stooped over his coffee. It was his check-book, and Rachel had not seen it since their travels.

That afternoon a not infrequent visitor arrived on his bicycle, to which was tied a bouquet of glorious roses instead of a lamp; this was Charles Langholm, the novelist, who had come to live in Delverton, over two hundred miles from his life-long haunts and the literary market-place, chiefly because upon a happy-go-lucky tour through the district he had chanced upon what he never tired of calling "the ideal rose-covered cottage of my dreams," though also for other reasons unknown in Yorkshire. His flat was abandoned before quarter-day, his effects transplanted at considerable cost, and ever since Langholm had been a bigoted countryman, who could not spend a couple of days in town without making himself offensive on the subject at his club, where he was nevertheless discreetly vague as to the exact locality of his rural paradise. Even at the club, however, it was admitted that his work had improved almost as much as his appearance; and he put it all down to the roses in which he lived embowered for so many months of the year. Such was their profusion that you could have filled a clothes-basket without missing one, and Langholm never visited rich or poor without a little offering out of his abundance.

"They may be coals to Newcastle," he would say to the Woodgates or the Steels, "but none of your Tyneside collieries are a patch on mine."

Like most victims of the artistic temperament, the literary Langholm was a creature of moods; but the very fact of a voluntary visit from him was sufficient guarantee of the humor in which he came, and this afternoon he was at his best. He had indeed been writing all day, and for many days past, and was filled with the curious exhilaration which accompanies an output too rapid and too continuous to permit a running sense of the defects. He was a ship with a fair wind, which he valued the more for the belts of calms and the adverse weather through which he had passed and must inevitably pass again; for the moment he was a happy man, though one with no illusion as to the present product of his teeming pen.

"It is nonsense," he said to Rachel, in answer to a question from that new and sympathetic friend, "but it is not such nonsense as to seem nothing else when one's in the act of perpetrating it, and what more can one want? It had to be done by the tenth of August, and by Jove it will be! A few weeks ago I didn't think it possible; but the summer has thawed my ink."

"Are you sure it isn't Mrs. Steel?" asked one of the Venables girls, who had also ridden over on their bicycles. "I heard you had a tremendously literary conversation when you dined with us."

"We had, indeed!" said Langholm, with enthusiasm. "And Mrs. Steel gave me one of the best ideas I ever had in my life; that's another reason why I'm racing through this rubbish – to take it in hand."

It was Sybil to whom he was speaking, but at this point Rachel plunged into the conversation with the sister, Vera, which required an effort, since the elder Miss Venables was a young lady who had cultivated languor as a sign of breeding and sophistication. Rachel, however, made the effort with such a will that the talk became general in a moment.

"I don't know how anybody writes books," was the elder young lady's solitary contribution; her tone added that she did not want to know.

"Nor I," echoed Sybil, "especially in a place like this, where nothing ever happens. If I wanted to write a novel, I should go to Spain – or Siberia – or the Rocky Mountains – where things do happen, according to all accounts."

"Young lady," returned the novelist, a twinkle in his eye, "I had exactly the same notion when I first began, and I remember what a much older hand said to me when I told him I was going down to Cornwall for romantic background. 'Young man,' said he, 'have you placed a romance in your mother's backyard yet?' I had not, but I did so at once instead of going to Cornwall, and sounder advice I never had in my life. Material, like charity, begins at home; nor need you suppose that nothing ever happens down here. That is the universal idea of the native about his or her own heath, but I can assure you it isn't the case at all. Only just now, on my way here, I saw a scene and a character that might have been lifted bodily out of Bret Harte."

Sybil Venables clamored for particulars, while her sister resigned herself to further weariness of the flesh. Rachel put down her cup and leant forward with curiously expectant eyes. They were sitting in the cool, square hall, with doors shut or open upon every hand, and the gilded gallery overhead. Statuettes and ferns, all reflected in the highly polished marble floor, added a theatrical touch which was not out of keeping with a somewhat ornate interior.

"It was the character," continued Langholm, "who was making the scene; and a stranger creature I have never seen on English earth. He wore what I believe they call a Crimean shirt, and a hat like a stage cowboy; and he informed all passers that he was knocking down his check!"

"What?" cried Rachel and Sybil in one breath, but in curiously different tones.

"Knocking down his check," repeated Langholm. "It's what they do in the far west or the bush or somewhere – but I rather fancy it's the bush – when they get arrears of wages in a lump in one check."

"And where did you see all this?" inquired Rachel, whose voice was very quiet, but her hazel eyes alight with a deeper interest than the story warranted.

"At the Packhorse on the York Road. I came that way round for the sake of the surface and the exercise."

"And did you see the check?"

"No, I only stopped for a moment, to find out what the excitement was about; but the fellow I can see now. You never set eyes on such a pirate – gloriously drunk and bearded to the belt. I didn't stop, because he was lacing into everybody with a cushion, and the local loafers seemed to like it."

"What a joke!" cried Sybil Venables.

"There is no accounting for taste," remarked her sapient sister.

"And he was belaboring them with a cushion, did you say?" added Rachel, with the slightest emphasis upon the noun.

"Well, it looked like one to me," replied Langholm, "but, on second thoughts, it was more like a bolster in shape; and now I know what it was! It has just dawned on me. It looked like a bolster done up in a blanket; but it was the swag that the tramps carry in Australia, with all their earthly goods rolled up in their bedding; and the fellow was an Australian swagsman, that's what he was!"

"Swagman," corrected Rachel, instinctively. "And pray what color was the blanket?" she made haste to add.

"Faded blue."

And, again from sheer force of instinct, Rachel gave a nod.

"Were you ever out there, Mrs. Steel?" inquired Langholm, carelessly. "I never was, but the sort of thing has been done to death in books, and I only wonder I didn't recognize it at once. Well, it was the last type one thought to meet with in broad daylight on an English country road!"

Had Langholm realized that he had put a question which he had no business to put? Had he convicted himself of a direct though unpremeditated attempt to probe the mystery of his hostess's antecedents, and were his subsequent observations designed to unsay that question in effect? If so, there was no such delicacy in the elder Miss Venables, who became quite animated at the sudden change in Rachel's face, and at her own perception of the cause.

"Have you been to Australia, Mrs. Steel?" repeated Vera, looking Rachel full in the eyes; and she added slyly, "I believe you have!"

There was a moment's pause, and then a crisp step rang upon the marble, as Mr. Steel emerged from his study.

"Australia, my dear Miss Venables," said he, "is the one country that neither my wife nor I have ever visited in our lives, and the last one that either of us has the least curiosity to see."

And he took his seat among them with a smile.

CHAPTER XIII

The Australian Room

It was that discomfort to man, that cruelty to beast, that outrage by unnatural Nature upon all her children – a bitter summer's day. The wind was in the east; great swollen clouds wallowed across the sky, now without a drop, now breaking into capricious showers of stinging rain; and a very occasional burst of sunlight served only to emphasize the evil by reminding one of the season it really was, or should have been, even if it did not entice one to the wetting which was the sure reward of a walk abroad. The Delverton air was strong and bracing enough, but the patron wind of the district bit to the bone through garments never intended for winter wear.

On such a day there could be few more undesirable abodes than Normanthorpe House, with its marble floors, its high ceilings, and its general scheme of Italian coolness and discomfort. It was a Tuesday, when Mr. Steel usually amused himself by going on 'Change in Northborough and lunching there at the Delverton Club. Rachel was thus not only physically chilled and depressed, but thrown upon her own society at its worst; and she missed that of her husband more than she was aware.

Once she had been a bright and energetic person with plenty of resources within herself; now she had singularly few. She was distraught and uneasy in her mind, could settle less and less to her singing or a book, and was the victim of an increasing restlessness of mind and limb. Others did not see it; she had self-control; but repression was no cure. And for all this there were reasons enough; but the fear of identification by the neighbors as the notorious Mrs. Minchin was no longer one of them.

No; it was her own life, root and branch, that had grown into the upas-tree which was poisoning existence for Rachel Steel. She was being punished for her second marriage as she had been punished for her first, only more deservedly, and with more subtle stripes. Each day brought a dozen tokens of the anomalous position which she had accepted in the madness of an hour of utter recklessness and desperation. Rachel was not mistress in her own house, nor did she feel for a moment that it was her own house at all. Everything was done for her; a skilled housekeeper settled the smallest details; and that these were perfect alike in arrangement and execution, that the said housekeeper was a woman of irreproachable tact and capability, and that she herself had never an excuse for concrete complaint, formed a growing though intangible grievance in Rachel's mind. She had not felt it at first. She had changed in these summer months. She wanted to be more like other wives. There was Morna Woodgate, with the work cut out for every hour of her full and happy days; but Morna had not made an anomalous marriage, Morna had married for love.

And to-day there was not even Morna to come and see her, or for her to go and see, for Tuesday afternoon was not one of the few upon which the vicar's wife had no settled duty or occupation in the parish. Rachel so envied her the way in which she helped her husband in his work; she had tried to help also, in a desultory way; but it is one thing to do a thing because it is a duty, and another thing to do it for something to do, as Rachel soon found out. Besides, Hugh Woodgate was not her husband. Rachel had the right feeling to abandon those half-hearted attempts at personal recreation in the guise of good works, and the courage to give Morna her reasons; but she almost regretted it this afternoon.

She had explored for the twentieth time that strange treasury known as the Chinese Room, a state apartment filled with loot brought home from the Flowery Land by a naval scion of the house of Normanthorpe, and somewhat cynically included in the sale. The idols only leered in Rachel's face, and the cabinets of grotesque design were unprovided with any key to their history of former uses. In sheer desperation Rachel betook herself to her husband's study; it was the first time she had crossed that threshold in his absence, but within were the books, and a book she must have.

These also had been purchased with the house. With few exceptions, they were ancient books in battered calf, which Steel had stigmatized as "musty trash" once when Rachel had asked him if she might take one. She had not made that request again; indeed, it was seldom enough that she had set foot inside the spacious room which the old books lined, and in which the master of the house disliked being disturbed. Yet it was anything but trash which she now discovered upon the dusty shelves.

There was *Tom Jones* in four volumes and the *Spectator* in eight, *Gil Blas* and the works of Swift, all with the long "s," and backs like polished oak; in the lower shelves were Hogarth and Gillray in rare folios; at every level and on either hand were books worth taking out.

But this was almost all that Rachel did; she took them out and put them in again, for that was her unsettled mood. She spent some minutes over the Swifts, but not sufficiently attracted to march off with them. The quaint, obsolete type of the various volumes attracted her more as a curiosity than as readable print; the coarse satires of the early masters of caricature and cartoon did not attract her at all. Rachel's upbringing had deprived her of the traditions, the superstitions, and the shibboleths which are at once a strength and a weakness of the ordinary English education; if, however, she was too much inclined to take a world's masterpiece exactly as she found it, her taste, such as it was, at all events was her own.

She had naturally an open mind, but it was not open now; it was full and running over with the mysteries and the perplexities of her own environment. Books would not take her out of herself; in them she could not hope to find a key to any one of the problems within problems which beset and tortured her. So she ran her hand along the dusty books, little dreaming that the key was there all the time; so in the end, and quite by chance, but for the fact that she was dipping into so many, she took out the right book, and started backward with it in her hand.

The book was *The Faerie Queene*, and Rachel had extracted it in a Gothic spirit, because she had once heard that very few living persons had read it from end to end; since she could not become interested in anything, she might as well be thoroughly bored. But she never opened the volume, for in the dark slit which it left something shone like a little new moon. Rachel put in her hand, and felt a small brass handle; to turn and pull it was the work of her hand without a guiding thought; but when tiers of books swung towards her with the opening door which they hid, it was not in human nature to shut that door again without so much as peeping in.

Rachel first peeped, then stepped, into a secret chamber as disappointing at the first glance as such a place could possibly be. It was deep in dust, and filled with packing-cases not half unpacked, a lumber-room and nothing more. The door swung to with a click behind her as Rachel stood in the midst of this uninteresting litter, and instinctively she turned round. That instant she stood rooted to the ground, her eyes staring, her chin fallen, a dreadful fear in every feature of her face.

It was not that her second husband had followed and discovered her; it was the face of her first husband that looked upon Rachel Steel, his bold eyes staring into hers, through the broken glass of a fly-blown picture-frame behind the door.

The portrait was not hanging from the wall, but resting against it on the floor. It was a photographic enlargement in colors, and the tinted eyes looked up at Rachel with all the bold assurance that she remembered so keenly in the perished flesh. She had not an instant's doubt about those eyes; they spoke in a way that made her shiver; and yet the photograph was that of a much younger man than she had married. It was Alexander Minchin with mutton-chop whiskers, his hair parted in the middle, and the kind of pin in the kind of tie which had been practically obsolete for years; it was none the less indubitably and indisputably Alexander Minchin.

And indeed that fact alone was enough to shake Rachel's nerves; her discovery had all the shock of an unwelcome encounter with the living. But it was the gradual appreciation of the true significance of her discovery that redoubled Rachel's qualms even as she was beginning to get the better of them. So they had been friends, her first husband and her second! Rachel stooped and looked hard at the enlargement, and there sure enough was the photographer's imprint. Yes, they had been friends in Australia, that country which John Buchanan Steel elaborately and repeatedly pretended never to have visited in all his travels!

Rachel could have smiled as she drew herself up with this point settled in her mind for ever; why, the room reeked of Australia! These cases had never been properly unpacked, they were overflowing with memorials of the life which she herself knew so well. Here a sheaf of boomerangs were peeping out; there was an old gray wide-awake, with a blue-silk fly-veil coiled above the brim; that was an Australian saddle; and those glass cases contained samples of merino wool. So it was in Australia as a squatter that Steel had made his fortune! But why suppress a fact so free from all discredit? These were just the relics of a bush life which a departing colonist might care to bring home with him to the old country. Then why cast them into a secret lumber-room whose very existence was unknown to the old Australian's Australian wife?

Rachel felt her brain reeling; and yet she was thankful for the light which had been vouchsafed to her at last. It was but a lantern flash through the darkness, which seemed the more opaque for that one thin beam of light; but it was something, a beginning, a clew. For the rest she was going straight to the man who had kept her so long in such unnecessary ignorance.

Why had he not told her about Australia, at all events? What conceivable harm could that have done? It would have been the strongest possible bond between them. But Rachel went further as she thought more. Why not have told her frankly that he had known Alexander Minchin years before she did herself? It could have made no difference after Alexander Minchin's death; then why had be kept the fact so jealously to himself? And the dead man's painted eyes answered "Why?" with the bold and mocking stare his wife could not forget, a stare which at that moment assumed a new and sinister significance in her sight.

Rachel looked upward through the window, which was barred, and almost totally eclipsed by shrubs; but a clout of sky was just visible under the architrave. It was a very gray sky; gray also was Rachel's face in the sudden grip of horror and surmise. Then a ragged edge of cloud caught golden fire, a glimmer found its way into the dust and dirt of the secret chamber, and Rachel relaxed with a slight smile but an exceedingly decided shake of the head. Thereafter she escaped incontinently, but successfully, as she had entered; closed the hidden door behind her, and restored *The Faerie Queene* very carefully to its place. Rachel no longer proposed to join the select band of those who have read that epic through.

CHAPTER XIV

Battle Royal

She went to her own rooms to think and to decide; and what she first thought and then decided was sensible enough. She was thankful she had not been caught like Fatima in the forbidden room; not that she lacked the courage to meet the consequences of her acts, but it would have put her in the wrong and at a disadvantage at the first crash of battle. And a battle royal Rachel quite expected; nor had she the faintest intention of disguising what she had done; but it was her husband who was to be taken aback, for a change.

The Steels dined alone, as usual, or as much alone as a man and his wife with a butler and two footmen are permitted to be at their meals. Steel was at his best after these jaunts of his to Northborough and the club. He would come home with the latest news from that centre of the universe, the latest gossip which had gone the rounds on 'Change and at lunch, the newest stories of Mr. Venables and his friends, which were invariably reproduced for Rachel's benefit with that slight but unmistakable local accent of which these gentry were themselves all unconscious. Steel had a wicked wit, and Rachel as a rule a sufficiently appreciative smile, but this was to-night either lacking altogether or of an unconvincing character. Rachel could never pretend, and her first spontaneous remark was when her glass filled up with froth.

"Champagne!" said she, for they seldom drank it.

"It has been such a wretched day," explained Steel, "that I ordered it medicinally. I am afraid it must have been perishing here, as it was in the town. This is to restore your circulation."

"My circulation is all right," answered Rachel, too honest even to smile upon the man with whom she was going to war. "I felt cold all the morning, but I have been warm enough since the afternoon."

And that was very true, for excitement had made her blood run hot in every vein; nor had Rachel often been more handsome, or less lovely, than she was to-night, with her firm lip and her brooding eye.

"There was another reason for the champagne," resumed her husband, very frankly for him, when at last they had the drawing-room to themselves. "I am in disgrace with you, I believe, and I want to hear from you what I have done."

"It is what you have not done," returned Rachel, as she stood imperiously before the lighted fire; and her bosom rose and fell, white as the ornate mantelpiece of Carrara marble which gleamed behind her.

"And what, may I ask, is my latest sin of omission?"

Rachel rushed to the point with a passionate directness that did her no discredit.

"Why have you pretended all these months that you never were in Australia in your life? Why did you never tell me that you knew Alexander Minchin out there?"

And she held her breath against the worst that he could do, being well prepared for him to lose first his color and then the temper which he had never lost since she had known him; to fly into a fury, to curse her up hill and down dale – in a word, to behave as her first husband had done more than once, but this one never. What Rachel did not anticipate was a smile that cloaked not a single particle of surprise, and the little cocksure bow that accompanied the smile.

"So you have found it out," said Steel, and his smile only ended as he sipped his coffee; even then there was no end to it in his eyes.

"This afternoon," said Rachel, disconcerted but not undone.

"By poking your nose into places which you would not think of approaching in my presence?"

"By the merest accident in the world!"

And Rachel described the accident, truth flashing from her eyes; in an instant her husband's face changed, the smile went out, but it was no frown that came in its stead.

"I beg your pardon, Rachel," said he, earnestly. "I suppose," he added, "that a man may call his wife by her Christian name for once in a way? I did so, however, without thinking, and because I really do most humbly beg your pardon for an injustice which I have done you for some hours in my own mind. I came home between three and four, and I heard you were in my study. You were not, but that book was out; and then, of course, I knew where you were. My hand was on the knob, but I drew it back. I wondered if you would have the pluck to do the tackling! And I apologize again," Steel concluded, "for I knew you quite well enough to have also known that at least there was no question about your courage."

"Then," said Rachel, impulsively, after having made up her mind to ignore these compliments, "then I think you might at least be candid with me!"

"And am I not?" he cried. "Have I denied that the portrait you saw is indeed the portrait of Alexander Minchin? And yet how easy that would have been! It was taken long before you knew him; he must have altered considerably after that. Or I might have known him under another name. But no, I tell you honestly that your first husband was a very dear friend of mine, more years ago than I care to reckon. Did you hear me?" he added, with one of his sudden changes of tone and manner. "A very dear friend, I said, for that he undoubtedly was; but was I going to ask you to marry a very dear friend of the man who deteriorated so terribly, and who treated you so ill?"

Delivered in the most natural manner imaginable, with the quiet confidence of which this man was full, and followed by a smile of conscious yet not unkindly triumph, this argument, like most that fell from his lips upon her ears, was invested with a value out of all proportion to its real worth; and Steel clinched it with one of those homely saws which are not disdained by makers of speeches the wide world over.

"Could you really think," he added, with one of his rarest and most winning smiles, "that I should be such a fool as to invite you to step out of the frying-pan into the fire?"

Rachel felt for a moment that she would like to say it was exactly what she had done; but even in that moment she perceived that such a statement would have been very far from the truth. And her nature was large enough to refrain from the momentary gratification of a bitter repartee. But he was too clever for her; that she did feel, whatever else he might be; and her only chance was to return to the plain questions with which she had started, demanding answers as plain. Rachel led up to them, however, with one or two of which she already knew the answer, thus preparing for her spring in quite the Old Bailey manner, which she had mastered subconsciously at her trial, and which for once was to profit a prisoner at the bar.

"Yet you don't any longer deny that you have been to Australia?"

"It is useless. I lived there for years."

"And you admit that you knew Alexander quite well out there?"

"Most intimately, in the Riverina, some fifteen or twenty years ago; he was on my station as almost everything a gentleman could be, up to overseer; and by that time he was half a son to me, and half a younger brother."

"But no relation, as a matter of fact?"

"None whatever, but my very familiar friend, as I have already told you."

"Then why in the world," Rachel almost thundered, "could you not tell me so in the beginning?"

"That is a question I have already answered."

"Then I have another. Why so often and so systematically pretend that you never were in Australia at all?"

"That is a question which I implore you not to press!"

The two answers, so like each other in verbal form, were utterly dissimilar in the manner of their utterance. Suddenly, and for the first time in all her knowledge of him, his cynical aplomb had fallen from the man like a garment. One moment he was brazening past deceit with a smiling face; the next, he was in earnest, even he, and that mocking voice vibrated with deep feeling.

"I should have thought all the more of you for being an Australian," continued Rachel, vaguely touched at the change in him, "I who am proud of being one myself. What harm could it have done, my knowing that?"

"You are not the only one from whom I have hidden it," said Steel, still in a low and altered voice.

"Yet you brought home all those keepsakes of the bush?"

"But I thought better of them, and have never even unpacked them all, as you must have seen for yourself."

"Yet your mysterious visitor of the other day – "

"Another Australian, of course; indeed, another man who worked upon my own run."

"And he knows why you don't want it known over here?"

"He does," said Steel, with grim brevity.

Rachel moved forward and pressed his hand impulsively. To her surprise the pressure was returned. That instant their hands fell apart.

"I beg your pardon in my turn," she said. "I can only promise you that I will never again reopen that wound – whatever it may be – and I won't even try to guess. I undertook not to try to probe your past, and I will keep my undertaking in the main; but where it impinges upon my own past I simply cannot! You say you were my first husband's close friend," added Rachel, looking her second husband more squarely than ever in the eyes. "Was that what brought you to my trial for his murder?"

He returned her look.

"It was."

"Was that what made you wish to marry me yourself?"

No answer, but his assurance coming back, as he stood looking at her under beetling eyebrows, over black arms folded across a snowy shirt. It was the wrong moment for the old Adam's return, for Rachel had reached the point upon which she most passionately desired enlightenment.

"I want to know," she cried, "and I insist on knowing, what first put it into your head or your heart to marry me – all but convicted – "

Steel held up his hand, glancing in apprehension towards the door.

"I have told you so often," he said, "and your glass tells you whenever you look into it. I sat within a few feet of you for the inside of a week!"

"But that is not true," she told him quietly; "trust a woman to know, if it were."

In the white glare of the electric light he seemed for once to change color slightly.

"If you will not accept my word," he answered, "there is no more to be said."

And he switched off a bunch of the lights that had beaten too fiercely upon him; but it only looked as if he was about to end the interview.

"You have admitted so many untruths in the last half hour," pursued Rachel, in a thrilling voice, "that you ought not to be hurt if I suspect you of another. Come! Can you look me in the face and tell me that you married me for love? No, you turn away – because you cannot! Then will you, in God's name, tell me why you did marry me?"

And she followed him with clasped hands, her beautiful eyes filled with tears, her white throat quivering with sobs, until suddenly he turned upon her as though in self-defence.

"No, I will not!" he cried. "Since the answer I have given you, and the obvious answer, is not good enough for you, the best thing you can do is to find out for yourself."

A truculent look came into Rachel's eyes, as they rested upon the smooth face so unusually agitated beneath the smooth silvery hair.

"I will!" she answered through her teeth. "I shall take you at your word, and find out for myself I will!"

And she swept past him out of the room.

CHAPTER XV

A Chance Encounter

There was now an open breach between the Steels, but no third person would have discerned any difference in their relations. It was a mere snapping of the threads across the chasm which had always separated Rachel from her second husband. The chasm had been plain enough to those who came much in contact with the pair, but the little threads of sympathy were invisible to the naked eye of ordinary observation. There was thus no outward change, for neither was there any outward rupture. It takes two to quarrel, and Steel imperturbably refused to make one. Rachel might be as trying as she pleased; no repulse depressed, no caprice annoyed him; and this insensibility was not the least of Steel's offences in the now jaundiced eyes of his wife.

Rachel felt as bitter as one only does against those who have inspired some softer feeling; the poison of misplaced confidence rankled in her blood. Her husband had told her much, but it was not enough for Rachel, and the little he refused to tell eliminated all the rest from her mind. There was no merit even in such frankness as he had shown, since her own, accidental discoveries had forced some measure of honesty upon him. He had admitted nothing which Rachel could not have deduced from that which she had found out for herself. She felt as far as ever from any satisfactory clew to his mysterious reasons for ever wishing to marry her. There lay the kernel of the whole matter, there the problem that she meant to solve. If her first husband was at the bottom of it, no matter how indirectly, and if she had been married for the dead man's sake, to give his widow a home, then Rachel felt that the last affront had been put upon her, and she would leave this man as she had been within an ace of leaving his friend. So ran the wild and unreasonable tenor of her thoughts. He had not married her for her own sake; it was not she herself who had appealed to him, after all. Curiosity might consume her, and a sense of deepening mystery add terrors of its own, but the resentful feeling was stronger than either of these, and would have afforded as strange a revelation as any, had Rachel dared to look deeper into her own heart.

If, on the other hand, she had already some conception of the truth about herself, it would scarcely lessen her bitterness against one who inspired in her emotions at once so complex and so painful. Suffice it that this bitterness was extreme in the days immediately following the scene between Rachel and her husband in the drawing-room after dinner. It was also unconcealed, and must have been the cause of many another such scene but for the imperturable temper and the singularly ruly tongue of John Buchanan Steel. And then, in those same days, there fell the two social events to which the bidden guests had been looking forward for some two or three weeks, and of which the whole neighborhood was to talk for years.

On the tenth of August the Uniackes were giving a great garden party at Hornby Manor, while the eleventh was the date of the first real dinner-party for which the Steels had issued invitations to Normanthorpe House.

The tenth was an ideal August day: deep blue sky, trees still untarnished in the hardy northern air, and black shadows under the trees. Rachel made herself ready before lunch, to which she came down looking quite lovely, in blue as joyous as the sky's, to find her husband as fully prepared, and not less becomingly attired, in a gray frock-coat without a ripple on its surface. They looked critically at each other for an instant, and then Steel said something pleasant, to which Rachel made practically no reply. They ate their lunch in a silence broken good-naturedly at intervals from one end of the table only. Then the Woodgates arrived, to drive with them to Hornby, which was some seven or eight miles away; and the Normanthorpe landau and pair started with, the quartette shortly after three o'clock.

Morning, noon, and afternoon of this same tenth of August, Charles Langholm, the minor novelist, never lifted his unkempt head from the old bureau at which he worked, beside an open window overlooking his cottage garden. A tumbler of his beloved roses stood in one corner of the writing space, up to the cuts in MSS., and roses still ungathered peeped above the window-sill and drooped from either side. But Langholm had a soul far below roses at the present moment; his neatly numbered sheets of ruled sermon-paper were nearing the five hundredth page; his hero and his heroine were in the full sweep of those emotional explanations which they had ingeniously avoided for the last three hundred at least; in a word, Charles Langholm's new novel is being finished while you wait. It is not one of his best; yet a moment ago there was a tear in his eye, and now he is grinning like a child at play. And at play he is, though he be paid for playing, and though the game is only being won after weeks and months of uphill labor and downhill joy.

At last there is the final ticking of inverted commas, and Charles

Langholm inscribes the autograph for which he is importuned once in a blue moon, and which the printer will certainly not set up at the foot of the last page; but the thing is done, and the doer must needs set his hand to it out of pure and unusual satisfaction with himself. And so, thank the Lord!

Langholm rose stiffly from the old bureau, where at his best he could lose all sense of time; for the moment he was bent double, and faint with fasting, because it was his mischievous rule to reach a given point before submitting to the physical and mental distraction of a meal. But to-day's given point had been the end of his book, and for some happy minutes Langholm fed on his elation. It was done at last, yet another novel, and not such a bad one after all. Not his best by any means, but perhaps still further from being his worst; and, at all events, the thing was done. Langholm could scarcely grasp that fact, though there was the last page just dry upon the bureau, and most of the rest lying about the room in galley-proofs or in typewritten sheets. Moreover, the publishers were pleased; that was the joke. It was nothing less to Langholm when he reflected that the final stimulus to finish this book had been the prospect and determination of at last writing one to please himself. And this reflection brought him down from his rosy clouds.

It was the day of the Uniacke's garden-party; they had actually asked the poor author, and the poor author had intended to go. Not that he either shone or revelled in society; but Mrs. Steel would be there, and he burned to tell her that he had finished his book, and was at last free to tackle hers; for hers at bottom it would be, the great novel by which the name of Langholm was to live, and which he was to found by Rachel Steel's advice upon the case of her namesake Rachel Minchin.

The coincidence of the Christian names had naturally struck the novelist, but no suspicion of the truth had crossed a mind too skilled in the construction of dramatic situations to dream of stumbling into one ready-made. It was thus with a heart as light as any feather that Langholm made a rapid and unwholesome meal, followed by a deliberate and painstaking toilet, after which he proceeded at a prudent pace upon his bicycle to Hornby Manor.

Flags were drooping from their poles, a band clashing fitfully through the sleepy August air, and carriages still sweeping into the long drive, when Langholm also made his humble advent. He was a little uneasy and self-conscious, and annoyed at his own anxiety to impart his tidings to Mrs. Steel, but for whom he would probably have stayed at home. His eye sought her eagerly as he set foot upon the lawn, having left his bicycle at the stables, and carefully removed the clips from his trousers; but before his vigilance could be rewarded he was despatched by his hostess to the tea-tent, in charge of a very young lady, detached for the nonce from the wing of a gaunt old gentleman with side whiskers and lantern jaws.

Fresh from his fagging task, Langholm did not know what on earth to say to the pretty schoolgirl, whose own shyness reacted on herself; but he was doing his best, and atoning in attentiveness for his shortcomings as a companion, when in the tent he had to apologize to a lady in blue, who turned out to be Rachel herself, with Hugh Woodgate at her side.

"Oh, no, we live in London," the young girl was saying; "only I go to the same school as Ida Uniacke, and I am staying here on a visit."

"I've finished it," whispered Langholm to Rachel, "this very afternoon; and now I'm ready for yours! I see," he added, dropping back into the attitude of respectful interest in the young girl; "only on a visit; and who was the old gentleman from whom I tore you away?"

The child laughed merrily.

"That was my father," she said; "but he is only here on his way to Leeds."

"You mustn't call it my book," remonstrated Rachel, while Woodgate waited upon both ladies.

"But it was you who gave me the idea of writing a novel round Mrs. Minchin."

"I don't think I did. I am quite sure it was your own idea. But one book at a time. Surely you will take a rest?"

"I shall correct this thing. It will depress me to the verge of suicide. Then I shall fall to upon my *magnum opus*."

"You really think it will be that?"

"It should be mine. It isn't saying much; but I never had such a plot as you have given me!"

Rachel shook her head in a last disclaimer as she moved away with the Vicar of Marley.

"Oh, Mr. Langholm, do you write books?" asked the schoolgirl, with round blue eyes.

"For my sins," he confessed. "But do you prefer an ice, or more strawberries and cream?"

"Neither, thank you. I've been here before," the young girl said with a jolly smile. "But I didn't know I should come back with an author!"

"Then we'll go out into the open air," the author said; and they followed Rachel at but a few yards' distance.

It was a picturesque if an aimless pageant, the smart frocks sweeping the smooth sward, the pretty parasols with the prettier faces underneath, the well-set-up and well-dressed men, with the old gray manor rising upon an eminence in the background, and a dazzling splash of scarlet and of brass somewhere under the trees. The band was playing selections from *The Geisha* as Langholm emerged from the tea-tent in Rachel's wake. Mrs. Venables was manoeuvring her two highly marriageable girls in opposite quarters of the field, and had only her own indefatigable generalship to thank for what it lost her upon this occasion. Mr. Steel and Mrs. Woodgate apparently missed the same thing through wandering idly in the direction of the band; but the tableau might have been arranged for the express benefit of Charles Langholm and the very young lady upon whom he was dancing laborious attendance.

Mrs. Uniacke had stepped apart from the tall old gentleman with the side whiskers, to whom she had been talking for some time, and had intercepted Rachel as she was passing on with Hugh Woodgate.

"Wait while I introduce you to my most distinguished guest, or rawther him to you," whispered Mrs. Uniacke, with the Irish brogue which rendered her slightest observation a delight to the appreciative. "Sir Baldwin Gibson – Mrs. Steel."

Langholm and the little Miss Gibson were standing close behind, and the trained eye of the habitual observer took in every detail of a scene which he never forgot. Handsome Mrs. Uniacke was clinching the introduction with a smile, which ended in a swift expression of surprise. Sir Baldwin had made an extraordinary pause, his hand half way to his hat, his lantern jaws fallen suddenly apart. Mrs. Steel, though slower at her part of the obvious recognition, was only a second slower, and thereupon stood abashed and ashamed in the eyes of all who saw; but only for another second at the most; then Sir Baldwin Gibson not only raised his hat, but held out his hand in a fatherly way, and as she took it Rachel's color changed from livid white to ruby red.

Yet even Rachel was mistress of herself so quickly that the one or two eye-witnesses of this scene, such as Mrs. Uniacke and Charles Langholm, who saw that it had a serious meaning, without dreaming what that meaning was, were each in hopes that no one else had seen as much as they. Sir Baldwin plunged at once into amiable and fluent conversation, and before many moments Rachel's replies were infected with an approximate assurance and ease; then Langholm turned to his juvenile companion, and put a question in the form of a fib.

"So that is your father," said he. "I seem, do you know, to know his face?"

Little Miss Gibson fell an easy prey.

"You probably do; he is the judge, you know!"

"The judge, is he?"

"Yes; and I wanted to ask you something just now in the tent. Did you mean the Mrs. Minchin who was tried for murder, when you were talking about your plot?"

Langholm experienced an unforeseen shock from head to heel; he could only nod.

"He was the judge who tried her!" the schoolgirl said with pardonable pride.

A lady joined them as they spoke.

"Do you really mean that that is Mr. Justice Gibson, who tried Mrs. Minchin at the Old Bailey last November?"

"Yes – my father," said the proud young girl.

"What a very singular thing! How do you do, Mr. Langholm? I didn't see it was you."

And Langholm found himself shaking hands with the aquiline lady to whom he had talked so little at the Upthorpe dinner-party; she took her revenge by giving him only the tips of her fingers now, and by looking deliberately past him at Rachel and her judge.

CHAPTER XVI

A Match for Mrs. Venables

That was absolutely all that happened at the Uniackes' garden-party. There was no scene, no scandal, no incident whatsoever beyond an apparently mutual recognition between Mrs. Steel and Mr. Justice Gibson. Of this there were not half-a-dozen witnesses, all of whom were given immediate reason to suppose that either they or the pair in question had made a mistake; for nothing could have surpassed the presence of mind and the kindness of heart with which Sir Baldwin Gibson chatted to the woman whom he had tried for her life within the year. And his charity continued behind her back.

"Odd thing," said Sir Baldwin to his hostess, at the earliest opportunity, "but for the moment I could have sworn that woman was some one else. May I ask who she is exactly?"

"Sure, Sir Baldwin," replied Mrs. Uniacke, "and that's what I thought we were to hear at last. It's who she is we none of us know. And what does it matter? She's pretty and nice, and I'm just in love with her; but then nobody knows any more about her husband, and so we talk."

A few more questions satisfied the judge that he could not possibly have been mistaken, and he hesitated a moment, for he was a pious man; but Rachel's face, combined with her nerve, had deepended an impression which was now nearly a year old, and the superfluous proximity of an angular and aquiline lady, to whom Sir Baldwin had not been introduced, but who was openly hanging upon his words, drove the good man's last scruple to the winds.

"Very deceptive, these likenesses," said he, raising his voice for the interloper's benefit; "in future I shall beware of them. I needn't tell you, Mrs. Uniacke, that I never before set eyes upon the lady whom I fear I embarrassed by behaving as though I had."

Rachel was not less fortunate in her companion of the moment which had so nearly witnessed her undoing. Ox-eyed Hugh Woodgate saw nothing inexplicable in Mrs. Steel's behavior upon her introduction to Sir Baldwin Gibson, and anything he did see he attributed to an inconvenient sense of that dignitary's greatness. He did not think the matter worth mentioning to his wife, when the Steels had dropped them at the Vicarage gate, after a pleasant but somewhat silent drive. Neither did Rachel see fit to speak of it to her husband. There was a certain unworthy satisfaction in her keeping something from him. But again she underrated his uncanny powers of observation, and yet again he turned the tables upon her by a sudden display of the very knowledge which she was painfully keeping to herself.

"Of course you recognized the judge?" said Steel, following his wife for once into her own apartments, where he immediately shut a door behind him and another in front of Rachel, who stood at bay before the glitter in his eyes.

"Of course," she admitted, with irritating nonchalance.

"And he you?"

"I thought he did at first; afterwards I was not so sure."

"But I am!" exclaimed Steel through his teeth.

Rachel's face was a mixture of surprise and incredulity.

"How can you know?" she asked coldly. "You were at least a hundred yards away at the time, for I saw you with Morna Woodgate."

"And do you think my sight is not good for a hundred yards," retorted Steel, "when you are at the end of them? I saw the whole thing – his confusion and yours – but then I did not know who he was. He must have been in the house when we arrived; otherwise I should have taken good care that you never met. I saw enough, however, to bring me up in time to see and hear more. I heard the way he was talking to you then; that was his damned good-nature, and he has us at his mercy all the same."

Rachel had never seen her husband in such a passion; indeed, she had never before known him in a state of mind to justify the use of such a word. He was paler than his wont, his eyes brighter, his lips more bloodless. Rachel experienced a strange sense of advantage, at once unprecedented and unforeseen, and with it an irresistible temptation to the sort of revenge which she knew to be petty at the time. But he had made her suffer; for once it was her turn. He could be cold as ice when she was not, could deny her his confidence when she all but fell upon her knees before him; he should learn what it was to be treated as he had treated her.

"I'm well aware of it," said Rachel, with a harsh, dry laugh, "though in point of fact I don't for a moment believe that he'll give me away. But really I don't think it matters if he does."

Steel stared; it was wonderful to her to see his face.

"It doesn't matter?" he repeated in angry astonishment.

"Not to me," rejoined Rachel, bitterly. "You tell me nothing. What can matter to me? When you can tell me why you felt compelled to marry me – when you have the courage to tell me that – other things may begin to matter again!"

Steel stared harder than before; he did not flinch, but his eyes seemed to hedge together as he stared, and the glittering light in them to concentrate in one baleful gleam. Yet it was not a cruel look; it was the look of a man who has sealed his lips upon one point for ever, and who views any questioning on that point as an attempt upon his treasury. There was more of self-defence than of actual hostility in the compressed lips, the bloodless face, the glaring eyes. Then, with a shrug, the look, the resentment, and the passion were shaken off, and Steel stepped briskly to the inner door, which he had shut in Rachel's path. Opening it, he bowed her through with a ceremony conspicuous even in their ceremonious relations.

But Rachel nursed her contrariety, even to the extent of a perverse satisfaction at her encounter with the judge, and a fierce enjoyment of its still possible consequences. The mood was neither logical nor generous, and yet it was human enough in the actual circumstances of the case. At last she had made him feel! It had taken her the better part of a year, but here at last was something that he really felt. And it had to do with her; it was impending disaster to herself which had brought about this change in her husband; she knew him too well not to acquit him of purely selfish solicitude for his own good name and comfortable status in a society for which he had no real regard. There was never a man less dependent upon the good opinion of other men. In absolute independence of character, as in sheer strength of personality, Steel stood by himself in the estimation of his wife. But he had deceived her unnecessarily for weeks and months. He had lied to her. He had refused her his whole confidence when she begged him for it, and when he knew how he could trust her. There was some deep mystery underlying their marriage, he could not deny it, yet he would not tell her what it was.

He had made her suffer needless pain; it was his turn. And yet, with all her resentment against him, and all her grim savoring of the scandal which he seemed to fear so much, there ran a golden thread of unacknowledged contentment in the conviction that those fears were all for her.

Outwardly she was callous to the last degree, reckless as on the day she made this marriage, and as light-hearted as it was possible to appear; but the excitement of the coming dinner-party was no small help to Rachel in the maintenance of this attitude. It was to be a very large dinner-party, and Rachel's first in her own house; in any case she must have been upon her mettle. Two dozen had accepted. The Upthorpe party was coming in force; if anybody knew anything, it would be Mrs. Venables. What would she do or say? Mrs. Venables was capable of doing or of saying anything. And what might not happen before the day was out?

It was a stimulating situation for one so curiously compact of courage and of nerves as the present mistress of Normanthorpe House; and for once she really was mistress, inspecting the silver with her own eyes, arranging the flowers with her own hands, and, what was more difficult, the order in which the people were to sit. She was thus engaged, in her own sanctum, when Mrs. Venables did the one thing which Rachel had not dreamt of her doing.

She called at three in the afternoon, and sent her name upstairs.

Rachel's heart made itself felt; but she was not afraid. Something was coming earlier than she had thought; she was chiefly curious to know what. Her first impulse was to have Mrs. Venables brought upstairs, and to invoke her aid in the arrangement of the table before that lady could open fire. Rachel disliked the great cold drawing-room, and felt that she must be at a disadvantage in any interview there. On the other hand, if this was a hostile visit, the visitor could not be treated with too much consideration. And so the servant was dismissed with word that her mistress would not be a moment; nor was Rachel very many. She glanced in a glass, but that was all; she might have been tidier, but not easily more animated, confident, and alert. She had reached the landing when she returned and collected all the cards which she had been trying to arrange; they made quite a pack; and Rachel laughed as she took them downstairs with her.

Mrs. Venables sat in solitary stiffness on the highest chair she had been able to find; neither Sybil nor Vera was in attendance; a tableful of light literature was at her elbow, but Mrs. Venables sat with folded hands.

"This is too good of you!" cried Rachel, greeting her in a manner redeemed from hypocrisy by a touch of irresistible irony. "You know my inexperience, and you have come to tell me things, have you not? You could not have come at a better time. How *do* you fit in twenty-six people at one table? I wanted to have two at each end, and it can't be done!"

Mrs. Venables suppressed a smile suggestive of some unconscious humor in these remarks, but sat more upright than ever in her chair, with a hard light in the bright brown eyes that stared serenely into Rachel's own.

"I cannot say I came to offer you my assistance, Mrs. Steel. I only take liberties with very intimate friends."

"Then I wonder what can have brought you!"

And Rachel returned both the smile and the stare with irritating self-control.

"I will tell you," said Mrs. Venables, weightily. "There is a certain thing being said of you, Mrs. Steel; and I wish to know from your own lips whether there is any truth in it or none."

Rachel held up her hands as quick as thought.

"My dear Mrs. Venables, you can't mean that you are bringing me a piece of unpleasant gossip on the very afternoon of my first dinner-party?"

"It remains with you," said Mrs. Venables, changing color at this hit, "to say whether it is mere gossip or not. You must know, Mrs. Steel, though we were all quite charmed with your husband from the moment he came among us, we none of us had the least idea where he came from nor have we yet."

"You are speaking for the neighborhood?" inquired Rachel, sweetly.

"I am," said Mrs. Venables.

"Town *and* county," murmured Rachel. "And you mean that nobody in the district knew anything at all about my husband?"

"Not a thing," said Mrs. Venables.

"And yet you called on him; and yet you took pity on him, poor lonely bachelor that he was!"

This shaft also left its momentary mark upon the visitor's complexion. "The same applies to you," she went on the more severely. "We had no idea who you were, either!"

"And now?" said Rachel, still mistress of the situation, for she knew so well what was coming.

"And now we hear, and I wish to know whether it is true or not. Were you, or were you not, the Mrs. Minchin who was tried last winter for her husband's murder?"

Rachel looked steadily into the hard brown eyes, until a certain hardness came into her own.

"I don't quite know what right you think you have to ask me such a question, Mrs. Venables. Is it the usual thing to question people who have made a second marriage – supposing I am one – about their first? I fancied myself that it was considered bad form; but then I am still very ignorant of the manners and customs in this part of the world. Since you ask it, however, you shall have your answer." And Rachel's voice rang out through the room, as she rose majestically from the chair which she had drawn opposite that of the visitor. "Yes, Mrs. Venables, I am that unhappy woman. And what then?"

"No wonder you were silent about yourself," said Mrs. Venables, in a vindictive murmur. "No wonder we never even heard – "

"And what then?" repeated Rachel, with a quiet and compelling scorn. "Does it put one outside the local pale to keep to oneself any painful incident in one's own career? Is an accusation down here the same thing as a conviction? Is there nothing to choose between 'guilty' and 'not guilty'?"

"You must be aware," proceeded Mrs. Venables, without taking any notice of these questions – "indeed, you cannot fail to be perfectly well aware – that a large proportion of the public was dissatisfied with the verdict in your case."

"Your husband, for one!" Rachel agreed, with a scornful laugh. "He would have come to see me hanged; he told me so at his own table."

"You never would have been at his table," retorted Mrs. Venables, with some effect, "if he or I had dreamt who you were; but now that we know, you may be quite sure that none of us will sit at yours."

And Mrs. Venables rose up in all her might and spite, her brown eyes flashing, her handsome head thrown back.

"Are you still speaking for the district?" inquired Rachel, conquering a recreant lip to put the question, and putting it with her finest scorn.

"I am speaking for Mr. Venables, my daughters, and myself," rejoined the lady with great dignity; "others will speak for themselves; and you will soon learn in what light you are regarded by ordinary people. It is a merciful chance that we have found you out – a merciful chance! That you should dare – you, about whom there are not two opinions among sensible people – that you should dare to come among us as you have done and to speak to me as you have spoken! But one thing is certain – it is for the last time."

With that Mrs. Venables sailed to the door by which she was to make her triumphant exit, but she stopped before reaching it. Steel stood before her on the threshold, and as he stood he closed the door behind him, and as he closed it he turned and took out the key. There was the other door that led through the conservatory into the garden. Without a word he crossed the room, shut that door also, locked it, and put the two keys in his pocket. Then at last he turned to the imprisoned lady.

"You are quite right, Mrs. Venables. It is the last conversation we are likely to have together. The greater the pity to cut it short!"

"Will you have the goodness to let me go?" the visitor demanded, white and trembling, but not yet unimpressive in her tremendous indignation.

"With the greatest alacrity," replied Steel, "when you have apologized to my wife."

Rachel stood by without a word.

"For what?" cried Mrs. Venables. "For telling her what the whole world thinks of her? Never; and you will unlock that door this instant, unless you wish my husband to – to – horsewhip you within an inch of your life!"

Steel merely smiled; he could well afford to do so, lithe and supple as he still was, with flabby Mr. Venables in his mind's eye.

"I might have known what to expect in this house," continued Mrs. Venables, in a voice hoarse with suppressed passion, "what unmanly and ungentlemanly behavior, what cowardly insults! I might have known!"

And she glanced from the windows to the bells.

"It is no use ringing," said Steel, with a shake of his snowy head, "or doing anything else of the sort. I am the only person on the premises who can let you out; your footman could not get in if he tried; but if you like I shall shout to him to try. As for insults, you have insulted my wife most cruelly and gratuitously, for I happen to have heard more than you evidently imagine. In fact, 'insult' is hardly the word for what even I have heard you say; let me warn you, madam, that you have sailed pretty close to the wind already in the way of indictable slander. You seem to forget that my wife was tried and acquitted by twelve of her fellow-countrymen. You will at least apologize for that forgetfulness before you leave this room."

"Never!"

Steel looked at his watch and sat down. "I begin to fear you are no judge of character, Mrs. Venables; otherwise you would have seen ere this which of us will have to give in sooner or later. I can only tell you which of us never will!"

And Rachel still stood by without a word.

CHAPTER XVII

Friends in Need

That afternoon the Vicar of Marley was paying house-to-house visits among his humbler parishioners. Though his conversation was the weak point to which attention has been drawn, Hugh Woodgate nevertheless possessed the not too common knack of chatting with the poor. He had the simplicity which made them kin, and his sympathy, unlike that of so many persons who consider themselves sympathetic, was not exclusively reserved for the death-bed and the ruined home. He wrote letters for the illiterate, found places for the unemployed, knew one baby from another as soon as their own mothers, and with his own hand sent to the local papers full reports of the village matches in which he rarely scored a run. Until this August afternoon he was not aware that he had made an actual enemy in all the years that he had spent in Delverton, first as an overworked Northborough curate, and latterly as one of the busiest country vicars in the diocese. But towards five o'clock, as Mr. Woodgate was returning to the Vicarage, a carriage and pair, sweeping past him in a cloud of dust, left the clergyman quite petrified on the roadside, his soft felt hat still in his hand; the carriage contained Mrs. Venables, who had simply stared him in the face when he took it off.

Woodgate was quite excited when he reached the Vicarage. Morna met him in the garden.

"Mrs. Venables cut me dead!" he cried while they were still yards apart.

"I am not surprised," replied Morna, who was in a state of suppressed excitement herself.

"But what on earth is the meaning of it?"

"She has just been here."

"Well?"

"She is not likely to come again. Oh, Hugh, I don't know how to tell you! If you agree with her for a moment, if you see any possible excuse for the woman, it will break my heart!"

Morna's fine eyes were filled with tears; the sight of them put out the flame that had leapt for once from stolid Hugh, and he took her hand in his own great soothing grasp.

"Come and sit down," he said, "and tell me all about it. Have I ever taken anybody's part against you, Morna, that you should think me likely to begin now?"

"No; but you would if you thought they were right and I was wrong."

Hugh reflected until they reached the garden-seat upon the lawn.

"Well, not openly, at all events," said he; "and not under any circumstances I can conceive in which Mrs. Venables was the other person."

"But she isn't the only other person; that is just it. Oh, Hugh, you do like Rachel, don't you?"

"I do," he said emphatically. "But surely you haven't been quarrelling with her?"

"No, indeed! And that is exactly why I *have* quarrelled with Mrs. Venables, because I wouldn't refuse to go to the dinner-party at Normanthorpe to-night!"

Woodgate was naturally nonplussed.

"Wouldn't refuse?" he echoed.

"Yes. She actually asked me not to go; and now I do believe she has gone driving round to ask everybody else!"

Woodgate's amazement ended in a guffaw.

"And that is what you quarrelled about!" he roared. "The woman must be mad. What reason did she give?"

"She had a reason, dear."

"But not a good one! There can be no excuse for such an action, let alone a good reason!"

Morna looked at her husband with sidelong anxiety, wondering whether he would say as much when he had heard all. She was sure enough of him. But as yet they had never differed on a point that mattered, and the one which was coming mattered infinitely to Morna.

"Hugh," she began, "do you remember being with Rachel yesterday at Hornby, when she was introduced to Sir Baldwin Gibson?"

"Perfectly," said Hugh.

"He is the judge, you know."

"Yes, yes."

"Did you think they looked as though they had ever seen each other before?"

The vicar revolved where he sat, looking his wife suddenly in the face, while a light broke over his own.

"Now you speak of it," he cried, "they did! It didn't strike me at the time. I was rather surprised at her being so nervous, but that never occurred to me as the explanation. Yet now I have no doubt about it. You don't mean to say he knows something against Mrs. Steel, and has been giving her away?"

"No, dear, the judge has not; but you were not the only one who saw the meeting; and other eyes are more suspicious than yours, Hugh. Darling, you would not think the worse of Rachel for keeping her past life to herself, would you, especially if it had been a very unhappy one?"

"Of course not; it is no business of ours."

"So you told Mrs. Venables the day she came to tell us Mr. Steel was married, and so I told her again this afternoon. However, that is not her main point, and there is another thing I am still surer you would never do. If a person had been put upon her trial, and found not guilty in open court, you would not treat her as though she had been found guilty, would you – even though the verdict had come as a surprise?"

"Of course I would not, Morna; no decent Christian would, I should hope! But do you mean to tell me that Mrs. Steel has been tried for something?"

"Yes; and by Justice Gibson!"

"Poor thing," said Hugh Woodgate, after a pause.

Morna took his hand.

"My dear, she is, or rather she was, Mrs. Minchin!"

"What! The woman who was tried for murdering her husband?"

"Yes – and acquitted."

"Good heavens!" exclaimed the vicar, and for a minute that was all. "Well," he continued, "I didn't read the case, and I am glad that I didn't, but I remember, of course, what was said about it at the time. But what does it matter what is said? I imagine the jury knew what they were about; they listened to the evidence for a week, I believe, which other people read in a few minutes. Of course they knew best! But how long have you known this, Morna?"

"Never until this afternoon; there was no reason why I should."

"Of course there was not."

"Then you agree with me, Hugh?"

And Morna was transfigured.

"Of course I agree with you! But I want to know more. Do you mean to tell me that a woman of education and ability, who calls herself a Christian, like Mrs. Venables, has actually backed out of this dinner-party on this account, and asked others to do the same?"

"She certainly asked me, point-blank," said Morna. "And when I refused, and persisted in my refusal, she flounced out in a rage, and must have cut you dead next minute."

"Incredible!" exclaimed Woodgate. "I mean, she must have had some further reason."

"Oh, but she had! I forgot to tell you in my anxiety to know what you thought. She came to me straight from Normanthorpe, where they had insulted her as she had never been insulted in her life before!"

"Who? Steel or his wife?"

"Mr. Steel, I fancy. Mrs. Venables had no name bad enough for him, but she brought it on herself, and I think more of him than I ever did before. You know that Mrs. Vinson, the Invernesses' new agent's wife?"

"I do. Langholm took her into dinner the night we dined at Upthorpe, and she was in the offing yesterday when Mrs. Steel was talking to the judge."

"Exactly! It appears that it was Mrs. Vinson who first suspected something, the very night you mention; and yesterday her suspicions were confirmed to her own satisfaction. At all events she felt justified in mentioning them to Mrs. Venables, who instantly drove over to ask Rachel to her face if there was any truth in the rumor that she was or had been Mrs. Minchin."

"Well?"

"Rachel told her it was perfectly true."

"Good!"

"And then the fat was in the fire; but what happened exactly it was impossible to gather from Mrs. Venables. I never saw a woman so beside herself with rage. She came in incoherent, and went out inarticulate! From the things she said of him, I could only guess that Mr. Steel had come upon the scene and insulted her as she deserved to be insulted. But I would give a good deal to know what did happen."

"Would you really?"

Morna started to her feet. The vicar rose more slowly, after sitting for some moments in mute confusion. It was Mrs. Steel who stood before them on their lawn, pale as death, and ten years older since the day before, yet with a smile upon her bloodless lips, which appeared indeed to express some faint irresistible amusement.

"Would you really like to know?" she repeated, standing at a distance from them, her great eyes travelling from one to the other. "It is strange, because I had come on purpose to tell you both that and all the rest – but especially all the rest – in which it seems Mrs. Venables has been before me." She paused an instant, and the corners of her sad mouth twitched just once. "What my husband did," said Rachel, "was to lock the doors and refuse to let her out until she had begged my pardon."

"I hope she did so," said Hugh Woodgate, with the emphasis which often atoned for the inadequacy of his remarks.

"In about three minutes," replied Rachel, dryly, with some pride, but no triumph in her tone.

Morna had not spoken. Now she took a quick step forward, her eyes brimming. But Rachel held up her hand.

"You are sure you realize who I am?"

"Yes, Rachel."

"Rachel Minchin!" added Rachel, harshly. "The notorious Mrs. Minchin – the Mrs. Minchin whom Mr. Venables would have come to see hanged!"

"Hush, Rachel, hush!"

"Then be honest with me – mind, honest – not kind! You would not have said what Mrs. Venables said to me; she said that all the world believed me guilty. You would not have said that, Morna; but are you sure you would not have said it in your heart? Can you look me in the face and tell me you don't believe it, like all the rest of the world?"

There was no faltering of the firm, sweet voice; it was only unutterably sad.

And Morna answered it only with a sob, as she flung her arms round Rachel's neck, while her husband waited with outstretched hand.

CHAPTER XVIII

"They which were Bidden"

The rose-covered cottage of Charles Langholm's dreams, which could not have come true in a more charming particular, stood on a wooded hill at the back of a village some three miles from Normanthorpe. It was one of two cottages under the same tiled roof, and in the other there lived an admirable couple who supplied all material wants of the simple life which the novelist led when at work. In his idle intervals the place knew him not; a nomadic tendency was given free play, and the man was a wanderer on the face of Europe. But he wandered less than he had done from London, finding, in his remote but fragrant corner of the earth, that peace which twenty years of a strenuous manhood had taught him to value more than downright happiness.

Its roses were not the only merit of this ideal retreat, though in the summer months they made it difficult for one with eyes and nostrils to appreciate the others. There was a delightful room running right through the cottage; and it was here that Langholm worked, ate, smoked, read, and had his daily being; his bath was in the room adjoining, and his bed in another adjoining that. Of the upper floor he made no use; it was filled with the neglected furniture of a more substantial establishment, and Langholm seldom so much as set foot upon the stairs. The lower rooms were very simply furnished. There was a really old oak bureau, and some solid, comfortable chairs. The pictures were chiefly photographs of other writers. There were better pictures deep in dust upstairs.

An artist in temperament, if not in attainment, Langholm had of late years found the ups and downs of his own work supply all the excitement that was necessary to his life; it was only when the work was done that his solitude had oppressed him; but neither the one nor the other had been the case of late weeks. His new book had been written under the spur of an external stimulus; it had not written itself, like all the more reputable members of the large but short-lived family to which it belonged. Langholm had not felt lonely in the breathing spaces between the later chapters. On the contrary, he would walk up and down among his roses with the animated face of one on the happy heights of intercourse with a kindred spirit, when in reality he was quite alone. But the man wrote novels, and withal believed in them at the time of writing. It was true that on one occasion, when the Steels came to tea, the novelist walked his garden with the self-same radiant face with which he had lately taken to walking it alone; but that also was natural enough.

The change came on the very day he finished his book, when Langholm made himself presentable and rode off to the garden-party at Hornby Manor in spirits worthy of the occasion. About seven of the same evening he dismounted heavily in the by-lane outside the cottage, and pushed his machine through the wicket, a different man. A detail declared his depression to the woman next door, who was preparing him a more substantial meal than Langholm ever thought of ordering for himself: he went straight through to his roses without changing his party coat for the out-at-elbow Norfolk jacket in which he had spent that summer and the last.

The garden behind the two cottages was all Langholm's. The whole thing, levelled, would not have made a single lawn-tennis court, nor yet a practice pitch of proper length. Yet this little garden contained almost everything that a garden need have. There were tall pines among the timber to one side, and through these set the sun, so that on the hottest days the garden was in sufficient shadow by the time the morning's work was done. There was a little grass-plot, large enough for a basket-chair and a rug. There was a hedge of Penzance sweet-brier opposite the backdoor and the window at which Langholm wrote, and yet this hedge broke down in the very nick and place to give the lucky writer a long glimpse across a green valley, with dim woods upon the opposite hill. And then there were the roses, planted by the last cottager – a retired gardener – a greater artist than his successor – a man who knew what roses were!

Over the house clambered a William Allen Richardson and two Gloires de Dijon, these last a-blowing, the first still resting from a profuse yield in June; in the southeast corner, a Crimson Rambler was at its ripe red height; and Caroline Testout, Margaret Dickson, La France, Madame Lambard, and Madame Cochet, blushed from pale pink to richest red, or remained coldly but beautifully white, at the foot of the Penzance briers. Langholm had not known one rose from another when he came to live among this galaxy; now they were his separate, familiar, individual friends, each with its own character in his eyes, its own charm for him; and the man's soul was the sweeter for each summer spent in their midst. But to-night they called to closed nostrils and blind eyes. And the evening sun, reddening the upper stems of the pines, and warming the mellow tiles of his dear cottage, had no more to say to Langholm's spirit than his beloved roses.

The man had emerged from the dreamy, artistic, aesthetic existence into which he had drifted through living alone amid so much simple beauty; he was in real, human, haunting trouble, and the manlier man for it already.

Could he be mistaken after all? No; the more he pondered, the more convinced he felt. Everything pointed to the same conclusion, beginning with that first dinner-party at Upthorpe, and that first conversation of which he remembered every word. Mrs. Steel was Mrs. Minchin – the notorious Mrs. Minchin – the Mrs. Minchin who had been tried for her husband's murder, and acquitted to the horror of a righteous world.

And he had been going to write a book about her, and it was she herself who had given him the idea!

But was it? There had been much light talk about Mrs. Steel's novel, and the plot that Mrs. Steel had given Langholm, but that view of the matter had been more of a standing joke than an intellectual bond between them. It was strange to think of it in the former light to-night.

Langholm recalled more than one conversation upon the same subject. It had had a fascination for Rachel, which somehow he was sorry to remember now. Then he recollected the one end to all these conversations, and his momentary regret was swept away by a rush of sympathy which it did him good to feel. They had ended invariably in her obtaining from him, on one cunning pretext or another, a fresh assurance of his belief in Mrs. Minchin's innocence. Langholm radiated among his roses as his memory convinced him of this. Rachel had not talked about her case and his plot for the morbid excitement of discussing herself with another, but for the solid and wholesome satisfaction of hearing yet again that the other disbelieved in her guilt.

And did he not? Langholm stood still in the scented dusk as he asked his heart of hearts the point-blank question. And it was a crisper step that he resumed, with a face more radiant than before.

Yes, analytical as he was, there at least he was satisfied with himself. Thank God, he had always been of one opinion on that one point; that he had made up his mind about her long before he knew the whilom Mrs. Minchin in the flesh, and had let her know which way almost as long before the secret of her identity could possibly have dawned upon him. Now, if the worst came to the worst, his sincerity at least could not be questioned. Others might pretend, others again be unconsciously prejudiced in favor of their friend; he at least was above either suspicion. Had he not argued her case with Mrs. Venables at the time, and had he not told her so on the very evening that they met?

Certainly Langholm felt in a strong position, if ever the worst came to the worst; it illustrated a little weakness, however, that he himself foresaw no such immediate eventuality. There had been a very brief encounter between two persons at a garden-party, and a yet more brief confusion upon either side. Of all this there existed but half-a-dozen witnesses, at the outside, and Langholm did not credit the other five with his own trained insight and powers of observation; he furthermore reflected that those others, even if as close observers as himself, could not possibly have put two and two together as he had done. And this was sound; but Langholm had a fatal knack of overlooking the lady whom he had taken in to dinner at Upthorpe Hall, and scarcely noticed at Hornby Manor. Cocksure as he himself was of the significance of that which he had seen with his own eyes, the observer flattered himself that he was the only real one present; remembered the special knowledge which he had to assist his vision; and relied properly enough upon the silence of Sir Baldwin Gibson.

The greater the secret, however, the more piquant the situation for one who was in it; and there were moments of a sleepless night in which Langholm found nothing new to regret. But he was in a quandary none the less. He could scarcely meet Mrs. Steel again without a word about the prospective story, which they had so often discussed together, and upon which he was at last free to embark; nor could he touch upon that theme without disclosing the new knowledge which would burn him until he did. Charles Langholm and Rachel Steel had two or three qualities in common: an utter inability to pretend was one, if you do not happen to think it a defect.

As a rule when he had finished a rapid bit of writing, Langholm sat down to correct, and a depressing task his spent brain always found it; but for once he let it beat him altogether. After a morning's tussle with one unfortunate chapter, the desperate author sent off the rest in their sins, and rode his bicycle to abolish thought. But that mild pastime fell lamentably short of its usual efficacy. It was not one of his heroines who was worrying the novelist, but a real woman whom he liked and her husband whom he did not. The husband it was who had finished matters by entering the field of speculation during the morning's work. It may he confessed that Langholm had not by any means disliked him the year before.

What was the secret of this second marriage on the part of one who had been so recently and so miserably married? Was it love? Langholm would not admit it for a moment. Steel did not love his wife, and there was certainly nothing to love in Steel. Langholm had begun almost to hate him; he told himself it was because Steel did not even pretend to love his wife, but let strangers see the abnormal terms on which they lived.

What, then, was the explanation – the history – the excuse? They were supposed to have married on the Continent; that was one of the few statements vouchsafed by Steel, and he happened to have made it in the first instance to Langholm himself. Was there any truth in it? And did Steel know the truth concerning his wife?

Your imaginative man is ever quick to form a theory based upon facts of his own involuntary invention. Langholm formed numerous theories and invented innumerable facts during the four-and-twenty hours of his present separation from the heroine and the villain of these romances. The likeliest of the lot was the idea that the pair had really met abroad, at some out-of-the-way place, where Rachel had been in hiding from the world, and that in her despair of receiving common justice from her kind, she had accepted the rich man without telling him who she was. His subsequent enlightenment was Langholm's explanation of Steel's coldness towards his wife.

He wondered if it was the kind of coldness that would ever be removed; if Steel believed her guilty, it never would. Langholm would not have admitted it, was not even aware of it in his own introspective mind, but he almost hoped that Steel was not thoroughly convinced of his wife's innocence.

The night of the dinner-party was so fine and the roads so clean that Langholm went off on his bicycle once more, making an incongruous figure in his dress-suit, but pedalling sedately to keep cool. Fortune, however, was against him, for they had begun clipping those northern hedgerows, and an ominous bumping upon a perfectly flat road led to the discovery of a puncture a long mile from Normanthorpe. Thence onward the unhappy cyclist had to choose between running beside his machine and riding on the rims, and between the two expedients arrived at last both very hot and rather late. But he thought he must be very late; for he neither met, followed, nor was followed by any vehicle whatsoever in the drive; and the door did not open before Langholm rang, as it does when they are still waiting for one. Then the house seemed strangely silent when the door did open, and the footman wore a curious expression as he ushered the late comer into an empty drawing-room. Langholm was now almost convinced that he had made some absurd mistake, and the impression was not removed by the entry of Steel with his napkin in one hand.

"I've mistaken the night!" exclaimed the perspiring author.

"Not a bit of it," replied Steel; "only we thought you weren't coming at all."

"Am I really so late as all that?"

And Langholm began to wish he had mistaken the night.

"No," said Steel, "only a very few minutes, and the sin is ours entirely. But we thought you were staying away, like everybody else."

"Like – everybody – else?"

"My dear fellow," said Steel, smiling on the other's bewilderment, "I humbly apologize for having classed you for an instant with the rank and file of our delightful neighbors; for the fact is that all but two have made their excuses at the last moment. The telegrams will delight you, one of these days!"

"There was none from me," declared Langholm, as he began to perceive what had happened.

"There was not; and my wife was quite confident that you would come; so the fault is altogether mine. Langholm, you were almost at her heels when she was introduced to the old judge yesterday?"

"I was."

"Have you guessed who she was – before she married me – or has anybody told you?"

"I have guessed."

Steel stood silent for an instant, his eyes resting in calm scrutiny upon the other, his mouth as firm and fixed, his face fresh as a young man's, his hair like spun silver in the electric light. Langholm looked upon the man who was looking upon him, and he could not hate him as he would.

"And do you still desire to dine with us?" inquired his host at last.

"I don't want to be in the way," faltered Langholm, "on a painful – "

"Oh, never mind that!" cried Steel. "Are you quite sure you don't want to cut our acquaintance?"

"You know I don't," said Langholm, bluntly.

"Then come in, pray, and take us as we are."

"One moment, Steel! All this is inconceivable; do you mean to say that your guests have thrown you over on account of – of – "

"My wife having been a certain Mrs. Minchin before she changed her name to Steel! Yes, every one of them, except our vicar and his wife, who are real good friends."

"I am another," said Langholm through his big mustache.

"The very servants are giving notice, one by one!"

"I am her servant, too!" muttered Langholm, as Steel stood aside to let him pass out first; but this time it was through his teeth, though from his heart, and the words were only audible to himself.

CHAPTER XIX

Rachel's Champion

The immediate ordeal proved less trying than Langholm was prepared to find it. His vivid imagination had pictured the long table, laid for six-and-twenty, with four persons huddled at one end; but the telegrams had come in time to have the table reduced to its normal size, and Langholm found a place set for him between Mrs. Woodgate and Mrs. Steel. He was only embarrassed when Rachel rose and looked him in the eyes before holding out her hand.

"Have you heard?" she asked him, in a voice as cold as her marble face, but similarly redeemed and animated by its delicate and distant scorn.

"Yes," answered Langholm, sadly; "yes, I have heard."

"And yet – "

He interrupted her in another tone.

"I know what you are going to say! I give you warning, Mrs. Steel, I won't listen to it. No 'and yets' for me; remember the belief I had, long before I knew anything at all! It ought not to be a whit stronger for what I guessed yesterday for myself, and what your husband has this minute confirmed. Yet it is, if possible, ten thousand times stronger and more sure!"

"I do remember," said Rachel, slowly; "and, in my turn, I believe what you say."

But her face did not alter as she took his hand; her own was so cold that he looked at her in alarm; and the whole woman seemed turned to stone. Yet the dinner went on without further hitch; it might have been the very smallest and homeliest affair, to which only these guests had been invited. Indeed, the menu had been reduced, like the table, by the unerring tact of Rachel's husband, so that there was no undue memorial to the missing one-and-twenty, and the whole ordeal was curtailed.

There was, on the other hand, no blinking what had happened, no pretence of ignoring the one subject which was in everybody's thoughts.

Thus Mrs. Woodgate exclaimed aloud, what she was thinking to herself, that she would never speak to Mrs. Venables again in all her life, and her husband told her across the table that she had better not. Rachel thereupon put in her word, to the effect that the Woodgates would cut themselves off from everybody if they made enemies of all who disbelieved in her, and she could not allow them to do anything of the kind. Steel, again, speculated upon the probable behavior of the Uniackes and the Invernesses, neither of these distinguished families having been invited to the dinner, for obvious reasons arising from their still recent return to the country. There was no effort to ignore the absorbing topic before the butler and his satellites, but the line was drawn in the right place, excluding as it did any reference to the rout of Mrs. Venables, and indeed all details whatsoever.

The butler, however, and in a less degree the footman, presented a rather interesting study during the course of this momentous meal, had the professional observer present been only a little less concerned for his hostess. The butler was a pompous but capable creature, whom Steel had engaged when he bought the place. Though speedily reduced to a more respectful servitude than he was accustomed to, the man had long since ceased to complain of his situation, which carried with it the highest wages and all arbitrary powers over his subordinates. On the steps, at her deferred departure, Mrs. Venables had screamed the secret of his mistress's identity into the butler's ear. The butler had risen with dignity to the occasion, and, after a brief interview, resigned on the spot with all his men. The mild interest was in the present behavior of these gentry, which was a rich blend of dignity and depression, and betrayed a growing doubt as to whether the sinking ship, that they had been so eager to abandon, was really sinking after all.

Certainly the master's manner could not have been very different at the head of his table as originally laid. It was not festive, it was neither unnaturally jocular nor showy in any way, but it was delightfully confident and serene. And the mistress was as calm in her way, though for once hers was the colder way, and it was the opinion of the pantry that she felt more than she showed; without a doubt Mrs. Woodgate had more work to restrain, now her tears for Rachel, and now her consuming indignation with the absentees.

"Your wife feels it as much as mine," said Steel to the vicar, when the gentlemen were alone at last; and one of them could have struck him for the speech, one who had insight and could feel himself.

"I wouldn't go so far as that," the good vicar rejoined. "But Morna feels it dreadfully. Dreadfully she feels it!"

"I almost wish we had kept the table as it was," pursued Steel over his cigar, "and had one of those flash-light photographs taken, as they do at all the twopenny banquets nowadays. All that was left of them – left of six-and-twenty!"

His flippant tone made Langholm writhe, and drove him into the conversation to change its tenor. He asked by whom the evil had come. "Surely not the judge?"

"No," said Steel, with emphasis. "Not that I have it for a fact, but I would put a thousand pounds upon his charity and his discretion in such a matter. A kinder and a sounder man does not exist, though I say it who never met him in my life. But I heard every word of my wife's trial, and I know the way the judge took the case. There were a heap of women witnesses, and her counsel was inclined to bully them; it was delightful to see the fatherly consideration that they received as compensation from the bench."

Langholm's breath was taken away. Here was an end to the likeliest theory that he had evolved that morning among his roses. Steel had not married his wife in ignorance of her life's tragedy; he had been present, and probably fallen in love with her, at her trial! Then why did he never behave as though he were in love? And why must he expatiate upon the judge's kindness to the female witnesses, instead of on the grand result of the trial over which he had presided? Did Steel himself entertain the faintest doubt about the innocence of his wife, whose trial he had heard, and whom he had married thereafter within a few months at the most? Langholm's brain buzzed, even while he listened to what Hugh Woodgate was saying.

"I am not surprised," remarked the vicar. "I remember once hearing that Sir Baldwin Gibson and Lord Edgeware were the two fairest judges on the bench; and why, do you suppose? Because they are both old athletes and Old Blues, trained from small boys to give their opponents every possible chance!"

Steel nodded an understanding assent. Langholm, however, who was better qualified to appreciate the vicar's point, took no notice of it.

"If it was not the judge," said he, "who in the world is it who has sprung this mine, I saw them meet, and as a matter of fact I did guess the truth. But I had special reasons. I had thought, God forgive me, of making something out of your wife's case, Steel, little dreaming it was hers, though I knew it had no ordinary fascination for her. But no one else can have known that."

"You talked it over with her, however?"

And Steel had both black eyes upon the novelist, who made his innocent admission with an embarrassment due entirely to their unnecessarily piercing scrutiny.

"You talked it over with her," repeated Steel, this time in dry statement of fact, "at least on one occasion, in the presence of a lady who had a prior claim upon your conversation. That lady was Mrs. Vinson, and it is she who ought to have a millstone hanged about her neck, and be cast into the sea. Don't look as though you deserved the same fate, Langholm! It would have been better, perhaps, if you had paid more attention to Vinson's wife and less to mine; but she is the last woman in the world to blame you – naturally! And now, if you are ready, we will join them, Woodgate."

Sensitive as all his tribe, and himself both gentle by nature and considerate of others according to his lights, which thoughtlessness might turn down or passion blur, but which burned steadily and brightly in the main, Charles Langholm felt stung to the soul by the last few words, in which Hugh Woodgate noticed nothing amiss. Steel's tone was not openly insulting, but rather that of banter, misplaced perhaps, and in poor taste at such a time, yet ostensibly good-natured and innocent of ulterior meaning. But Langholm was not deceived. There was an ulterior meaning to him, and a very unpleasant one withal. Yet he did not feel unjustifiably insulted; he looked within, and felt justly rebuked; not for anything he had said or done, but for what he found in his heart at that moment. Langholm entered the drawing-room in profound depression, but his state of mind was no longer due to anything that had just been said.

The scene awaiting him was surely calculated to deepen that dejection. Rachel had left the gentlemen with the proud mien and the unbroken spirit which she had maintained at table without trace of effort; they found her sobbing on Morna Woodgate's shoulder, in distress so poignant and so pitiful that even Steel stopped short upon the threshold. In an instant she was on her feet, the tears still thick in her noble eyes, but the spirit once more alight behind the tears.

"Don't go!" she begged them, in a voice that pierced one heart at least.

"Stop and help me, for God's sake! I can't bear it. I am not strong enough. I can only pretend to bear it, for an hour, before the servants. Even that has almost maddened me, the effort, and the shame."

"The shame is on others," said Steel, gravely enough now, "and not on you. And who are those others, I should like to know? And what does it matter what they think or say? A hole-and-corner district like this is not the world!"

Rachel shook her head sadly; her beautiful eyes were dry now, and only the more lustrous for the tears that they had shed. Langholm saw nothing else.

"But it is the world," she asserted. "It is part of the world, and the same thing would happen in any other part. It would happen in London, and everywhere else as soon as I became known. And henceforth I mean to be known!" cried Rachel, wilfully; "there shall be no more hiding who I was, or am; that is the way to make them think the worst when they find out. But is it not disgraceful? I was acquitted, and yet I am to be treated as though I had been merely pardoned. Is that not a disgrace to common humanity?"

"Humanity is not so common as you imagine," remarked Steel.

"It is un-Christian!" cried Hugh Woodgate, with many repetitions of the epithet.

Langholm said nothing. His eyes never left Rachel's face. Neither did she meet them for an instant, nor had she a look for Hugh Woodgate or even for his wife. It was to her husband that Rachel had spoken every word; it was nearest him she stood, in his face only that she gazed.

"Are you going to let the disgrace continue?" she asked him, fiercely.

His answer was natural enough.

"My dear Rachel, what can I do? I never dreamt that it would come out here; it is by the merest fluke that it did."

"But I want it to come out," cried Rachel; "if you mean the fact of my trial and my acquittal. It was a mistake ever to hide either for a moment. Henceforth they shall be no secret."

"Then we cannot prevent the world from thinking and saying what it likes, however uncharitable and unjust. Do be reasonable, and listen to reason, though God knows you can be in no mood for such cold comfort! But I have done my best; I will do my best again. I will sell this place to-morrow. We will go right away somewhere else."

"And then the same thing will happen there! Is that all you can suggest, you who married me after hearing with your own ears every scrap of evidence that they could bring against me?"

"Have you anything better to suggest yourself, Rachel?"

"I have," she answered, looking him full and sternly in the face, in the now forgotten presence of their three guests. "Find out who *is* guilty, if you really want people to believe that I am not!"

Steel did not start, though there came a day when one at least of the listening trio felt honestly persuaded that he had; as a matter of fact, his lips came more closely together, while his eyes searched those of his wife with a wider stare than was often seen in them, but for two or three seconds at most, before dropping in perplexity to the floor.

"How can I, Rachel?" her husband asked quietly, indeed gently, yet with little promise of acquiescence in his tone. "I am not a detective, after all."

But that was added for the sake of adding something, and was enough to prove Steel ill at ease, to the wife who knew him as no man ever had.

"A detective, no!" said she, readily enough. "But you are a rich man; you could employ detectives; you could clear your wife, if you liked."

"Rachel, you know very well that you are cleared already."

"That is your answer, then!" she cried scornfully, and snatched her eyes from him at last, without waiting for a denial. She was done with him, her face said plainly; he looked at her a moment, then turned aside with a shrug.

But Rachel's eyes went swiftly round the room; they alighted for an instant upon Morna Woodgate, leaning forward upon the sofa where they had sat together, eager, enthusiastic, but impotent as a woman must be; they passed over the vicar, looking stolid as usual, and more than a little puzzled; but at last they rested on Langholm's thin, stooping figure, with untidy head thrust forward towards her, and a light in his dreamy eyes that kindled a new light in her own.

"You, Mr. Langholm!" cried Rachel, taking a quick, short step in his direction. "You, with your plots and your problems that nobody can solve; don't you think you could unravel this one for me?"

Her eyes were radiant now, and their radiance all for him. Langholm felt the heart swimming in his body, the brain in his head. A couple of long-legged strides to meet her nine-tenths of the way, and he had taken Rachel's hand before her husband and her friends.

"Before God," said Langholm, "I'll try!"

Their hands met only to part. There was a sardonic laugh from Rachel's husband.

"Do you forbid me?" demanded Langholm, turning upon him.

"Far from it," said Steel. "I shall be most interested to see you go to work."

"Is that a challenge?"

The two men faced each other, while the third man and the women looked on. It had sounded like a challenge to all but the vicar, though neither of the others had had time to think so before they heard the word and recognized its justice.

"If you like," said Steel, indifferently.

"I accept it as such," rejoined Langholm, dogging the other with his eyes. "And find him I will – the guilty man – if I never write another line – and if the villain is still alive!"

CHAPTER XX

More Haste

There are eminent men of action who can acquit themselves with equal credit upon the little field of letters, as some of the very best books of late years go to prove. The man of letters, on the other hand, capable of cutting a respectable figure in action, is, one fears, a much rarer type. Langholm was essentially a man of letters. He was at his best among his roses and his books, at his worst in unforeseen collision with the rougher realities of life. But give him time, and he was not the man to run away because his equipment for battle was as short as his confidence in himself; and perhaps such courage as he possessed was not less courageous for the crust of cowardice (mostly moral) through which it always had to break. Langholm had one other qualification for the quest to which he had committed himself, but for which he was as thoroughly unsuited by temperament as by the whole tenor of his solitary life. In addition to an ingenious imagination (a quality with its own defects, as the sequel will show), he had that capacity for taking pains which has no disadvantageous side, though in Langholm's case, for one, it was certainly not a synonym for genius.

It was 3.45 on the Monday afternoon when he alighted at King's Cross, having caught the 9.30 from Northborough after an early adieu to William Allen Richardson and the rest. Langholm made sure of the time before getting into his hansom at the terminus.

"Drive hard," he said, "to the Capital and Counties Bank in Oxford Street."

And he was there some minutes before the hour.

"I want to know my exact balance, if it is not too much trouble to look it up before you close."

A slip of paper was soon put into Langholm's hand, and at a glance he flushed to the hat with pleasure and surprise, and so regained his cab. "The Cadogan Hotel, in Sloane Street," he cried through the trap; "and there's no hurry, you can go your own pace."

Nor was there any further anxiety in Langholm's heart. His balance was a clear hundred more than he had expected to find it, and his whole soul sang the praises of a country life. Unbusinesslike and unmethodical as he was, in everything but the preparation of MS., such a discovery could never have been made in town, where Langholm's expenditure had marched arm-in-arm with his modest earnings.

"And it can again," he said recklessly to himself, as he decided on the best hotel in the field of his investigations, instead of lodgings; "thank God, I have enough to run this racket till the end of the year at least! If I can't strike the trail by then – "

He lapsed into dear reminiscence and dearer daydreams, their common scene some two hundred miles north; but to realize his lapse was to recover from it promptly. Langholm glanced at himself in the little mirror. His was an honest face, and it was an honest part that he must play, or none at all. He leaned over the apron and interested himself in the London life that was so familiar to him still. It was as though he had not been absent above a day, yet his perceptions were sharpened by his very absence of so many weeks. The wood pavement gave off a strong but not unpleasant scent in the heavy August heat; it was positively dear to the old Londoner's nostrils. The further he drove upon his southwesterly course, the emptier were the well-known thoroughfares. St. James's Street might have been closed to traffic; the clubs in Pall Mall were mostly shut. On the footways strolled the folk whom one only sees there in August and September, the entire families from the country, the less affluent American, guide book in hand. Here and there was a perennial type, the pale actor with soft hat and blue-black chin, the ragged sloucher from park to park. Langholm could have foregathered with one and all, such was the strange fascination of the town for one who was twice the man among his northern roses. But that is the kind of mistress that London is to those who have once felt her spell; you may forget her by the year, but the spell lies lurking in the first whiff of the wood pavement, the first flutter of the evening paper on the curb; and even in the cab you wonder how you have borne existence elsewhere.

The hotel was very empty, and Langholm found not only the best of rooms at his disposal, but that flattering quality of attention which awaits the first comer when few come at all. He refreshed himself with tea and a bath, and then set out to reconnoitre the scene of the already half-forgotten murder. He had a vague though sanguine notion that his imaginative intuition might at once perceive some possibility which had never dawned upon the academic intelligence of the police.

Of course he remembered the name of the street, and it was easily found. Nor had Langholm any difficulty in discovering the house, though he had forgotten the number. There were very few houses in the street, and only one of them was empty and to let. It was plastered with the bills of various agents, and Langholm noted down the nearest of these, whose office was in King's Road. He would get an order to view the house, and would explore every inch of it that very night. But his bath and his tea had made away with the greater part of an hour; it was six o'clock before Langholm reached the house-agent's, and the office was already shut.

He dined quietly at his hotel, feeling none the less that he had made a beginning, and spent the evening looking up Chelsea friends, who were likely to be more conversant than himself with all the circumstances of Mr. Minchin's murder and his wife's arrest; but who, as might have been expected, were one and all from home.

In the morning the order of his plans were somewhat altered. It was essential that he should have those circumstances at his fingers' ends, at least so far as they had transpired in open court. Langholm had read the trial at the time with the inquisitive but impersonal interest which such a case inspires in the average man. Now he must study it in a very different spirit, and for the nonce he repaired betimes to the newspaper room at the British Museum.

By midday he had mastered most details of the complex case, and made a note of every name and address which had found their way into the newspaper reports. But there was one name which did not appear in any account. Langholm sought it in bound volume after bound volume, until even the long-suffering attendants, who trundle the great tomes from their shelves on trolleys, looked askance at the wanton reader who filled in a new form every five or ten minutes. But the reader's face shone with a brighter light at each fresh failure. Why had the name he wanted never come up in open court? Where was the evidence of the man who had made all the mischief between the Minchins? Langholm intended having first the one and then the other; already he was on the spring to a first conclusion. With a caution, however, which did infinite credit to one of his temperament, the amateur detective determined to look a little further before leaping even in his own mind.

Early in the afternoon he was back in Chelsea, making fraudulent representations to the house-agent near the Vestry Hall.

"Not more than ninety," repeated that gentleman, as he went through his book, and read out particulars of several houses at about that rental;

144

but the house which Langholm burned to see over was not among the number.

"I want a quiet street," said the wily writer, and named the one in which it stood. "Have you nothing there?"

"I have one," said the agent with reserve, "and it's only seventy."

"The less the better," cried Langholm, light-heartedly. "I should like to see that one."

The house-agent hesitated, finally looking Langholm in the face.

"You may as well know first as last," said he, "for we have had enough trouble about that house. It was let last year for ninety; we're asking seventy because it is the house in which Mr. Minchin was shot dead. Still want to see it?" inquired the house-agent, with a wry smile.

It was all Langholm could do to conceal his eagerness, but in the end he escaped with several orders to view, and the keys of the house of houses in his pocket. No caretaker could be got to live in it; the agent seemed half-surprised at Langholm's readiness to see over it all alone.

About an hour later the novelist stood at a door whose name and number were not inscribed upon any of the orders obtained by fraud from the King's Road agent. It was a door that needed painting, and there was a conspicuous card in the ground-floor window. Langholm tugged twice in his impatience at the old-fashioned bell. If his face had been alight before, it was now on fire, for by deliberate steps he had arrived at the very conclusion to which he had been inclined to jump. At last came a slut of the imperishable lodging-house type.

"Is your mistress in?"

"No."

"When do you expect her?"

"Not before night."

"Any idea what time of night?"

The untidy child had none, but at length admitted that she had orders to keep the fire in for the landlady's supper. Langholm drew his own deduction. It would be little use in returning before nine o'clock. Five hours to wait! He made one more cast before he went.

"Have you been here long, my girl?"

"Going on three months."

"But your mistress has been here some years?"

"I believe so."

"Are you her only servant?"

"Yes."

And five hours to wait for more!

It seemed an infinity to Langholm as he turned away. But at all events the house had not changed hands. The woman he would eventually see was the woman who had given invaluable evidence at the Old Bailey.

CHAPTER XXI

Worse Speed

Langholm returned to his hotel and wrote a few lines to Rachel. It had been arranged that he was to report progress direct to her, and as often as possible; but it was a very open arrangement, in which Steel had sardonically concurred. Yet, little as there was to say, and for all his practice with the pen, it took Langholm the best part of an hour to write that he believed he had already obtained a most important clew, which the police had missed in the most incredible manner, though it had been under their noses all the time. So incredible did it appear, however, even to himself, when written down, that Langholm decided not to post this letter until after his interview with the Chelsea landlady.

To kill the interval, he went for his dinner to the single club to which he still belonged. It was a Bohemian establishment off the Strand, and its time-honored name was the best thing about it in this member's eyes. He was soon cursing himself for coming near the place while engaged upon his great and sacred quest. Not a "clubable" person himself, as that epithet was understood in this its home, Langholm was not a little surprised when half-a-dozen men (most of whom he barely knew) rose to greet him on his appearance in the smoking-room. But even with their greetings came the explanation, to fill the newcomer with a horror too sudden for concealment.

It appeared that Mrs. Steel's identity with the whilom Mrs. Minchin had not only leaked out in Delverton. Langholm gathered that it was actually in one of that morning's half-penny papers, at which he had not found time to glance in his hot-foot ardor for the chase. For the moment he was shocked beyond words, and not a little disgusted, to discover the cause of his own temporary importance.

"Talk of the devil!" cried a comparative crony. "I was just telling them that you must be the 'well-known novelist' in the case, as your cottage was somewhere down there. Have you really seen anything of the lady?"

"Seen anything of her?" echoed a journalist to whom Langholm had never spoken in his life. "Why, can't you see that he bowled her out himself and came up straight to sell the news?"

Langholm took his comparative crony by the arm.

"Come in and dine with me," he said; "I can't stand this! Yes, yes, I know her well," he whispered, as they went round the screen which was the only partition between pipes and plates; "but let me see what that scurrilous rag has to say while you order. I'll do the rest, and you had better make it a bottle of champagne."

The "scurrilous rag" had less to say than Langholm had been led to expect. He breathed again when he had read the sequence of short but pithy paragraphs. Mrs. Minchin's new name was not given after all, nor that of her adopted district; while Langholm himself only slunk into print as "a well-known novelist who, oddly enough, was among the guests, and eye-witness of a situation after his own heart." The district might have been any one of the many manufacturing centres in "the largest of shires," which was the one geographical clew vouchsafed by the half-penny paper. Langholm began to regret his readiness to admit the impeachment with which he had been saluted; it was only in his own club that he would have been pounced upon as the "well-known novelist"; but it was some comfort to reflect that even in his own club his exact address was not known, for his solicitor paid his subscription and sent periodically for his letters. Charles Langholm had not set up as hermit by halves; he had his own reasons for being thorough there. And it was more inspiriting than the champagne to feel that no fresh annoyance was likely to befall the Steels through him.

"It's not so bad as I thought," said Langholm, throwing the newspaper aside as his companion, whose professional name was Valentine Venn, finished with the wine-card.

"Dear boy," said Venn, "it took a pal to spot you. Alone I did it! But I wish you weren't so dark about that confounded cottage of yours; the humble mummer would fain gather the crumbs that fall from the rich scribe's table, especially when he's out of a shop, which is the present condition of affairs. Besides, we might collaborate in a play, and make more money apiece in three weeks than either of us earns in a fat year. That little story of yours – "

"Never mind my little stories," said Langholm, hastily; "I've just finished a long one, and the very thought of fiction makes me sick."

"Well, you've got facts to turn to for a change, and for once they really do seem as strange as the other thing. Lucky bargee! Have you had her under the microscope all the summer? Ye gods, what a part of Mrs. – "

"Drink up," said Langholm, grimly, as the champagne made an

opportune appearance; "and now tell me who that fellow is who's opening the piano, and since when you've started a musical dinner."

The big room that the screen divided had a grand piano in the dining half, for use upon those Saturday evenings for which the old club was still famous, but rarely touched during the working days of the week. Yet even now a dark and cadaverous young man was raising the top of the piano, slowly and laboriously, as though it were too heavy for him. Valentine Venn looked over his shoulder.

"Good God!" said he. "Another fact worth most folks' fiction – another coincidence you wouldn't dare to use!"

"Why – who is it?"

Venn's answer was to hail the dark, thin youth with rude geniality. The young fellow hesitated, almost shrank, but came shyly forward in the end. Langholm noted that he looked very ill, that his face was as sensitive as it was thin and pale, but his expression singularly sweet and pleasing.

"Severino," said Venn, with a play-actor's pomp, "let me introduce you to Charles Langholm, the celebrated novelist – 'whom not to know is to argue yourself unknown.'"

"Which is the champion *non sequitur* of literature," added Langholm, with literary arrogance, as he took the lad's hand cordially in his own, only to release it hurriedly before he crushed such slender fingers to their hurt.

"Mr. Langholm," pursued Venn, "is the hero of that paragraph" – Langholm kicked him under the table – "that – that paragraph about his last book, you know. Severino, Langholm, is the best pianist we have had in the club since I have been a member, and you will say the same yourself in another minute. He always plays to us when he drops in to dine, and you may think yourself lucky that he has dropped in to-night."

"But where does the coincidence come in?" asked Langholm, as the young fellow returned to the piano with a rather sad shake of the head.

"What!" cried Venn, below his breath; "do you mean to say you are a friend of Mrs. Minchin's, or whatever her name is now, and that you never heard of Severino?"

"No," replied Langholm, his heart in an instantaneous flutter. "Who is he?"

"The man she wanted to nurse the night her husband was murdered – the cause of the final row between them! His name was kept out of the papers, but that's the man."

Langholm sat back in his chair. To have spent a summer's day in stolid search for traces of this man, only to be introduced to the man himself by purest chance in the evening! It was, indeed, difficult to believe; nor was persuasion on the point followed by the proper degree of gratitude in Langholm for a transcendent stroke of fortune. In fact, he almost resented his luck; he would so much rather have stood indebted to his skill. And there were other causes for disappointment, as in an instant there were things more incredible to Langholm than the everyday coincidence of a chance meeting with the one person whom one desires to meet.

"So that's the man!" he echoed, in a tone that might have told his companion something, only the fingers which Langholm had feared to crush had already fallen upon the keys, with the strong, tender, unerring touch of a master, and the impressionable player was swaying with enthusiasm on his stool.

"And can't he play?" whispered Valentine Venn, as though it were the man's playing alone that they were discussing.

Yet even the preoccupied novelist had to listen and nod, and then listen again, before replying.

"He can," said Langholm at length. "But why was it that they took such pains to keep his name out of the case?"

"They didn't. It would have done no good to drag him in. The poor devil was at death's door at the time of the murder."

"But is that a fact?"

Venn opened his eyes.

"Supposing," continued Langholm, speaking the thing that was not in his mind with the deplorable facility of the professional story-teller – "supposing that illness had been a sham, and they had really meant to elope under cover of it!"

"Well, it wasn't."

"I dare say not. But how do you know? They ought to have put him in the box and had his evidence."

"He was still too ill to be called," rejoined Venn. "But I'll take you at your word, dear boy, and tell you exactly how I do know all about his illness. You see that dark chap with the cigar, who's just come in to listen? That's Severino's doctor; it was he who put him up here; and I'll introduce you to him, if you like, after dinner."

"Thank you," said Langholm, after some little hesitation; "as a matter of fact, I should like it very much. Venn," he added, leaning right across the little table, "I know the woman well! I believe in her absolutely, on every point, and I mean to make her neighbors and mine do the same. That is my object – don't give it away!"

"Dear boy, these lips are sealed," said Valentine Venn.

But a very little conversation with the doctor sufficed to satisfy Langholm's curiosity, and to remove from his mind the wild prepossession which he had allowed to grow upon it with every hour of that wasted day. The doctor was also one of the Bohemian colony in Chelsea, and by no means loath to talk about a tragedy of which he had exceptional knowledge, since he himself had been one of the medical witnesses at each successive stage of the investigations. He had also heard on the other side of the screen, that Langholm was the novelist referred to in a paragraph which had of course had a special interest for him; and, as was only fair, Langholm was interrogated in his turn. What was less fair, and indeed ungrateful in a marked degree, was the way in which the original questioner parried all questions put to himself; and he very soon left the club. On his way out, he went into the writing-room, and, tearing into little pieces a letter which he had written that afternoon, left the fragments behind him in the waste-paper basket.

His exit from the room was meanwhile producing its sequel in a little incident which would have astonished Langholm considerably. Severino had been playing for nearly an hour on end, had seemed thoroughly engrossed in his own fascinating performance, and quite oblivious of the dining and smoking going on around him according to the accepted ease and freedom of the club. Yet no sooner was Langholm gone than the pianist broke off abruptly and joined the group which the other had deserted.

"Who is that fellow?" said Severino, in English so perfect that the slight Italian accent only added a charm to his gentle voice. "I did not catch the name."

It was repeated, with such additions as may be fairly made behind a man's back.

"A dashed good fellow, who writes dashed bad novels," was one of these.

"You forget!" said another. "He is the 'well-known novelist' who is going the rounds as a neighbor and friend of Mrs. – "

Looks from Venn and the doctor cut short the speech, but not before its import had come home to the young Italian, whose hollow cheeks flushed a dusky brown, while his sunken eyes caught fire. In an instant he was on his feet, with no attempt to hide his excitement, and still less to mask the emotion that was its real name.

"He knows her, do you tell me? He knows Mrs. Minchin – "

"Or whatever her name is now; yes; so he says."

"And what is her name?"

"He won't say."

"Nor where she lives?"

"No."

"Then where does he live?"

"None of us know that either; he's the darkest horse in the club."

Venn agreed with this speaker, some little bitterness in his tone. Another stood up for Langholm.

"We should be as dark," said he, "if we had married Gayety choristers, and they had left us, and we went in dread of their return!"

They sum up the life tragedies pretty pithily, in these clubs.

"He was always a silly ass about women," rejoined Langholm's critic, summing up the man. "So it's Mrs. Minchin now!"

The name acted like magic upon young Severino. His attention had wandered. In an instant it was more eager than before.

"If you don't know where he lives in the country," he burst out, "where is he staying in town?"

"We don't know that either."

"Then I mean to find out!"

And the pale musician rushed from the room, in pursuit of the man who had been all day pursuing him.

CHAPTER XXII

The Darkest Hour

The amateur detective walked slowly up to Piccadilly, and climbed on top of a Chelsea omnibus, a dejected figure even to the casual eye. He was more than disappointed at the upshot of his wild speculations, and in himself for the false start that he had made. His feeling was one of positive shame. It was so easy now to see the glaring improbability of the conclusion to which he had jumped in his haste, at the first promptings of a too facile fancy. And what an obvious idea it had been at last! As if his were the only brain to which it could have occurred!

Langholm could have laughed at his late theory if it had only entailed the loss of one day, but it had also cost him that self-confidence which was the more valuable in his case through not being a common characteristic of the man. He now realized the difficulties of his quest, and the absolutely wrong way in which he had set about it. His imagination had run away with him. It was no case for the imagination. It was a case for patient investigation, close reasoning, logical deduction, all arts in which the imaginative man is almost inevitably deficient.

Langholm, however, had enough lightness of temperament to abandon an idea as readily as he formed one, and his late suspicion was already driven to the four winds. He only hoped he had not shown what was in his mind at the club. Langholm was a just man, and he honestly regretted the injustice that he had done, even in his own heart, and for ever so few hours, to a thoroughly innocent man.

And all up Piccadilly this man was sitting within a few inches of him, watching his face with a passionate envy, and plucking up courage to speak; he only did so at Hyde Park Corner, where an intervening passenger got down.

Langholm was sufficiently startled at the sound of his own name, breaking in upon the reflections indicated, but to find at his elbow the very face which was in his mind was to lose all power of immediate reply.

"My name is Severino," explained the other. "I was introduced to you an hour or two ago at the club."

"Ah, to be sure!" cried Langholm, recovering. "Odd thing, though, for we must have left about the same time, and I never saw you till this moment."

Severino took the vacant place by Langholm's side. "Mr. Langholm," said he, a tremor in his soft voice, "I have a confession to make to you. I followed you from the club!"

"*You* followed *me?*"

Langholm could not help the double emphasis; to him it seemed a grotesque turning of the tables, a too poetically just ending to that misspent day. It was all he could do to repress a smile.

"Yes, I followed you," the young Italian repeated, with his taking accent, in his touching voice; "and I beg your pardon for doing so – though I would do the same again – I will tell you why. I thought that you were talking about me while I was strumming to them at the club. It is possible, of course, that I was quite mistaken; but when you went out I stopped at once and asked questions. And they told me you were a friend of – a great friend of mine – of Mrs. Minchin!"

"It is true enough," said Langholm, after a pause. "Well?"

"She was a very great friend of mine," repeated Severino. "That was all."

And he sighed.

"So I have heard," said Langholm, with sympathy. "I can well believe it, for I might almost say the same of her myself."

The 'bus toiled on beside the park. The two long lines of lights rose gently ahead until they almost met, and the two men watched them as they spoke.

"Until to-day," continued Severino, "I did not know whether she was dead or alive."

"She is both alive and well."

"And married again?"

"And married again."

There was a long pause. The park ended first.

"I want you to do me a great favor," said Severino in Knightsbridge. "She was so good to me! I shall never forget it, and yet I have never been able to thank her. I nearly died – it was at that time – and when I remembered, she had disappeared. I beg and beseech you, Mr. Langholm, to tell me her name, and where she is living now!"

Langholm looked at his companion in the confluence of lights at the Sloane Street corner. The pale face was alight with passion, the sunken eyes ablaze. "I cannot tell you," he answered, shortly.

"Is it your own name?"

"Good God, no!"

And Langholm laughed harshly.

"Will you not even tell me where she lives?"

"I cannot, without her leave; but if you like I will tell her about you."

There was no answer as they drove on. Then of a sudden Langholm's arm was seized and crushed by bony fingers.

"I am dying," the low voice whispered hoarsely in his ear. "Can't you see it for yourself? I shall never get better; it might be a year or two, it may be weeks. But I want to see her again and make sure. Yes, I love her! There is no sense in denying it. But it is all on my side, and I am dying, and she has married again! What harm can it do anybody if I see her once more?"

The sunken eyes were filled with tears. There were more tears in the hollow voice. Langholm was deeply touched.

"My dear fellow," he said, "I will let her know. No, no, not that, of course! But I will write to her at once – to-night! Will that not do?"

Severino thanked him, with a heavy sigh. "Oh, don't get down," he added, as Langholm rose. "I won't talk about her any more."

"I am staying in this street," explained Langholm, guardedly.

"And these are my lodgings," rejoined the other, pulling a letter from his pocket, and handing the envelope to Langholm. "Let me hear from you, for pity's sake, as soon as you hear from her!"

Langholm sauntered on the pavement until the omnibus which he had left was no longer distinguishable from the general traffic of the thoroughfare. The address on the envelope was that of the lodging-house at which he was to have called that night. He was glad now that his luck had not left him to find Severino for himself; the sense of fatuity would have been even keener than it was. In a way he now felt drawn to the poor, frank boy who had so lately been the object of his unjust and unfounded suspicions. There was a new light in which to think of him, a new bond between them, a new spring of sympathy or jealousy, if not of both. But Langholm was not in London to show sympathy or friendship for any man. He was in London simply and solely upon his own great quest, in which no man must interrupt him. That was why he had been so guarded about his whereabouts – though not guarded enough – and why he watched the omnibus out of sight before entering his hotel. The old Londoner had forgotten how few places there are at which one can stay in Sloane Street.

A bad twenty-four hours was in store for him.

They began well enough with the unexpected discovery that an eminent authority on crime and criminals, who had been a good friend to Langholm in his London days, was still in town. The novelist went round to his house that night, chiefly because it was not ten minutes' walk from the Cadogan Hotel, and with little hope of finding anybody at home. Yet there was his friend, with the midnight lamp just lighted, and so kind a welcome that Langholm confided in him on the spot. And the man who knew all the detectives in London did not laugh at the latest recruit to their ranks; but smile he did.

"I'll tell you what I might do," he said at length. "I might give you a card that should get you into the Black Museum at New Scotland Yard, where they would show you any relics they may have kept of the Minchin murder; only don't say why you want to see them. Every man you see there will be a detective; you may come across the very fellows who got up the case; if so, they may tell you what they think of it, and you should be able to find out whether they're trying again. Here you are, Langholm, and I wish you luck. Doing anything to-morrow night?"

Langholm could safely say that he was not.

"Then dine with me at the Rag at seven, and tell me how you get on. It must be seven, because I'm off to Scotland by the night mail. And I don't want to be discouraging, my dear fellow, but it is only honest to say that I think more of your chivalry than of your chances of success!"

At the Black Museum they had all the trophies which had been produced in court; but the officer who acted as showman to Langholm admitted that they had no right to retain any of them. They were Mrs. Minchin's property, and if they knew where she was they would of course restore everything.

"But the papers say she isn't Mrs. Minchin any longer," the officer added. "Well, well! There's no accounting for taste."

"But Mrs. Minchin was acquitted," remarked Langholm, in tone as impersonal as he could make it.

"Ye-es," drawled his guide, dryly. "Well, it's not for us to say anything about that."

"But you think all the more, I suppose?"

"There's only one opinion about it in the Yard."

"But surely you haven't given up trying to find out who really did murder Mr. Minchin?"

"We think we did find out, sir," was the reply to that.

So they had given it up! For a single second the thought was stimulating; if the humble author could succeed where the police had failed! But the odds against such success were probably a million to one, and Langholm sighed as he handled the weapon with which the crime had been committed, in the opinion of the police.

"What makes you so certain that this was the revolver?" he inquired, more to satisfy his conscience by leaving no question unasked than to voice any doubt upon the point.

The other smiled as he explained the peculiarity of the pistol; it had been made in Melbourne, and it carried the bullet of peculiar size which had been extracted from Alexander Minchin's body.

"But London is full of old Australians," objected Langholm, for objection's sake.

"Well, sir," laughed the officer, "you find one who carries a revolver like this, and prove that he was in Chelsea on the night of the murder, with a motive for committing it, and we shall be glad of his name and address. Only don't forget the motive; it wasn't robbery, you know, though her ladyship was so sure it was robbers! There's the maker's name on the barrel. I should take a note of it, sir, if I was you!"

That name and that note were all that Langholm had to show when he dined with the criminologist at his service club the same evening. The amateur detective looked a beaten man already, but he talked through his teeth of inspecting the revolvers in every pawnbroker's shop in London.

"It will take you a year," said the old soldier, cheerfully.

"It seems the only chance," replied the despondent novelist. "It is a case of doing that or nothing."

"Then take the advice of an older fogey than yourself, and do nothing! You are quite right to believe in the lady's innocence; there is no excuse for entertaining any other belief, still less for expressing it. But when you come to putting salt on the real culprit, that's another matter. My dear fellow, it's not the sort of thing that you or I could hope to do on our own, even were the case far simpler than it is. It was very sporting of you to offer for a moment to try your hand; but if I were you I should confess without delay that the task is far beyond you, for that's the honest truth."

Langholm walked back to his hotel, revolving this advice. Its soundness was undeniable, while the source from which it came gave it exceptional weight and value. It was an expert opinion which no man in his senses could afford to ignore, and Langholm felt that Mrs. Steel also ought at least to hear it before building on his efforts. The letter would prepare her for his ultimate failure, as it was only fair that she should be prepared, and yet would leave him free to strain every nerve in any fresh direction in which a chance ray lit the path. But it would be a difficult letter to write, and Langholm was still battling with the first sentence when he reached the Cadogan.

"A gentleman to see me?" he cried in surprise. "What gentleman?"

"Wouldn't leave his name, sir; said he'd call again; a foreign gentleman, he seemed to me."

"A delicate-looking man?"

"Very, sir. You seem to know him better than he knows you," added the hall-porter, with whom Langholm had made friends. "He wasn't certain whether it was the Mr. Langholm he wanted who was staying here, and he asked to look at the register."

"Did you let him see it?" cried Langholm, quickly.

"I did, sir."

"Then let me have another look at it, please!"

It was as Langholm feared. Thoughtlessly, but naturally enough, when requested to put his own name in the book, he had also filled in that full address which he took such pains to conceal in places where he was better known. And that miserable young Italian, that fellow Severino, had discovered not only where he was staying in town, but where he lived in the country, and his next discovery would be Normanthorpe House and its new mistress! Langholm felt enraged; after his own promise to write to Rachel, a promise already fulfilled, the unhappy youth might have had the decency to refrain from underhand tricks like this. Langholm felt inclined to take a cab at once to Severino's lodgings, there to relieve his mind by a very plain expression of his opinion. But it was late; and perhaps allowances should be made for a sick man with a passion as hopeless as his bodily state; in any case he would sleep upon it first.

But there was no sleep for Charles Langholm that night, nor did the thought of Severino enter his head again; it was suddenly swept aside and as suddenly replaced by that of the man who was to fill the novelist's mind for many a day.

Idly glancing up and down the autographed pages of the hotel register, as his fingers half-mechanically turned leaf after leaf backward, Langholm's eye had suddenly caught a name of late as familiar to him as his own.

It was the name of John Buchanan Steel.

And the date was the date of the Minchin murder.

CHAPTER XXIII

Dawn

The hall-porter was only too ready for further chat. It was the dull season, and this visitor was one of a variety always popular in the quieter hotels; he was never above a pleasant word with the servants. Yet the porter stared at Langholm as he approached. His face was flushed, and his eyes so bright that there would have been but one diagnosis by the average observer. But the porter knew that Langholm had come in sober, and that for the last twenty minutes he had sat absorbed in the hotel register.

"I see," said Langholm – and even his voice was altered, which made the other stare the harder – "I see that a friend of mine stayed here just upon a year ago. I wonder if you remember him?"

"If it was the off-season, sir, I dare say I shall."

"It was in September, and his name was Steel."

"How long did he stay?"

"Only one night, I gather – an elderly gentleman with very white hair."

The porter's face lighted up.

"I remember him, sir! I should think I did! A very rich gentleman, I should say; yes, he only stayed the one night, but he gave me a sovereign when he went away next day."

"He is very rich," said Langholm, repressing by main force a desire to ask a string of questions. He fancied that the porter was not one who needed questioning, and his patience had its immediate reward.

"I remember when he arrived," the man went on. "It was late at night, and he hadn't ordered his room. He came in first to see whether we could give him one. I paid the cab myself and brought in his bag."

"He had just arrived from the country, I presume?"

The porter nodded.

"At King's Cross, by the 10.45, I believe; but it must have been a good bit late, for I was just coming off duty, and the night-porter was just coming on."

"Then you didn't see any more of Mr. Steel that night?"

"I saw him go out again," said the porter, dryly, "after he had something to eat, for we are short-handed in the off-season, and I stopped up myself to see he got it. I didn't see him come in the second time."

Langholm could hardly believe his ears. To cover his excitement he burst out laughing.

"The old dog!" he cried. "Do you know if he ever came in at all?"

"Between two and three, I believe," said the porter in the same tone.

Langholm laughed again, but asked no more questions, and in a little he was pacing his bedroom floor, with fevered face and tremulous stride, as he was to continue pacing it for the greater part of that August night.

Yet it was not a night spent in thought, but rather in intercepting and in casting out the kind of thoughts that chased each other through the novelist's brain. His imagination had him by the forelock once more, but this time he was resisting with all his might. It meant resistance to the strongest attribute that he possessed. The man's mind was now a picture-gallery and now a stage. He thought in pictures and he saw in scenes. It was no fault of Langholm's, any more than it was a merit. Imagination was the predominant force of his intellect, as in others is the power of reasoning, or the gift of languages, or the mastery of figures. Langholm could no more help it than he could change the color of his eyes, but to-night he did his best. He had mistaken invention for discovery once already. He was grimly determined not to let it happen twice.

To suspect Steel because he chanced to have been in the neighborhood of Chelsea on the night of the murder, and absent from his hotel about the hour of its committal, was not less absurd than his first suspicion of the man who could be proved to have been lying between life and death at the time. There had been something to connect the dead man with Severino. There was nothing within Langholm's knowledge to connect him with Steel. Yet Steel was the most mysterious person that he had ever met with outside the pages of his own novels. No one knew where he had made his money. He might well have made it in Australia; they might have known each other out there. Langholm suddenly remembered the Australian swagman whom he had seen "knocking down his check" at a wayside inn within a few miles of Normanthorpe, and Steel's gratuitously explicit statement that neither he nor his wife had ever been in Australia in their lives. There was one lie at least, then why not two? Yet, the proven lie might have been told by Steel simply to anticipate and allay any possible suspicion of his wife's identity. That was at least conceivable. And this time Langholm sought the conceivable explanation more sedulously than the suspicious circumstance.

He had been far too precipitate in all that he had done hitherto, from the Monday morning up to this Wednesday night. His departure on the Monday had been in itself premature. He had come away without seeing the Steels again, whereas he should have had an exhaustive interview with one or both of them before embarking upon his task. But Steel's half-hostile and half-scornful attitude was more than Langholm could trust his temper to endure, and he had despaired of seeing Mrs. Steel alone. There were innumerable points upon which she could have supplied him with valuable information. He had hoped to obtain what he wanted from the fuller reports of the trial; but that investigation had been conducted upon the supposition that his wife, and no other, had caused the death of Alexander Minchin. No business friend of the deceased had been included among the witnesses, and the very least had been made of his financial difficulties, which had formed no part of the case for the Crown.

Langholm, however, his wits immensely quickened by the tonic of his new discovery, began to see possibilities in this aspect of the matter, and, as soon as the telegraph offices were open, he despatched a rather long message to Mrs. Steel, reply paid. It was simply to request the business address of her late husband, with the name and address of any partner or other business man who had seen much of him in the City. If the telegram were not intercepted, Langholm calculated that he should have his reply in a couple of hours, and one came early in the forenoon: –

"Shared office 2 Adam's Court Old Broad Street with a Mr. Crofts his friend but not mine Rachel Steel."

Langholm looked first at the end, and was thankful to see that the reply was from Rachel herself. But the penultimate clause introduced a complication. It must have some meaning. It would scarcely be a wholly irrelevant expression of dislike. Langholm, at all events, read a warning in the words – a warning to himself not to call on Mr. Crofts as a friend of the dead man's wife. And this increased the complication, ultimately suggesting a bolder step than the man of letters quite relished, yet one which he took without hesitation in Rachel's cause. He had in his pocket the card of the detective officer who had shown him over the Black Museum; luckily it was still quite clean; and Langholm only wished he looked the part a little more as he finally sallied forth.

Mr. Crofts was in, his small clerk said, and the sham detective followed the real one's card into the inner chamber of the poky offices upon the third floor. Mr. Crofts sat aghast in his office chair, the puzzled picture of a man who feels his hour has come, but who wonders which of his many delinquencies has come to light. He was large and florid, with a bald head and a dyed mustache, but his coloring was an unwholesome purple as the false pretender was ushered in.

"I am sorry to intrude upon you, Mr. Crofts," began Langholm, "but I have come to make a few inquiries about the late Alexander Minchin, who, I believe, once – "

"Quite right! Quite right!" cried Crofts, as the purple turned a normal red in his sanguine countenance. "Alexander Minchin – poor fellow – to be sure! Take a seat, Inspector, take a seat. Happy to afford you any information in my power."

If Mr. Crofts looked relieved, however, as many a decent citizen might under similar visitation, it was a very real relief to Langholm not to have been found out at a glance. He took the proffered seat with the greater readiness on noting how near it was to the door.

"The death of Mr. Minchin is, as you know, still a mystery – "

"I didn't know it," interrupted Crofts, who had quite recovered his spirits. "I thought the only mystery was how twelve sane men could have acquitted his wife."

"That," said Langholm, "was the opinion of many at the time; but it is one which we are obliged to disregard, whether we agree with it or not. The case still engages our attention, and must do so until we have explored every possible channel of investigation. What I want from you, Mr. Crofts, is any information that you can give me concerning Mr. Minchin's financial position at the time of his death."

"It was bad," said Mr. Crofts, promptly; "about as bad as it could be. He had one lucky flutter, and it would have been the ruin of him if he had lived. He backed his luck for more than it was worth, and his luck deserted him on the spot. Yes, poor old devil!" sighed the sympathetic Crofts: "he thought he was going to make his pile out of hand, but in another week he would have been a bankrupt."

"Had you known him long, Mr. Crofts?"

"Not six months; it was down at Brighton we met, quite by chance, and got on talking about Westralians. It was I put him on to his one good spec. His wife was with him at the time – couldn't stand the woman! She was much too good for me and my missus, to say nothing of her own husband. I remember one night on the pier – "

"I won't trouble you about Brighton, Mr. Crofts," Langholm interrupted, as politely as he could. "Mr. Minchin was not afterwards a partner of yours, was he?"

"Never; though I won't say he mightn't have been if things had panned out differently, and he had gone back to Westralia with some capital. Meanwhile he had the run of my office, and that was all."

"And not even the benefit of your advice?"

"He wouldn't take it, once he was bitten with the game."

Thus far Langholm had simply satisfied his own curiosity upon one or two points concerning a dead man who had been little more than a name to him hitherto. His one discovery of the least potential value was that Minchin had evidently died in difficulties. He now consulted some notes jotted down on an envelope upon his way to the City.

"Mr. Minchin, as you are aware," resumed Langholm, "was, like his wife, an Australian by birth. Had he many Australian friends here in London?"

"None at all," replied Mr. Crofts, "that I am aware of."

"Nor anywhere else in the country, think you?"

"Not that I remember."

"Not in the north of England, for example?"

Thus led, Mr. Crofts frowned at his desk until an enlightened look broke over his florid face.

"By Jove, yes!" said he. "Now you speak of it, there *was* somebody up north – a rich man, too – but he only heard of him by chance a day or so before his death."

"A rich man, you say, and an Australian?"

"I don't know about that, but it was out there they had known each other, and Minchin had no idea he was in England till he saw it in the paper a day or two before his death."

"Do you remember the name?"

"No, I don't, for he never told it to me; fact is, we were not on the best of terms just at the last," explained Mr. Crofts. "Money matters – money matters – they divide the best of friends – and to tell you the truth he owed me more than I could afford to lose. But the day before the last day of his life he came in and said it was all right, he'd square up before the week was out, and if that wasn't good enough for me I could go to the devil. Of course I asked him where the money was coming from, and he said from a man he'd not heard of for years until that morning, but he didn't say how he'd heard of him then, only that he must be a millionaire. So then I asked why a man he hadn't seen for so long should pay his debts, but Minchin only laughed and swore that he'd make him. And that was the last I ever heard of it; he sat down at that desk over yonder and wrote to his millionaire there and then, and took it out himself to post. It was the last time I saw him alive, for he said he wasn't coming back till he got his answer, and it was the last letter he ever wrote in the place."

"On that desk, eh?" Langholm glanced at the spare piece of office furniture in the corner. "Didn't he keep any papers here?" he added.

"He did, but you fellows impounded them."

"Of course we did," said Langholm, hastily. "Then you have nothing of his left?"

"Only his pen, and a diary in which he hadn't written a word. I slipped them into a drawer with his papers, and there they are still."

Langholm felt disappointed. He had learnt so much, it was tantalizing not to learn a little more. If he could only make sure of that millionaire friend of Minchin! In his own mind he was all but sure, but his own mind was too elastic by half.

Crofts was drumming on the blotting-pad in front of him; all of a sudden Langholm noticed that it had a diary attached.

"Minchin's diary wasn't one like yours, was it?" he exclaimed.

"The same thing," said Mr. Crofts.

"Then I should like to see it."

"There's not a word written in it; one of you chaps overhauled it at the time."

"Never mind!"

"Well, then, it's in the top long drawer of the desk he used to use – if my clerk has not appropriated it to his own use."

Langholm held his breath as he went to the drawer in question. In another instant his breath escaped him in a sigh of thankfulness. The "Universal Diary" (for the year before) was there, sure enough. And it was attached to a pink blotter precisely similar to that upon which Mr. Crofts still drummed with idle fingers.

"Anything more I can show you?" inquired that worthy, humorously.

Langholm was gazing intently, not at the diary, but at the pink blotting-paper. Suddenly he looked up.

"You say that was the last letter he ever wrote in your office?"

"The very last."

"Then – yes – you can show me a looking-glass if you have one!"

Crofts had a small one on his chimney-piece.

"By the Lord Harry," said he, handing it, "but you tip-top 'tecs are a leery lot!"

CHAPTER XXIV

One who was not Bidden

Langholm went north next morning by the ten o'clock express from King's Cross. He had been but four nights in town, and not four days, yet to Langholm they might have been weeks, for he had never felt so much and slept so little in all his life. He had also done a good deal; but it is the moments of keen sensation that make up the really crowded hours, and Langholm was to run the gamut of his emotions before this memorable week was out. In psychological experience it was to be, for him, a little lifetime in itself; indeed, the week seemed that already, while it was still young, and comparatively poor in incident and surprise.

He had bought magazines and the literary papers for his journey, but he could concentrate his mind on nothing, and only the exigencies of railway travelling kept him off his legs. Luckily for Langholm, however, sleep came to him when least expected, in his cool corner of the corridor train, and he only awoke in time for luncheon before the change at York. His tired brain was vastly refreshed, but so far he could not concentrate it, even on the events of these eventful days. He was still in the thick of them. A sense of proportion was as yet impossible, and a consecutive review the most difficult of intellectual feats. Langholm was too excited, and the situation too identical with suspense, for a clear sight of all its bearings and potentialities; and then there was the stern self-discipline, the determined bridling of the imagination, in which he had not yet relaxed. Once in the night, however, in the hopeless hours between darkness and broad day, he had seen clearly for a while, and there and then pinned his vision down to paper. It concerned only one aspect of the case, but this was how Langholm found that he had stated it, on taking out his pocket-book during the final stages of his journey –

PROVISIONAL CASE AGAINST ------------

1. *Was in Sloane Street on the night of the murder, at an hotel about a mile from the house in which the murder was committed. This can be proved.*

2. *Left hotel shortly after arrival towards midnight, believed to have returned between two and three, and would thus have been absent at*

very time at which crime was committed according to medical evidence adduced at trial. But exact duration of absence from hotel can he proved.

3. *Knew M. in Australia, but was in England unknown to M. till two mornings before murder, when M. wrote letter on receipt of which ------------ came up to town (arriving near scene of murder as above stated, about time of commission). All this morally certain and probably capable of legal proof.*

4. *"So then I asked why a man he hadn't seen for so long should pay his debts; but M. only laughed and swore, and said he'd make him." C. could be subpoenaed to confirm if not to amplify this statement to me, with others to effect that it was for money M. admitted having written to "a millionaire."*

5. *Attended Mrs. M.'s trial throughout, thereafter making her acquaintance and offering marriage without any previous private knowledge whatsoever of her character or antecedents.*

POSSIBLE MOTIVES

------------ is a human mystery, his past life a greater one. He elaborately pretends that no part of that past was spent in Australia.

M. said he knew him there; also that "he'd make him" – pay up!

Blackmail not inconsistent with M.'s character.

Men have died as they deserved before to-day for threatening blackmail.

Possible Motive for Marriage

Atonement of the Guilty to the Innocent.

As Langholm read and re-read these precise pronouncements, with something of the detachment and the mild surprise with which he occasionally dipped into his own earlier volumes, he congratulated himself upon the evidently lucid interval which had produced so much order from the chaos that had been his mind. Chaotic as its condition still was, that orderly array of impression, discovery, and surmise, bore the test of conscientious reconsideration. And there was nothing that Langholm felt moved to strike out in the train; but, on the other hand, he saw the weakness of his case as it stood at present, and was helped to see it by the detective officer's remark to him at Scotland Yard: "You find one [old Australian] who carries a revolver like this, and prove that he was in Chelsea on the night of the murder, with a motive for committing it, and we shall be glad of his name and address." Langholm had found the old Australian who could be proved to have been in Chelsea, or thereabouts, on the night in question; but the pistol he could not hope to find, and the motive was mere surmise.

And yet, to the walls of the mind that he was trying so hard to cleanse from prejudice and prepossession – to school indeed to an inhuman fairness – there clung small circumstances and smaller details which could influence no one else, which would not constitute evidence before any tribunal, but which weighed more with Langholm himself than all the points arrayed in his note-book with so much primness and precision.

There was Rachel's vain appeal to her husband, "Find out who *is* guilty if you want people to believe that I am not." Why should so natural a petition have been made in vain, to a husband who after all had shown some solicitude for his wife's honor, and who had the means to employ the best detective talent in the world? Langholm could only conceive one reason: there was nothing for the husband to find out, but everything for him to hide.

Langholm remembered the wide-eyed way in which Steel had looked at his wife before replying, and the man's embarrassment grew automatically in his mind. His lips had indeed shut very tight, but unconscious exaggeration made them tremble first.

And then the fellow's manner to himself, his defiant taunts, his final challenge! Langholm was not sorry to remember the last; it relieved him from the moral incubus of the clandestine and the underhand; it bid him go on and do his worst; it set his eyes upon the issue as between himself and Steel, and it shut them to the final possibilities as touching the woman in the case.

So Langholm came back from sultry London to a world of smoke and rain, with furnaces flaring through the blurred windows, and the soot laid with the dust in one of the grimiest towns in the island; but he soon shook both from his feet, and doubled back upon the local line to a rural station within a mile and a half of his cottage. This distance he walked by muddy ways, through the peculiarly humid atmosphere created by a sky that has rained itself out and an earth that can hold no more, and came finally to his dripping garden by the wicket at the back of the cottage. There he stood to inhale the fine earthy fragrance which atoned somewhat for a rather desolate scene. The roses were all washed away. William Allen Richardson clung here and there, in the shelter of the southern eaves, but he was far past his prime, and had better have perished with the exposed beauties on the tiny trees. The soaking foliage had a bluish tinge; the glimpse of wooded upland, across the valley through the gap in the hedge of Penzance briers, lay colorless and indistinct as a faded print from an imperfect negative. A footstep crunched the wet gravel at Langholm's back.

"Thank God you've got back, sir!" cried a Yorkshire voice in devout accents; and Langholm, turning, met the troubled face and tired eyes of the woman next door, who kept house for him while living in her own.

"My dear Mrs. Brunton," he exclaimed, "what on earth has happened? You didn't expect me earlier, did you? I wired you my train first thing this morning."

"Oh, no, it isn't that, sir. It's – it's the poor young gentleman – "

And her apron went to her eyes.

"What young gentleman, Mrs. Brunton?"

"Him 'at you saw i' London an' sent all this way for change of air! He wasn't fit to travel half the distance. I've been nursing of him all night and all day too."

"A young gentleman, and sent by me?" Langholm's face was blank until a harsh light broke over it. "What's his name, Mrs. Brunton?"

"I can't tell you, sir. He said he was a friend of yours, and that was all before he took ill. He's been too bad to answer questions all day. And then we knew you'd soon be here to tell us."

"A foreigner, I suppose?"

"I should say he was, sir."

"And did he really tell you I had sent him?"

"Well, I can't say he did, not in so many words, but that was what I thought he meant. It was like this, sir," continued Mrs. Brunton, as they stood face to face on the wet gravel: "just about this time yesterday I was busy ironing, when my nephew, the lad you used to send with letters, who's here again for his summer holidays, comes to me an' says, 'You're wanted.' So I went, and there was a young gentleman looking fit to drop. He'd a bag with him, and he'd walked all the way from Upthorpe station, same as I suppose you have now; but yesterday was the hottest day we've had, and I never did see living face so like the dead. He had hardly life enough to ask if this was where you lived; and when I said it was, but you were away, he nodded and said he'd just seen you in London; and he was sure he might come in and rest a bit. Well, sir, I not only let him do that, but you never will lock up anything, so I gave him a good sup o' your whiskey too!"

"Quite right," said Langholm – "and then?"

"It seemed to pull him together a bit, and he began to talk. He wanted to know about all the grand folks round about, where they lived and how long they'd lived there. At last he made me tell him the way to Normanthorpe House, after asking any amount of questions about Mr. and Mrs. Steel; it was hard work not to tell him what had just come out, but I remembered what you said before you went away, sir, and I left that to others."

"Good!" said Langholm. "But did he go to Normanthorpe?"

"He started, though I begged him to sit still while we tried to get him a trap from the village; and his self-will nearly cost him his life, if it doesn't yet. He was hardly out of sight when we see him come staggering back with his handkerchief up to his mouth, and the blood dripping through his fingers into the road."

"A hemorrhage!"

"Yes, sir, yon was the very word the doctor used, and he says if he has another it'll be all up. So you may think what a time I've had! If he's a friend of yours, sir, I'm sure I don't mind. In any case, poor gentleman – "

"He is a friend of mine," interrupted Langholm, "and we must do all we can for him. I will help you, Mrs. Brunton. You shall have your sleep to-night. Did you put him into my room?"

"No, sir, your bed wasn't ready, so we popped him straight into our own; and now he has everything nice and clean and comfortable as I could make it. If only we can pull him through, poor young gentleman, between us!"

"God bless you for a good woman," said Langholm, from his heart; "it will be His will and not your fault if we fail. Yes, I should like to see the poor fellow, if I may."

"He is expecting you, sir. He told Dr. Sedley he must see you the moment you arrived, and the doctor said he might. No, he won't know you're here yet, and he can't have heard a word, for our room is at t'front o' t'house."

"Then I'll go up alone, Mrs. Brunton, if you won't mind."

Severino was lying in a high, square bed, his black locks tossed upon a spotless pillow no whiter than his face; a transparent hand came from under the bedclothes to meet Langholm's outstretched one, but it fell back upon the sick man's breast instead.

"Do you forgive me?" he whispered, in a voice both hoarse and hollow.

"What for?" smiled Langholm. "You had a right to come where you liked; it is a free country, Severino."

"But I went to your hotel – behind your back!"

"That was quite fair, my good fellow. Come, I mean to shake hands, whether you like it or not."

And the sound man took the sick one's hand with womanly tenderness; and so sat on the bed, looking far into the great dark sinks of fever that were human eyes; but the fever was of the brain, for the poor fellow's hand was cool.

"You do not ask me why I did it," came from the tremulous lips at last.

"Perhaps I know."

"I will tell you if you are right."

"It was to see her again – your kindest friend – and mine," said Langholm, gently.

"Yes! It was to see her again – before I die!"

And the black eyes blazed again.

"You are not going to die," said Langholm, with the usual reassuring scorn.

"I am. Quite soon. On your hands, I only fear. And I have not seen her yet!"

"You shall see her," said Langholm, tenderly, gravely. He was rewarded with a slight pressure of the emaciated hand; but for the first time he suspected that all the scrutiny was not upon one side – that the sick youth was trying to read him in his turn.

"I love her!" at last cried Severino, in rapt whispers. "Do you hear me? I love her! I love her! What does it matter now?"

"It would matter to her if you told her," rejoined Langholm. "It would make her very unhappy."

"Then I need not tell her."

"You must not, indeed."

"Very well, I will not. It is a promise, and I keep my promises; it is only when I make none – "

"That's all right," said Langholm, smiling.

"Then you will bring her to me?"

"I shall have to see her first, and the doctor."

"But you will do your best? That is why I am here, remember! I shall tell the doctor so myself."

"I will do my best," said Langholm, as he rose.

A last whisper followed him to the door.

"Because I worship her!" were the words.

CHAPTER XXV

A Point to Langholm

"I am glad you have come back," said Dr. Sedley with relief. "Of course eventually he will require trained nursing, either here or somewhere else; there is only one end to such a case, but it needn't come yet, unless he has another hemorrhage. I understand you offered him your cottage while you were away, but there was some muddle, and he came before they were ready for him? It was like your kindness, my dear fellow, only never you send another consumptive to the northeast coast or anywhere near it! As to his seeing any ladies who like to look him up, by all means, only one at a time, and they mustn't excite him. Your return, for example, has been quite enough excitement for to-day, and I should keep him quiet for the next twenty-four hours."

The doctor had called within an hour of the return of Langholm, who repeated these stipulations upstairs, with his own undertaking in regard to Rachel. He would write that night and beg her to call the following day. No, he preferred writing to going to see her, and it took up far less time. But he would write at once. And, as he went downstairs to do so then and there, Langholm asked himself whether an honorable man could meet the Steels again without reading to their faces the notes that he had made in London and conned in the train.

This letter written, there was a small pile of them awaiting attention on top of the old bureau; and Langholm sat glancing at proofs and crumpling up press-cuttings until he needed a lamp. The letter that he kept to the last looked like one of the rare applications for his autograph which he was not too successful to welcome as straws showing the wind of popular approval. In opening the envelope, however, he noticed that it bore the Northborough postmark, also that the handwriting was that of an illiterate person, and his very surname misspelt. The contents were as follows:

"Northborough, August 18, 189 – .

"MR. LANGHAM, Sir,

"I here as you are on the tracks of them that murdered Alexander Minchin, if you want to know of them that had a Reason for doing it I can give you the straight Tip.

"I have been out to your place to-night, but you are only due home to-morrow night, therefore I will be your way again to-morrow night, but will only come to the cross-roads as your old girl look suspichious last night and this is on the strickt Q.T.

"Till to-morrow night then at the cross-roads near your place, from nine to ten to-morrow night, when you will here of something to your advantage.

"Believe your's faithly,

"JOHN WILLIAM ABEL."

Langholm could not guess who this man Abel might be, but idly imagined him one of the innumerable drinking drones who stood about the street corners of Northborough from morning till night throughout the year. This one had more information than the common run, with perhaps more cunning and ingenuity to boot. Langholm deemed it discreet not to mention the matter to his dear "old girl" of disrespectful reference, who served him an excellent supper at eight o'clock. And little better than an hour later, having seen the invalid once more, and left him calm and comfortable for the night, the novelist sallied forth to meet his unknown correspondent.

It was a dark night, for the rain was by no means over, though not actually falling at the moment; and the cross-roads, which lay low, with trees in all four angles, was a dark spot at full moon. As he approached with caution, rapping the road with his stick in order to steer clear of the ditch, Langholm wished he had come on his bicycle, for the sake of the light he might have had from its lamp; but a light there was, ready waiting for him, though a very small and feeble one; for his illiterate correspondent was on the ground before him, with a cutty-pipe in full blast.

"Name of Langholm?" said a rather rollicking voice, with a rank puff and a shower of sparks, as the cautious steps followed the rapping stick.

"That's it," said Langholm; "if yours is Abel, I have got your letter."

"You have, have you?" cried the other, with the same jovial familiarity. "And what do you think of it?"

The glowing pipe lit a wild brown beard and mustache, thickly streaked with gray, a bronzed nose, and nothing more. Indeed, it was only at each inhalation that so much stood out upon the surrounding screen of impenetrable blackness. Langholm kept his distance, stick in hand, his gaunt figure as invisible as the overhanging trees; but his voice might have belonged to the most formidable of men.

"As yet," said he, sternly, "I think very little of either you or your letter. Who are you, and what do you mean by writing to me like that?"

"Steady, mister, you do know my name!" remonstrated the man, in rather more respectful tones. "It's Abel – John William – and as much at your service as you like if you take him proper; but he comes from a country where Jack isn't the dirt under his master's feet, and you're no master o' mine."

"I don't want to be, my good fellow," rejoined Langholm, modifying his own manner in turn. "Then you're not a Northborough man?"

"Not me!"

"I seem to have heard your voice before," said Langholm, to whom the wild hair on the invisible face was also not altogether unfamiliar. "Where do you come from?"

"A little place called Australia."

"The devil you do!"

And Langholm stood very still in the dark, for now he knew who this man was, and what manner of evidence he might furnish, and against whom. The missing links in his own secret chain, what if these were about to be given to him by a miracle, who had discovered so much already by sheer chance! It seemed impossible; yet his instinct convinced Langholm of the nature of that which was to come. Without another word he stood until he could trust himself to speak carelessly, while the colonist made traditional comparisons between the old country as he found it and the one which he wished he had never left.

"I know you," said Langholm, when he paused. "You're the man I saw 'knocking down your check,' as you called it, at an inn near here called the Packhorse."

"I am so!" cried the fellow, with sudden savagery. "And do you know where I got the check to knock down? I believe he's a friend of yours;

it's him I've come to talk to you about to-night, and he calls himself Steel!"

"Isn't it his real name?" asked Langholm, quickly.

"Well, for all I know, it is. If it isn't, it ought to be!" added Abel, bitterly.

"You knew him in Australia, then?"

"Knew him? I should think I did know him! But who told you he was ever out there? Not him, I'll warrant!"

"I happen to know it," said Langholm, "that's all. But do you mean to tell me that it was Mr. Steel to whom you referred in your letter?"

"I do so!" cried Abel, and clinched it with an oath.

"You said 'they.'"

"But I didn't mean anybody else."

Langholm lowered his voice. Neither foot nor hoof had passed or even sounded in the distance. There was scarcely a whisper of the trees; an ordinary approach could have been heard for hundreds of yards, a stealthy one for tens. Langholm had heard nothing, though his ears were pricked. And yet he lowered his voice.

"Do you actually hint that Mr. Steel has or could have been a gainer by Mr. Minchin's death?"

Abel pondered his reply.

"What I will say," he declared at length, "is that he might have been a loser by his life!"

"You mean if Mr. Minchin had gone on living?"

"Yes – amounts to the same thing, doesn't it?"

"You are not thinking of – of Mrs. Steel?" queried Langholm, after pausing in his turn.

"Bless you, no! She wasn't born or thought of, so far as we was concerned, when we were all three mates up the bush."

"Ah, all three!"

"Steel, Minchin, and me," nodded Abel, as his cutty glowed.

"And you were mates!"

"Well, we were and we weren't: that's just it," said Abel, resentfully. "It would be better for some coves now, if we'd all been on the same footin' then. But that we never were. I was overseer at the principal out-station – a good enough billet in its way – and Minchin was overseer in at the homestead. But Steel was the boss, damn him, trust Steel to be the boss!"

"But if the station was his?" queried Langholm. "I suppose it was a station?" he added, as a furious shower of sparks came from the cutty.

"Was it a station?" the ex-overseer echoed. "Only about the biggest and the best in the blessed back-blocks – that's all! Only about half the size of your blessed little old country cut out square! Oh, yes, it was his all right; bought it for a song after the bad seasons fifteen year ago, and sold it in the end for a quarter of a million, after making a fortune off of his clips alone. And what did I get out of it?" demanded Abel, furiously. "What was my share? A beggarly check same as he give me the other day, and not a penny more!"

"I don't know how much that was," remarked Langholm; "but if you weren't a partner, what claim had you on the profits?"

"Aha! that's tellings," said Abel, with a sudden change both of tone and humor; "that's what I'm here to tell you, if you really want to know! Rum thing, wasn't it? One night I turn up, like any other swaggy, humping bluey, and next week I'm overseer on a good screw (I will say that) and my own boss out at the out-station. Same way, one morning I turn up at his grand homestead here – and you know what! It was a check for three figures. I don't mind telling you. It ought to have been four. But why do you suppose he made it even three? Not for charity, you bet your boots! I leave it to you to guess what for."

The riddle was perhaps more easily solvable by an inveterate novelist than by the average member of the community. It was of a kind which Langholm had been concocting for many years.

"I suppose there is some secret," said he, taking a fresh grip of his stick, in sudden loathing of the living type which he had only imagined hitherto.

"Ah! You've hit it," purred the wretch.

"It is evident enough, and always has been, for that matter," said Langholm, coldly. "And so you know what his secret is!"

"I do, mister."

"And did Mr. Minchin?"

"He did."

"You would tell him, of course?"

The sort of scorn was too delicate for John William Abel, yet even he seemed to realize that an admission must be accompanied by some form of excuse.

"I did tell him," he said, "for I felt I owed it to him. He was a good friend to me, was Mr. Minchin; and neither of us was getting enough for all we did. That was what I felt; to have his own way, the boss'd ride roughshod over us both, and he himself only – but that's tellings again. You must wait a bit, mister! Mr. Minchin hadn't to wait so very long, because I thought we could make him listen to two of us, so one night I told him what I knew. You could ha' knocked him down with a feather. Nobody dreamt of it in New South Wales. No, there wasn't a hand on the place who would have thought it o' the boss! Well, he was fond of Minchin, treated him like a son, and perhaps he wasn't such a good son as he might have been. But when he told the boss what I told him, and made the suggestion that I thought would come best from a gent like him – "

"That you should both be taken into partnership on the spot, I suppose?" interrupted Langholm.

"Well, yes, it came to something like that."

"Go on, Abel. I won't interrupt again. What happened then?"

"Well, he'd got to go, had Mr. Minchin! The boss told him he could tell who he liked, but go he'd have to; and go he did, with his tail between his legs, and not another word to anybody. I believe it was the boss who started him in Western Australia."

"Not such a bad boss," remarked Langholm, dryly; and the words set him thinking a moment on his own account. "And what happened to you?" he added, abandoning reflection by an effort.

"I stayed on."

"Forgiven?"

"If you like to put it that way."

"And you both filed the secret for future use!"

"Don't talk through your neck, mister," said Abel, huffily. "What are you drivin' at?"

"You kept this secret up your sleeve to play it for all it was worth in a country where it would be worth more than it was in the back-blocks? That's all I mean."

"Well, if I did, that's my own affair."

"Oh, certainly. Only you came here at your own proposal in order, I suppose, to sell this secret to me?"

"Yes, to sell it."

"Then, you see, it is more or less my affair as well."

"It may be," said Abel, doggedly. And his face was very evil as he struck a match to relight his pipe; but before the flame Langholm had stepped backward, with his stick, that no superfluous light might fall upon his thin wrists and half-filled sleeves.

"You are sure," he pursued, "that Mr. Minchin was in possession of this precious secret at the time of his death?"

"I told it him myself. It isn't one you would forget."

"Was it one that he could prove?"

"Easily."

"Could I?"

"Anybody could."

"Well, and what's your price?"

"Fifty pounds."

"Nonsense! I'm not a rich man like Mr. Steel."

"I don't take less from anybody – not much less, anyhow!"

"Not twenty in hard cash?"

"Not me; but look here, mister, you show me thirty and we'll see."

The voice drew uncomfortably close. And there were steps upon the cross-roads at last; they were those of one advancing with lumbering gait and of another stepping nimbly backward. The latter laughed aloud.

"Did you really think I would come to meet the writer of a letter like yours, at night, in a spot like this, with a single penny-piece in my pocket? Come to my cottage, and we'll settle there."

"I'm not coming in!"

"To the gate, then. It isn't three hundred yards from this. I'll lead the way."

Langholm set off at a brisk walk, his heart in his mouth. But the lumbering steps did not gain upon him; a muttered grumbling was their only accompaniment; and in minute they saw the lights. In another minute they were at the wicket.

"You really prefer not to come in?"

There was a sly restrained humor in Langholm's tone.

"I do – and don't be long."

"Oh, no, I shan't be a minute."

There were other lights in the other cottage. It was not at all late. A warm parallelogram appeared and disappeared as Langholm opened his door and went in. Was it a sound of bolts and bars that followed?

Abel was still wondering when his prospective paymaster threw up the window and reappeared across the sill.

"It was a three-figured check you had from Mr. Steel, was it?"

"Yes – yes – but not so loud!"

"And then he sent you to the devil to do your worst?"

"That's your way of putting it."

"I do the same – without the check."

And the window shut with a slam, the hasp was fastened, and the blind pulled down.

CHAPTER XXVI

A Cardinal Point

The irresistible discomfiture of this ruffian did not affect the value of the evidence which he had volunteered. Langholm was glad to remember that he had volunteered it; the creature was well served for his spite and his cupidity; and the man of peace and letters, whose temperament shrank from contention of any kind, could not but congratulate himself upon an incidental triumph for which it was impossible to feel the smallest compunction. Moreover, he had gained his point. It was enough for him to know that there was a certain secret in Steel's life, upon which the wretch Abel had admittedly traded, even as his superior Minchin had apparently intended to do before him. Only those two seemed to have been in this secret, and one of them still lived to reveal it when called upon with authority. The nature of the secret mattered nothing in the meanwhile. Here was the motive, without which the case against John Buchanan Steel must have remained incomplete. Langholm added it to his notes – and trembled!

He had compunction enough about the major triumph which now seemed in certain store for him; the larger it loomed, the less triumphant and the more tragic was its promise. And, with all human perversity, an unforeseen and quite involuntary sympathy with Steel was the last complication in Langholm's mind.

He had to think of Rachel in order to harden his heart against her husband; and that ground was the most dangerous of all. It was strange to Langholm to battle against *that* by the bedside of a weaker brother fallen in the same fight. Yet it was there he spent the night. He had scarcely slept all the week. It was a comfort to think that this vigil was a useful one.

Severino slept fitfully, and Langholm had never a long stretch of uninterrupted thought.

But before morning he had decided to give Steel a chance. It was a vague decision, dependent on the chance that Steel gave him when they met, as meet they must. Meanwhile Langholm had some cause for satisfaction with the mere resolve; it defined the line that he took with a somewhat absurd but equally startling visitor, who waited upon him early in the forenoon, in the person of the Chief

Constable of Northborough.

This worthy had heard of Langholm's quest, and desired to be informed of what success, if any, he had met with up to the present. Langholm opened his eyes.

"It's my own show," he protested.

"Would you say that if you had got the man? I doubt it would be our show then!" wheezed the Chief Constable, who was enormously fat.

"It would be Scotland Yard's," admitted Langholm, "perhaps."

"Unless you got him up here," suggested the fat official. "In that case you would naturally come to me."

Langholm met his eyes. They were very small and bright, as the eyes of the obese often are, or as they seem by contrast with a large crass face. Langholm fancied he perceived a glimmer of his own enlightenment, and instinctively he lied.

"We are not likely to get him up here," he said. "This is about the last place where I should look!"

The Chief Constable took his departure with a curious smile. Langholm began to feel uneasy; his unforeseen sympathy with Steel assumed the form of an actual fear on his behalf. Severino was another thorn in his side. He knew that Rachel had been written to, and fell into a fever of impatience and despair because the morning did not bring her to his bedside. She was not coming at all. She had refused to come – or her husband would not allow it. So he must die without seeing her again! The man was as unreasonable as sick men will be; nothing would console him but Langholm's undertaking to go to Normanthorpe himself after lunch and plead in person with the stony-hearted lady or her tyrannical lord. This plan suited Langholm well enough. It would pave the way to the "chance" which he had resolved to give to Rachel's husband.

That resolve was not weakened by successive encounters, first with a policeman near the entrance gates, next with a trespasser whom Langholm rightly took for another policeman in plain clothes, and finally with the Woodgates on their way from the house. The good couple welcomed him with a warmth beyond his merits.

"Oh, what a blessing you have come!" cried Morna, whose kind eyes discovered a tell-tale moisture. "Do please go up and convince Mrs. Steel that you can't be rearrested on a charge on which you have already been tried and acquitted!"

"But of course you can't," said Langholm. "Who has put that into her head, Mrs. Woodgate?"

"The place is hemmed in by police."

"Since when?" asked Langholm, quickly.

"Only this morning."

Langholm held his tongue. So the extortioner Abel, outwitted by the amateur policeman, had gone straight to the professional force! The amateur had not suspected him of such resource.

"I don't think this has anything to do with Mrs. Steel," he said at last; "in fact, I think I know what it means, and I shall be only too glad to reassure her, if I can."

But his own face was not reassuring, as Hugh Woodgate plainly told him in the first words which the vicar contributed to the discussion.

"I have been finding out things – I have not been altogether unsuccessful – but the things are rather on my mind," the author explained. "How does Steel take the development, by the way?"

"As a joke!" cried Morna, with indignation; her husband was her echo both as to words and tone; but Langholm could only stare.

"I must see him," he exclaimed, decisively. "By the way, once more, do you happen to know whether Mrs. Steel got a letter from me this morning, Mrs. Woodgate?"

"Yes, she did," answered Morna at once. Her manner declared her to be not unacquainted with the contents of the letter, and Langholm treated the declaration as though spoken.

"And is she not going to see that poor fellow?" he asked.

"At once," said Morna, "and I am going with her. She is to call for me with the phaeton at three."

"Do you know anything about him, Mrs. Woodgate?"

"All."

"Then I can only commend him to the sympathy which I know he has already. And I will talk to Mr. Steel while you are gone."

The first sentence was almost mechanical. That matter was off Langholm's mind, and in a flash it was fully occupied with the prospect before himself. He lifted the peak of his cap, but, instead of remounting his bicycle, he wheeled it very slowly up the drive. The phaeton was at the door when Langholm also arrived, and Rachel herself ran out to greet him on the steps – tall and lissome, in a light-colored driving cloak down to her heels, and a charming hat – yet under it a face still years older than the one he wore in his heart, though no less beautiful in its distress.

"I hardly dare ask you!" she gasped, her hand trembling in his. "Have you found out – anything at all?"

"A little."

And he opened his hand so that hers must drop.

"Oh, but anything is better than nothing! Come in and tell me – quick!"

"Bravo!" added an amused voice from the porch.

It was Steel, spruce and serene as ever, a pink glow upon his mobile face, a pink flower in his reefer jacket, a jaunty Panama straw covering his white hairs, and buckskin shoes of kindred purity upon his small and well-shaped feet. Langholm greeted him in turn, only trusting that the tremors which had been instantly communicated to his own right hand might not be detected by the one it was now compelled to meet.

"I came to tell Mr. Steel," said Langholm, a little lamely.

"Excellent!" murmured that gentleman, with his self-complacent smile.

"But am I not to hear also?" demanded Rachel.

"My dear Mrs. Steel, there is very little to tell you as yet. I only wish there were more. But one or two little points there are – if you would not mind my first mentioning them to your husband?"

"Oh, of course."

There was no pique in the tone. There was only disappointment – and despair.

"You manage a woman very prettily," remarked Steel, as they watched the phaeton diminish down the drive like a narrow Roman road.

"You are the first who ever said so," rejoined the novelist, with a rather heavy sigh.

"Well, let us have a cigar and your news. I confess I am interested. A stroll, too, would be pleasanter than sitting indoors, don't you think? The thickest walls have long ears, Langholm, when every servant in the place is under notice. The whole lot? Oh, dear, yes – every mother's son and daughter of them. It is most amusing; every one of them wants to stay and be forgiven. The neighbors are little better. The excuses they have stooped to make, some of them! I suppose they thought that we should either flee the country or give them the sanguinary satisfaction of a double suicide. Well, we are not going to do either one or the other; we are agreed about that, if about nothing else. And my wife has behaved like a trump, though she wouldn't like to hear me say so; it is her wish that we should sit tighter than if nothing had happened, and not even go to Switzerland as we intended. So we are advertising for a fresh domestic crew, and we dine at Ireby the week after next. It is true that we got the invitation before the fat fell into the fire, but I fancy we may trust the Invernesses not to do anything startling. I am interested, however, to see what they will do. It is pretty safe to be an object-lesson to the countryside, one way or the other."

During this monologue the pair had strolled far afield with their cigars, and Langholm was beginning to puff his furiously. At first he had merely marvelled at the other's coolness; now every feeling in his breast was outraged by the callousness, the flippancy, the cynicism of his companion. There came a moment when Langholm could endure the combination no longer. Steel seemed disposed to discuss every aspect of the subject except that of the investigations upon which his very life might depend. Langholm glanced at him in horror as they walked. The broad brim of his Panama hat threw his face in shadow to the neck; but to Langholm's heated imagination, it was the shadow of the black cap and of the rope itself that he saw out of the corners of his eyes. It was the shadow that had lit upon the wife the year before, happily to lift forever; now it was settling upon the husband; and it rested with Langholm – if it did rest with him – and how could he be sure? His mind was off at a tangent. He was not listening to Steel; without ceremony he interrupted at last.

"I thought you came out to listen to me?"

"My dear fellow," cried Steel, "and so, to be sure, I did! Why on earth did you let me rattle on? Let me see – the point was – ah, yes! Of course, my dear Langholm, you haven't really anything of any account to tell? I considered you a Quixote when you undertook your quest; but I shall begin to suspect a dash of Munchausen if you tell me you have found out anything in the inside of a week!"

"Nevertheless," said Langholm, grimly, "I have."

"Anything worth finding out?"

"I think so."

"You don't mean to tell me you have struck a clew?"

"I believe I can lay hands upon the criminal," said Langholm, as quietly as he could. But he was the more nervous man of the two.

The other simply stood still and stared his incredulity. The stare melted into a smile. "My dear fellow!" he murmured, in a mild blend of horror and reproof, as though it were the fourth dimension that Langholm claimed to have discovered. It cost the discoverer no small effort not to cry out that he could lay hands on him then and there. The unspoken words were gulped down, and a simple repetition substituted at the last.

"I could swear to him myself," added Langholm. "It remains to be seen whether there is evidence enough to convict."

"Have you communicated with the police?"

"Not yet."

"They seem to have some absurd bee in their helmet down here, you know."

"They don't get it from me."

It was impossible any longer to doubt the import of Langholm's earnest and rather agitated manner. He was doing his best to suppress his agitation, but that strengthened the impression that he had indeed discovered something which he himself honestly believed to be the truth. There was an immediate alteration in the tone and bearing of his host.

"My dear fellow," he said, "forgive my levity. If you have really found out anything, it is a miracle; but miracles do happen now and then. Here's the pond, and there's the boathouse behind those rhododendrons. Suppose you tell me the rest in the boat? We needn't keep looking over our shoulders in the middle of the pond!"

For an instant Langholm dreamt of the readiest and the vilest resource; in another he remembered, not only that he could swim, but the insidious sympathy for this man which a darker scoundrel had sown in his heart. It had grown there like Jonah's gourd; only his flippancy affected it; and Steel was far from flippant now. Langholm signed to him to lead the way, and in a very few minutes they were scaring the wildfowl in mid-water, Steel sculling from the after thwart, while Langholm faced him from the crimson cushions.

"I thought," said the latter, "that I would like to tell you what sort of evidence I could get against him before – before going any further. I – I thought it would be fair."

Steel raised his bushy eyebrows the fraction of an inch. "It would be fairest to yourself, I agree. Two heads are better than one, and – well, I'm open to conviction still, of course."

But even Langholm was not conscious of the sinister play upon words; he had taken out his pocket-book, and was nervously turning to the leaves that he had filled during his most sleepless night in town.

"Got it all down?" said Steel.

"Yes," replied Langholm, without raising his eyes; "at least I did make some notes of a possible – if not a really damning – case against the man I mean."

"And what may the first point be?" inquired Steel, who was gradually drifting back into the tone which Langholm had resented on the shore; he took no notice of it now.

"The first point," said Langholm, slowly, "is that he was in Chelsea, or at least within a mile of the scene of the murder, on the night that it took place."

"So were a good many people," remarked Steel, smiling as he dipped the sculls in and out, and let his supple wrists fall for the feather, as though he were really rowing.

"But he left his – he was out at the time!" declared Langholm, making his amended statement with all the meaning it had for himself.

"Well, you can't hang him for that."

"He will have to prove where he was, then."

"I am afraid it will be for you to prove a little more first."

Langholm sat very dogged with his notes. There had been a pause on Steel's part; there was a thin new note in his voice. Langholm was too grimly engrossed to take immediate heed of either detail, or to watch the swift changes in the face which was watching him. And there he lost most of all.

"The next point is that he undoubtedly knew Minchin in Australia – "

"Aha!"

"That he was and is a rich man, whereas Minchin was then on the verge of bankruptcy, and that Minchin only found out that he was in England thirty-six hours before his own death, when he wrote to his old friend for funds."

"And you have really established all that!"

Steel had abandoned all pretence of rowing; his tone was one of admiration, in both senses of the word, and his dark eyes seemed to penetrate to the back of Langholm's brain.

"I can establish it," was the reply.

"Well! I think you have done wonders; but you will have to do something more before they will listen to you at Scotland Yard. What about a motive?"

"I was coming to that; it is the last point with which I shall trouble you

191

for the present." Langholm took a final glance at his notes, then shut the pocket-book and put it away. "The motive," he continued, meeting Steel's eyes at last, with a new boldness in his own – "the motive is self-defence! There can be no doubt about it; there cannot be the slightest doubt that Minchin intended blackmailing this man, at least to the extent of his own indebtedness in the City of London."

"Blackmailing him?"

There was a further change of voice and manner; and this time nothing was lost upon Charles Langholm.

"There cannot be the slightest doubt," he reiterated, "that Minchin was in possession of a secret concerning the man in my mind, which secret he was determined to use for his own ends."

Steel sat motionless, his eyes upon the bottom of the boat. It was absolutely impossible to read the lowered face; even when at length he raised it, and looked Langholm in the eyes once more, the natural inscrutability of the man was only more complete than ever.

"So that is your case!" said he.

And even his tone might have been inspired either by awe or by contempt, so truly rang the note between the two.

"I should be sorry to have to meet it," observed Langholm, "if I were he."

"I should find out a little more," was the retort, "if I were you!"

"And then?"

"Oh, then I should do my duty like a man – and take all the emoluments I could."

The sneer was intolerable. Langholm turned the color of brick.

"I shall!" said he through his mustache. "I have consulted you; there will be no need to do so again. I shall make a point of taking you at your word. And now do you mind putting me ashore?"

A few raindrops were falling when they reached the landing-stage; they hurried to the house, to find that Langholm's bicycle had been removed from the place where he had left it by the front entrance.

"Don't let anybody trouble," he said, ungraciously enough, for he was still smarting from the other's sneer. "I can soon find it for myself."

Steel stood on the steps, his midnight eyes upon Langholm, the glint of a smile in those eyes, but not the vestige of one upon his lips.

"Oh, very well," said he. "You know the side-door near the billiard-room? They have probably put it in the first room on the left; that is where we keep ours – for we have gone in for them at last. Good-by, Langholm; remember my advice."

And, that no ceremony should be lost between them, the host turned on his heel and disappeared through his own front door, leaving Langholm very angry in the rain.

But anger was the last emotion for such an hour; the judge might as well feel exasperated with the prisoner at the bar, the common hangman with the felon on the drop. Langholm only wished that, on even one moment's reflection, he could rest content in so primitive and so single a state of mind. He knew well that he could not, and that every subtle sort of contest lay before him, his own soul the arena. In the meantime let him find his bicycle and get away from this dear and accursed spot; for dear it had been to him, all that too memorable summer; but now of a surety the curse of Cain brooded over its cold, white walls and deep-set windows like sunken eyes in a dead face.

Langholm found the room to which he had been directed; in fact, he knew it of old. And there were the two new Beeston Humbers; but their lustrous plating and immaculate enamel did not shame his own old disreputable roadster, for the missing machine certainly was not there. Langholm was turning away when the glazed gun-rack caught his eye. Yes, this was the room in which the guns were kept. He had often seen them there. They had never interested him before. Langholm was no shot. Yet now he peered through the glass – gasped – and opened one of the sliding panels with trembling hand.

There on a nail hung an old revolver, out of place, rusty, most conspicuous; and at a glance as like the relic in the Black Museum as one pea to another. But Langholm took it down to make sure. And the maker's name upon the barrel was the name that he had noted down at the Black Museum; the point gained, the last of the cardinal points postulated by the official who had shown him round.

The fortuitous discoverer of them all was leaving like a thief – more and more did Langholm feel himself the criminal – when the inner door opened and Steel himself stood beaming sardonically upon him.

"Sorry, Langholm, but I find I misled you about the bicycle. They had taken it to the stables. I have told them to bring it round to the front."

"Thank you."

"Sure you won't wait till the rain is over?"

"No, thank you."

"Well, won't you come through this way?"

"No, thank you."

"Oh, all right! Good-by, Langholm; remember my advice."

It was an inglorious exit that Langholm made; but he was thinking to himself, was there ever so inglorious a triumph? He knew not what he had said; there was only one thing that he did know. But was the law itself capable of coping with such a man?

CHAPTER XXVII

The Whole Truth

"Have the ladies gone?"

Langholm had ridden a long way round, through the rain, in order to avoid them; nor was there any sign of the phaeton in the lane; yet these were his first whispered words across the wicket, and he would not venture to set foot upon the noisy wet gravel without Mrs. Brunton's assurance that the ladies had been gone some time.

"And they've left him a different man," she added. "But what have you been doing to get wet like that? Dear, dear, dear! I do call it foolish of yer! Well, sir, get out o' them nasty wet things, or I shall have you to nurse an' all!"

The kind, blunt soul bustled to bring him a large can of scalding water, and Langholm bathed and changed before going near the invalid. He also felt another man. The thorough wetting had cooled his spirit and calmed his nerves. His head still ached for sleep, but now it was clear enough. If only his duty were half as plain as the mystery that was one no more! Yet it was something to have solved the prime problem; nay, everything, since it freed his mind for concentration upon his own immediate course. But Langholm reckoned without his stricken guest next door; and went up presently, intending to stay five or ten minutes at the most.

Severino lay smiling, like a happy and excited child. Langholm was sorry to detect the excitement, but determined to cut his own visit shorter than ever. It was more pleasing to him to note how neat and comfortable the room was now, for that was his own handiwork, and the ladies had been there to see it. The good Bruntons had moved most of their things into the room to which they had themselves migrated. In their stead were other things which Langholm had unearthed from the lumber in his upper story, dusted, and carried down and up with his own hands. Thus at the bedside stood a real Chippendale table, with a real Delft vase upon it, filled with such roses as had survived the rain. A drop of water had been spilt upon the table from the vase, and there was something almost fussy in the way that Langholm removed it with his handkerchief.

"Oh," said Severino, "she quite fell in love with the table you found for me, and Mrs. Woodgate wanted the vase. They were wondering if Mrs. Brunton would accept a price."

"They don't belong to Mrs. Brunton," said Langholm, shortly.

"No? Mrs. Woodgate said she had never noticed them in your room. Where did you pick them up?"

Langholm looked at the things, lamps of remembrance alight beneath his lowered eyelids. "The table came from a little shop on Bushey Heath, in Hertfordshire, you know. We – I was spending the day there once ... you had to stoop to get in at the door, I remember. The vase is only from Great Portland Street." The prices were upon his lips; both had been bargains, a passing happiness and pride.

"I must remember to tell them when they come to-morrow," said Severino. "They are the sort of thing a woman likes."

"They are," agreed Langholm, his lowered eyes still lingering on the table and the vase "the sort of thing a woman likes ... So these women are coming again to-morrow, are they?"

The question was quite brisk, when it came.

"Yes, they promised."

"Both of them, eh?"

"Yes, I hope so!" The sick man broke into eager explanations. "I only want to see her, Langholm! That's all I want. I don't want her to myself. What is the good? To see her and be with her is all I want – ever. It has made me so happy. It is really better than if she came alone. You see, as it is, I can't say anything – that matters. Do you see?"

"Perfectly," said Langholm, gently.

The lad lay gazing up at him with great eyes. Langholm fancied their expression was one of incredulity. Twilight was falling early with the rain; the casement was small, and further contracted by an overgrowth of creeper; those two great eyes seemed to shine the brighter through the dusk. Langholm could not make his visit a very short one, after all. He felt it would be cruel.

"What did you talk about, then?" he asked.

A small smile came with the answer, "You!"

"Me! What on earth had you to say about me?"

"I heard all you had been doing."

"Oh, that."

"You know you didn't tell me, that evening in town."

"No, I was only beginning, then."

It seemed some months ago – more months since that very afternoon.

"Have you found out anything?"

Langholm hesitated.

"Yes."

Why should he lie?

"Do you mean to say that you have any suspicion who it is?" Severino was on his elbow.

"More than a suspicion. I am certain. There can be no doubt about it. A pure fluke gave me the clew, but every mortal thing fits it."

Severino dropped back upon his pillow. Langholm seemed glad to talk to him, to loosen his tongue, to unburden his heart ever so little. And, indeed, he was glad.

"And what are you going to do about it?"

"That's my difficulty. She must be cleared before the world. That is the first duty – if it could be done without – making bad almost worse!"

"Bad – worse? How could it, Langholm?"

No answer.

"Who do you say it is?"

No answer again. Langholm had not bargained to say anything to anybody just yet.

Severino raised himself once more upon an elbow.

"I must know!" he said.

Langholm rose, laughing.

"I'll tell you who I thought it was at first," said he, heartily. "I don't mind telling you that, because it was so absurd; and I think you'll be the first to laugh at it. I was idiot enough to think it might be you, my poor, dear chap!"

"And you don't think so still?" asked Severino, harshly. He had not been the first to laugh.

"Of course I don't, my dear fellow."

"I wish you would sit down again. That's better. So you know it is some one else?"

"So far as one can know anything."

"And you are going to try to bring it home to this man?"

"I don't know. The police may save me the trouble. I believe they are on the same scent at last. Meanwhile, I have given him as fair a warning as a man could wish."

Severino lay back yet again in silence and deep twilight. His breath came quickly. A shiver seemed to pass through the bed.

"You needn't have done that," he whispered at last.

"I thought it was the fair thing to do."

"Yet you needn't have done it – because – your first idea was right!"

"Right?" echoed Langholm, densely. "My first idea was – right?"

"You said you first thought it was I who killed – her husband."

"It couldn't have been!"

"But it was."

Langholm got back to his feet. He could conceive but one explanation of this preposterous statement. Severino's sickness had extended to his brain. He was delirious. This was the first sign.

"Where are you going?" asked the invalid, querulously, as his companion moved towards the door.

"When was the doctor here last?" demanded Langholm in return.

There was silence for a few moments, and then a faint laugh, that threatened to break into a sob, from the bed.

"I see what you think. How can I convince you that I have all my wits about me? I'd rather not have a light just yet – but in my bag you'll find a writing-case. It is locked, but the keys are in my trouser's pocket. In my writing-case you will find a sealed envelope, and in that a fuller confession than I shall have breath to make to you. Take it downstairs and glance at it – then come back."

"No, no," said Langholm, hoarsely; "no, I believe you! Yes – it was my first idea!"

"I hardly knew what I was doing," Severino whispered. "I was delirious then, if you like! Yet I remember it better than anything else in all my life. I have never forgotten it for an hour – since it first came back!"

"You really were unconscious for days afterwards?"

"I believe it was weeks. Otherwise, you must know – she will be the first to believe – I never could have let her – "

"My poor, dear fellow – of course – of course."

Langholm felt for the emaciated hand, and stroked it as though it had been a child's. Yet that was the hand that had slain Alexander Minchin! And Langholm thought of it; and still his own was almost womanly in the tender pity of its touch.

"I want to tell you," the sick lad murmured. "I wanted to tell her – God knows it – and that alone was why I came to her the moment I could find out where she was. No – no – not that alone! I am too ill to pretend any more. It was not all pretence when I let you think it was only

199

passion that drove me down here. I believe I should have come, even if I had had nothing at all to tell her – only to be near her – as I was this afternoon! But the other made it a duty. Yet, when she came this afternoon, I could not do my duty. I had not the courage. It was too big a thing just to be with her again! And then the other lady – I thanked God for her too – for she made it impossible for me to speak. But to you I must ... especially after what you say."

The man came out in Langholm's ministrations. "One minute," he said; and returned in two or three with a pint of tolerable champagne. "I keep a few for angel's visits," he explained; "but I am afraid I must light the candle. I will put it at the other side of the room. Do you mind the tumbler? Now drink, and tell me only what you feel inclined, neither more nor less."

"It is all written down," began Severino, in better voice for the first few drams: "how I first heard her singing through the open windows in the summer – only last summer! – how she heard me playing, and how afterwards we came to meet. She was unhappy; he was a bad husband; but I only saw it for myself. He was nice enough to me in his way – liked to send round for me to play when they had anybody there – but there was only one reason why I went. Oh, yes ... the ground she trod on ... the air she breathed! I make no secret of it now; if I made any then, it was because I knew her too well, and feared to lose what I had got. And yet – that brute, that bully, that coarse – "

He checked himself by an effort that stained his face a sickly brown in the light of the distant candle. Langholm handed him the tumbler, and a few more drams went down to do the only good – the temporary good – that human aid could do for Severino now. His eyes brightened. He lay still and silent, collecting strength and self-control.

"I was ill; she brought me flowers. I never had any constitution – trust a Latin race for that – and I became very ill indeed. With a man like you, a chill at worst; with me, pneumonia in a day. Then she came to see me herself, saw the doctor, got in all sorts of things, and was coming to nurse me through the night herself. God bless her for the thought alone! I was supposed not to know; they thought I was unconscious already. But I kept conscious on purpose, I could have lived through anything for that alone. And she never came!

"My landlady sat up instead. She is another of the kindest women on earth; she thought far more of me than I was ever worth, and it was she who screened me through thick and thin during the delirium that followed, and after that. She did not tell the whole truth at the trial; may there be no mercy for me hereafter if the law is not merciful to that staunch soul! She has saved my life – for this! But that night – it was her second in succession – and she had been with me the whole long day – that night she fell asleep beside me in the chair. I can hear her breathing now.

"Dear soul, how it angered me at the time! It made me fret all the more for – her. Why had she broken faith? I knew that she had not. Something had kept her; had he? I had hoped he was out of the way; he left her so much. He was really on the watch, as you may know. At last I got up and went to the window. And all the windows opposite were in darkness except theirs."

Langholm sprang to his feet, but sat down again as suddenly.

"Go on!"

"What is it that you thought, Langholm?"

"I believe I know what you did. That's all."

"What? Tell me, please, and then I will tell you."

"All those garden walls – they connect."

"Yes? Yes?"

"You got through your window, climbed upon your wall, and ran along to the lights. It occurred to you suddenly; it did to me when I went over the house the other day."

Severino lay looking at the imaginative man.

"And yet you could suspect another after that!"

"Ah, there is some mystery there alsohought it was the fair thing to . But it is strange, indeed, to think that I was right in the beginning!"

"I did not know what I was doing," resumed the young Italian, who, like many a clever foreigner, spoke more precise English than any Englishman; that, with an accent too delicate for written reproduction, alone would have betrayed him. "I still have very little recollection of what happened between my climbing out of our garden and dropping into theirs. I remember that my feet were rather cold, but that is about all.

"It was near midnight, as you know, and the room it happened in – the study – had the brightest light of all. An electric lamp was blazing on the writing-table at the window, and another from a bracket among the books. The window was as wide open as it would go, the lower sash thrown right up; it was just above the scullery window, which is half underground, and has an outside grating. The sill was only the height of one's chin. I can tell you all that now, but at the time I knew very little until I was in the room itself. Thank you, I will take another sip. It does me more good than harm to tell you. But you will find it all written down."

Langholm set down the glass and replenished it. The night had fallen without. The single candle in the farthest corner supplied the only light; in it the one man sat, and the other lay, their eyes locked.

"I spilt the ink as I was creeping over the desk. That is an odd thing to remember, but I was looking for something to wipe it up with when I heard their voices upstairs."

"You heard them both?"

"Yes – quarrelling – and about me! The first thing I heard was my own name. Then the man came running down. But I never tried to get away. The doors were all open. I had heard something else, and I waited to tell him what a liar he was! But I turned out the lights, so that she should not hear the outcry, and sure enough he shut both doors behind him (you would notice there were two) before he turned them on again. So there we stood.

"'Don't let her hear us,' were my first words; and we stood and cursed each other under our breath. I don't know why he didn't knock me down, or rather I do know; it was because I put my hands behind my back and invited him to do it. I was as furious as he was. I forgot that there was anything the matter with me, but when I began telling him that there had been, he looked as though he could have spat in my face. It was no use going on. I could not expect him to believe a word.

"At last he told me to sit down in the chair opposite his chair, and I said, 'With pleasure.' Then he said, 'We'd better have a drink, because only one of us is coming out of this room alive,' and I said the same thing again. He was full of drink already, but not drunk, and my own head was as light as air. I was ready for anything. He unlocked a drawer and took a brace of old revolvers from the case in which I put them away again. I locked up the drawer afterwards, and put his keys back in his pocket, before losing my head and doing all the rest that the police saw through at a glance. Sit still, Langholm! I am getting the cart before the horse. I was not so guilty as you think. They may hang me if they like, but it was as much his act as mine.

"He stood with his back to me, fiddling with the revolvers for a good five minutes, during which time I heard him tear his handkerchief in two, and wondered what in the world he was going to do next. What he did was to turn round and go on fiddling with the pistols behind his back. Then he held out one in each hand by the barrel, telling me to take my choice, that he didn't know which was which himself, but only one of them was loaded. And he had lapped the two halves of his handkerchief round the chambers of each in such a way that neither of us could tell when we were going to fire.

"Then he tossed for first shot, and made me call, and I won. So he sat down in his chair and finished his drink, and told me to blaze across at him from where I sat in the other chair. I tried to get out of it, partly because I seemed to have seen more good in Minchin in those last ten minutes than in all the months that I had known him; he might be a brute, but he was a British brute, and all right about fair play. Besides, for the moment, it was difficult to believe he was serious, or even very angry. But I, on my side, was more in a dream than not, or he would not have managed me as he did. He broke out again, cursed me and his wife, and swore that he would shoot her too if I didn't go through with it. You can't think of the things he was saying when – but I believe he said them on purpose to make me. Anyhow I pulled at last, but there was only a click, and he answered with another like lightning. That showed me how he meant it, plainer than anything else. It was too late to get out. I set my teeth and pulled again ..."

"Like the clash of swords," whispered Langholm, in the pause.

Severino moved his head from side to side upon the pillow.

"No, not that time, Langholm. There was such a report as might have roused the neighborhood – you would have thought – but I forgot to tell you he had shut the window and run up some shutters, and even drawn the curtains, to do for the other houses what the double doors did for his own. When the smoke lifted, he was lying back in his chair as though he had fallen asleep ...

"I think the worst was waiting for her to come down. I opened both doors, but she never came. Then I shut them very quietly – and utterly lost my head. You know what I did. I don't remember doing half. It was the stupid cunning of a real madman, the broken window, and the things up the chimney. I got back as I had come, in the way that struck you as possible when you were there, and I woke my landlady getting in. I believe I told her everything on the spot, and that it was the last sense I spoke for weeks; she nursed me day and night that I might never tell anybody else."

So the story ended, and with it, as might have been expected, the unnatural strength which had sustained the teller till the last; he had used up every ounce of it, and he lay exhausted and collapsed. Langholm became uneasy.

Severino could not swallow the champagne which Langholm poured into his mouth.

Langholm fetched the candle in high alarm – higher yet at what it revealed.

Severino was struggling to raise himself, a deadly leaden light upon his face.

"Raise me up – raise me up."

Langholm raised him in his arms.

"Another – hemorrhage!" said Severino, in a gasping whisper.

And his blood dripped with the words.

Langholm propped him up and rushed out shouting for Brunton – for Mrs. Brunton – for anybody in the house. Both were in, and the woman came up bravely without a word.

"I'll go for the doctor myself," said Langholm. "I shall be quickest."

And he went on his bicycle, hatless, with an unlit lamp.

But the doctor came too late.

CHAPTER XXVIII

In the Matter of a Motive

That was between eight and nine o'clock at night; before ten an outrageous thought occurred to the man with the undisciplined imagination. It closed his mind to the tragedy of an hour ago, to the dead man lying upstairs, whose low and eager voice still went on and on in his ears. It was a thought that possessed Langholm like an unclean spirit from the moment in which he raised his eyes from the last words of the manuscript to which the dead man had referred.

In the long, low room that Langholm lived in a fire was necessary in damp weather, irrespective of the season. It was on the fire that his eyes fell, straight from the paper in his hand ...

No one else had read it. There was an explicit assurance on the point. The Chelsea landlady had no idea that such a statement was in existence; she would certainly have destroyed it if she had known; and further written details convinced Langholm that the woman would never speak of her own accord. There were strange sidelights on the feelings which the young Italian had inspired in an unlikely breast; a mother could have done no more to shield him. On the night of the acquittal, for example, when he was slowly recovering in her house, it had since come to the writer's knowledge that this woman had turned Mrs. Minchin from her door with a lying statement as to his whereabouts. This he mentioned to confirm his declaration that he always meant to tell the truth to Rachel, that it was his first resolve in the early stages of his recovery, long before he knew of her arrest and trial, and that this woman was aware of that resolve as of all else. But he doubted whether she could be made to speak, though he hoped that for his sake she would. And Langholm grinned with set teeth as he turned back to this passage: he would be diabolically safe.

It was only an evil thought. He did not admit it as a temptation. Yet how it stuck, and how it grew!

There was the fire, as though lit on purpose; in a minute the written evidence could be destroyed for ever; and there was no other kind. Dead men tell no tales, and live men only those that suit them!

It all fitted in so marvellously. To a villain it would have been less a temptation than a veritable gift of his ends. Langholm almost wished he were a villain.

There was Steel. Something remained for explanation there, but there really was a case against him. The villain would let that case come on; the would-be villain did so in his own ready fancy, and the end of it was a world without Steel but not without his wife; only, she would be Steel's wife no more.

And this brought Langholm to his senses. "Idiot!" he said, and went out to his wet paths and ruined roses. But the ugly impossible idea dogged him even there.

"If Steel had been guilty – but he isn't, I tell you – no, but if he had been, just for argument, would she ever have looked – hush! – idiot and egotist! – No, but *would* she? And could you have made her happy if she had? – Ah, that's another thing ... I wonder! – It is worth wondering about; you know you have failed before. Yes, yes, yes; do you think I forget it? No, but I must remind you. Are you the type to make women happy, women with anything in them, women with nerves? Are you not moody, morbid, uneven, full of yourself? – No, of my work. It comes to the same thing for the woman. Could you have made her happy? – yes or no! If no, then pull yourself together and never think of it. Isn't it always better to be the good friend than the tiresome husband, and, if you care for her, to show her your best side instead of all your sides? I thought so! Then thank your stars, and – never again!"

So the two voices, that are only one voice, within Langholm that night, in the heavy fragrance of his soaking garden, under the half-shut eye of a waning moon; and, having conquered him, the voice of sense and sanity reminded him of his reward: "Remember, too, how you promised to serve her; and how, if less by management than good luck, you have, after all, performed the very prodigy you undertook. Go and tell her. I should go to-night. No, it is never too late to bring good news. I should jump on my bicycle and go now!"

The old moon's eye drooped also over Normanthorpe House, out of the clearest sky that there had been for days. The Steels were strolling on the sweep of the drive before the house, out for outing's sake for the first time that day, and together for the sake of being together for the first time that month. There was something untoward in the air. In fact, there was suspicion, and Rachel was beginning to suspect what that suspicion was. She could not say absolutely that she did not entertain it herself for a single instant. She had entertained and had dismissed the thought a good many times. Why had he never told her his real motive in marrying her? Some subtle motive there had been; why could he never tell her what it was? Then there was his intimacy with her first husband, which she had only discovered by chance, after the most sedulous concealment on his part. And, finally, there was the defiant character of his challenge to Langholm, as it were to do his worst (not his best) as a detective.

On the other hand, there was that woman's instinct which no wise woman disregards; and Rachel's instinct had never confirmed her fancies in this matter. But within the last few hours her point of view had totally changed. Her husband was suspected. He said so laughingly himself. He was in a certain danger. Her place was by his side. And let it be remembered that, before his absolute refusal to answer her crucial question about his prime motive for the marriage, Rachel had grown rather to like that place.

They had been strolling quite apart, though chatting amiably. Rachel had not dreamt of putting her hand within his arm, as she had sometimes done towards the end before their quarrel. Yet she did it again now, the very moment his quicker vision descried the cyclist in the drive.

"I hope they are not going to run me in to-night," he said. "If they do, I shall run *them* in for riding without a light. So it's Langholm! Well, Langholm, put salt on him yet?"

"On whom?"

"Your murderer, of course."

"I have his confession in my pocket."

It was the first time that Rachel had known her husband taken visibly aback.

"Good God!" he cried. "Then you don't think it's me any longer?"

"I know it is not. Nevertheless, Mrs. Steel must prepare for a shock."

Rachel was shocked. But her grief and horror, though both were real and poignant, were swept away for that hour at least by the full tide of her joy.

It was a double joy. Not only would Rachel be cleared for ever before the world, but her husband would stand exonerated at her side. The day of unfounded suspicions, of either one of them, by the other or by the world, that day at least was over once for all.

Her heart was too full for many explanations; she lingered while Langholm told of his interview with Abel, and then left him to one with her husband alone.

Langholm thereupon spoke more openly of his whole case against Steel, who instantly admitted its strength.

"But I owe you an apology," the latter added, "not only for something I said to you this afternoon, more in mischief than in malice, which I would nevertheless unsay if I could, but for deliberately manufacturing the last link in your chain. I happened to buy both my revolvers and Minchin's from a hawker up the country; his were a present from me; and, as they say out there, one pair was the dead spit of the other. This morning when I found I was being shadowed by these local heroes, it occurred to me for my own amusement to put one of my pair in a thoroughly conspicuous place, and this afternoon I could not resist sending you to the room to add it to your grand discoveries. You see, I could have proved an alibi for the weapon, at all events, during my trip to town a year ago. Yes, poor Minchin wrote to me, and I went up to town by the next train to take him by surprise. How you got to know of his letter I can't conceive. But it carried no hint of blackmail. I think you did wonders, and I hope you will forgive me for that little trap; it really wasn't set for you. It is also perfectly true that I stayed at the Cadogan and was out at that particular time. I went there because it was the one decent hotel I knew of in those parts, which was probably your own reason, and I was out reconnoitring my old friend's house because I knew him for an inveterate late-bird, and he did not write as though marriage had improved his habits. In fact, as you know, he had gone to the dogs altogether."

This reminded Langholm of the hour.

"It is late now," said he, "and I must be off. Poor Severino had not a relation in this country that I know of. There will be a great deal to do to-morrow."

Steel at once insisted on bearing all expenses; that would be the lightest part, he said. "You have done so much!" he added. "By the way, you can't go without saying good-night to my wife. She has still to thank you."

"I don't want to be thanked."

"But for you the truth might never have come out."

"Still I shall be much happier if she never speaks of it again."

"Very well, she shall not – on one condition."

"What is that?"

"Langholm, I thought last summer we were to be rather friends? I don't think that of many people. May I still think it of you?"

"If you will," said Langholm. "I – I don't believe I ever should have brought myself to give you away!"

"You behaved most fairly, my dear fellow. I shall not forget it, nor the way you scored off the blackmailer Abel. If it is any satisfaction to you, I will tell you what his secret was. Nay, I may as well; and my wife, I must tell her too, though all these months I have hidden it from her; but I have no doubt he took it to the police when you failed him. It is bound to get about, but I can live it down as I did the thing itself. Langholm, like many a better man, I left my country for my country's good. Never mind the offence; the curious can hunt up the case, and will perhaps admit there have been worse. But that man and I were transported to Western Australia on the same vessel in '69."

"And yet," said Langholm – they were not quite his next words – "and yet you challenged me to discover the truth! I still can't understand your attitude that night!"

Steel stood silent.

"Some day I may explain it to you," he said. "I am only now going to explain it to my wife."

The men shook hands.

And Langholm rode on his bicycle off the scene of the one real melodrama of a life spent in inventing fictitious ones; and if you ask what he had to show for his part in it, you may get your answer one day from his work. Not from the masterpiece which he used to talk over with Mrs. Steel, for it will never be written; not from any particular novel or story, much less in the reproduction of any of these incidents, wherein he himself played so dubious a part; but perhaps you will find your answer in a deeper knowledge of the human heart, a stronger grasp of the realities of life, a keener sympathy with men and (particularly) with women, than formerly distinguished this writer's books. These, at all events, are some of the things which Charles Langholm has to show, if he will only show them. And in the meantime you are requested not to pity him.

Steel went straight to his wife. Tears were still in her eyes, but such tears, and such eyes! It cost him an effort to say what he had to say, and that was unusual in his case.

"Rachel," he said at length, in a tone as new as his reluctance, "I am going to answer the question which you have so often asked me. I am going to answer it with perfect honesty, and very possibly you will never speak to me again. I shall be sorry for both our sakes if you do anything precipitate, but in any case you shall act as you think best. You know that I was exceedingly fond of Alec Minchin as a young man; now, I am not often exceedingly fond of anybody, as you may also know by this time. Before your trial I was convinced that you had killed my old friend, whom I was so keen to see again that I came up to town by the very first train after getting his letter. You had robbed me of the only friend I had in England at the very moment when he needed me and I was on my way to him. I could have saved his ship, and you had sent both him and it to the bottom! That, I say candidly, was what I thought."

"I don't blame you for thinking it before the trial," said Rachel. "It seems to have been the universal opinion."

"I formed mine for myself, and I had a particular reason for forming it," continued Steel, with a marked vibration in his usually unemotional voice. "I don't know which to tell you first.... Well, it shall be that reason. On the night of the murder do you remember coming downstairs and going or rather looking into the study – at one o'clock in the morning?"

Rachel recoiled in her chair.

"Heavens!" she cried. "How can you know that?"

"Did you hear nothing as you went upstairs again?"

"I don't remember."

"Not a rattle at the letter-box?"

"Yes! Yes! Now I do remember. And it was actually you!"

"It was, indeed," said Steel, gravely. "I saw you come down, I saw you peep in – all dread and reluctance! I saw you recoil, I saw the face with which you shut those doors and put out the lights. And afterwards I learned from the medical evidence that your husband must have been dead at that time; one thing I knew, and that was that he was not shot during the next hour and more, for I waited about until half-past two in the hope that he would come out. I was not going to ring and bring you down again, for I had seen your face, and I still saw your light upstairs."

"So you thought I had come down to see my handiwork!"

"To see if he was really dead. Yes, I thought that afterwards. I could not help thinking it, Rachel."

"Did it never occur to you that I might have thought he was asleep?"

"Yes, that has struck me since."

"You have not thought me guilty all along, then?"

"Not all along."

"Did you right through my trial?"

"God forgive me – yes, I did! And there was one thing that convinced me more than anything else; that was when you told the jury that the occasion of your final parting upstairs was the last time you saw poor Alec alive."

"But it was," said Rachel. "I remember the question. I did not know how to answer it. I could not tell them I had seen him dead but fancied him only asleep; that they would never have believed. So I told the simple truth. But it upset me dreadfully."

"That I saw. You expected cross-examination."

"Yes; and I did not know whether to stick to the truth or to lie!"

"I can read people sometimes," Steel continued after a pause. "I guessed your difficulty. Surely you must see the only conceivable inference?"

"I did see it."

"And, seeing, do you not forgive?"

"Yes, that. But you married me while you still thought me guilty. I forgive you for denying it at the time. I suppose that was necessary. But you have not yet told me why you did it."

"Honestly, Rachel, it was largely fascination – "

"But not primarily."

"No."

"Then let me hear the prime motive at last, for I am tired of trying to guess it!"

Steel stood before his wife as he had never stood before her yet, his white head bowed, his dark eyes lowered, hands clasped, shoulders bent, the suppliant and the penitent in one.

"I did it to punish you," he said. "I thought some one must – I felt I could have hanged you if I had spoken out what I had seen – and I – married you instead!"

His eyes were on the ground. When he raised them she was smiling through unshed tears. But she had spoken first.

"It was not a very terrible motive, after all," she had said; "at least, it has not been such a very terrible – punishment!"

"No; but that was because I did the very last thing I ever thought of doing."

"And that was?"

"To fall in love with you at the beginning!"

Rachel gave a little start.

"Although you thought me guilty?"

"That made no difference at all. But I have thought it less and less, until, on the night you appealed first to me and then to Langholm – on